THE LOST TESTAMENT

THE LOST TESTAMENT

BRIAN L. THOMPSON

Copyright © 2010 by Brian L. Thompson

Great Nation Publishing
3828 Salem Road #56
Covington, GA 30016

www.greatnationpublishing.com
email: info@greatnationpublishing.com

All rights reserved. No part of this publication may be reproduced, stored in a retrieval system or transmitted, in any form, or by any means, electronic, mechanical, recorded, photocopied, or otherwise, without the prior permission of the copyright owner, except by a reviewer who may quote brief passages in a review.

This book is a work of fiction. Names, characters, places and incidents are products of the author's imagination. Any resemblance to actual events or persons, living or dead, is purely coincidental.

Printed in the United States of America

ISBN: 978-0-578-05549-7

Library of Congress Control Number: 2010912054

ACKNOWLEDGEMENTS

To my Lord and Savior Jesus Christ for teaching me the importance of overcoming obstacles and embracing my calling, no matter the cost.

My wife, best friend, and business partner Heather for her many sacrifices to make this work possible. I could not have done it without your constant encouragement, inspiration, input, and support.

A special thanks to my pastor and spiritual father, Bishop Eddie L. Long; my editor, Steven Manchester; Stephanie Perry-Moore; my parents Bradley and Barbara for their unwavering support, and for all those who continue to contribute to and believe in what God is calling me to do.

Watch for *The Revelation Gate* in 2011.

We are the Lost Testament.

This work is dedicated to the memories of my maternal grandmother, Beatrice Thompson, and a spiritual father, James Darien.

ONE

THURSDAY EVENING, JUNE 21, 1962

PREDESTINATION ideas and Calvinist theories irked Darrion James just as bad as sitting through poorly-acted cinema. Regardless, his insensitive clergyman peer steered their telephone conversation toward the subject aimed at convincing him otherwise. Confronted with these beliefs, Darrion questioned how a pastor could believe God permitted sin with one hand but offered salvation to those pre-selected with the other. And, since history's details had already been predestined, wasn't mankind little more than flesh-and-blood marionettes? Then, prayer and church services become pointless routine and life was a scripted, torturous existence. Why not just *die*?

The theological grandstand silenced the proselyte, who hung up without rebuttal or farewell. This was best. Burying seven years in cardboard boxes could no longer wait and would take most of the night. At noon tomorrow, a pair of newlyweds driving cross-country planned to settle into the second-floor duplex apartment. He agreed to leave the place swept and clean by 9:00. Otherwise, the sheriff would follow through with eviction at 10:00. Darrion would leave without protest. After all, the landlord, himself a divorcé driven to bankruptcy, agreed not to sue for three months of back rent.

But the separation cost Darrion far more than just financial ruin, which he'd experienced to some degree since birth.

As his in-laws came from old money, Jayne, his ex-wife, never adequately adjusted to the culture shock of being *regular*, though it was her decision alone to break protocol and marry for *love* and not money or influence. Maintaining affluence in marriages of substance was not the Carpenter's style. But Daniel, his father-in-law, deviated from tradition himself in a way, arranging for Darrion to assume a nearby pastorate that paid well. After the revelation of an affair, however, the church board members presented a case against their pastor for fraud. They fired him without ceremony or severance, and if he did not protest, lawyers would never have to get involved.

From there, no other place of worship in the surrounding area entertained hiring him, regardless of its need. He'd explained that he did not hide anything about his background, but just did not *disclose* it. Daniel did not see the difference, nor had the church board.

Late that night, exactly when he was not sure, clumsy feet stumbled across the hardwood floor en route to the kitchen. Nothing valuable remained in the apartment. Whatever Jayne had left he'd pawned to pay overdue accounts. Whatever the intruder sought, if just a fight; Darrion had nothing.

Almost simultaneous to Jayne's ungainly flourish through the doorway, he detected a strong aroma of liquor. She balanced herself against the kitchen table where her ex-husband rested and slumped into the closest chair. Darrion stared at the finely-coiffed mess attempting to muffle the rising belch in her mouth to no avail, which amused him. Carpenters sprouted from rich Irish stock. Both sexes held their liquor well, but not Jayne. At their wedding reception, he discovered her talking to an ice sculpture after two glasses of champagne. Unlike tonight's somber showing, which promised to progressively deteriorate, much merriment took place that night.

Suppressed emotions simmered beneath the surface of the silent pair. Darrion played his straight, while hers boiled over. He did not grant Jayne his shoulder as she disintegrated into sobbing fits before his eyes. Nor did he soften in response. He would not offer Kleenex to blot the mascara running rampant – no, not even if it swelled to an Olympic-sized pool on the floor and they both drowned in it. She stumbled to the bathroom alone and used the rough toilet paper, as he could not afford their customary brand. When Jayne reemerged, her face stripped clean of its expensive trappings, some equilibrium had returned to her form. Still, no words passed between them, as Darrion flitted from box-to-box. Given that she'd forced the last face-to-face into mediation, she bided her time. Moments later, near the point of exasperation, her resolve finally broke. "Don't you want to know why I'm here?"

Resisting the urge to curse, Darrion laughed. He dug into his left pocket, produced a threadbare leather wallet and tossed it onto the kitchen table. "The one anniversary gift you gave me that you forgot. It belongs to you. But the cash is mine."

Belittled, Jayne palmed the wallet and walked it over to him. "That's fair, I deserve that, but I don't want this or your money."

Darrion received it. "Then what *do* you want? I've got a lot of packing to do."

She forced a gentle smile. "That's part of why I'm here." From her designer pocketbook, she produced a number of large bills. "Call the landlord first thing in the morning and give him this. It's the back rent, plus next month's."

Incredulous, Darrion verified the amount. "Where did you get this kind of money?"

"You know where I got it from. I asked him to make some calls for you, too."

"Not that easy," he interjected. "Another couple rented the apartment."

"So, find another one. There's enough there for a deposit and then some. Blow some of it on yourself, if you feel like it."

Darrion considered the proposal. With that kind of head start and a positive word on the job front, he could start fresh in the town, even though the matter of his reputation and her father's true motives lingered. "Daniel wouldn't just do that. He ruined me in the first place. What did you do, tell him the *truth*?"

She bit her lip, pensively. "I *couldn't*. He'd...never look at me the same way."

Darrion pressed the wad of cash into Jayne's hand. Her eyes dropped. The money might as well be covered in the blood of his self-respect and dignity.

Fresh tears trailed down her bare cheeks. "What I've done to you... it's terrible," she said with compunction. "I rarely eat or sleep. I can't function. I need your forgiveness and I thought you'd give it to me if I made things right. *That* is what I told him. Let me fix the damage I caused, honey. Take it all. I could care less what you do with it."

Darrion's eyes narrowed. His distrust sent a dull ache into Jayne's chest. "Then, I'll go to him and tell him the truth. I'll say... 'Daddy, I'm the one who broke up my marriage, not Darrion,' and we'll leave together, I don't care where. I'll do it. Besides, Ben and I, we...it ended right before our mediation." She drew close to Darrion and caressed his face, which he secretly loathed. "I *never* stopped loving you and if you think you might still love me, we'll go, just you and me, far away – wherever you want. Just give us another chance. You'll trust me again, in time. I'll earn it back. I swear it on my mother's grave."

They kissed, tenderly. Jayne sensed a faint longing behind Darrion's lips and fed it with swelling passion, but he backed away.

"Let me call a taxicab for you," he offered in post-protracted silence.

His ex-wife turned away, wantonly swabbing the skin beneath her nose with a tissue until it reddened. "Nothing runs past midnight and it's a quarter past one."

Darrion absent-mindedly checked his bare wrist, where the white gold, diamond and polished limestone anniversary watch used to reside. After composing herself, Jayne produced the timepiece from her front pocket. Unlike the money, receiving it did not track footprints across his pride, as her father had nothing to do with it. "I actually missed having this."

Jayne fished her car keys out of her purse. "I'll be on my way then."

"Not like that, you're not. I'll run you home. You can pick up the car in the morning."

He led Jayne by the elbow down the cobbled stone path, walking close enough to balance her, but not enough to communicate romantic motives. At the end of the curbed sidewalk, they parted company, each to a different side of a sedan inexplicably parked half of a block away in the dark. Jayne tried to hide the quarter-full bottle lying on the passenger side, but fumbled it the more she attempted discretion. For an hour prior to their meeting, she'd swilled it and contemplated what she'd done over the past few months to change his perception of her. With no such luck – she'd apologized, offered him money, disavowed her adulterous affair and volunteered to leave everything to go with him to parts unknown. *What more can he want?*

The noiseless atmosphere made the drive to her father's estate – a ten minute trip at regular speed – seem like an hours-long journey in her still dulled and hazy mind. She contemplated mashing his foot against the pedal. *Can't he drive faster?*

When the sedan pulled into the gated entrance and around to the ranch home Daniel built for her on the sprawling property, she relaxed. Darrion saw her to the door and leaned in, and calculating the threat of just a platonic peck on the cheek, he reversed field at the last moment and returned to the idling car. He drove away.

"Goodbye," she whispered, placing a hand over her mouth. She wondered, after tomorrow, if she would ever see him again.

Having an awareness of time jumpstarted his energy. By ten minutes to 2:00, he was back to packing and doubly exhausted. An extra pair of hands would have helped, but not at the cost of conversation. After rounding together items he could do without and placing them into trash bags, he repeated the process until the apartment had been packed and only cleaning remained. Sometime after 4:00, he conked out on the mattress until constant knocking at the door awakened him at 9:00 a.m. sharp. He prayed it was the cavalry and not an overambitious sheriff.

"Good morning!" With sunglasses perched in the blonde up-do above her bangs, Jayne handed him a white paper bag and a cup of steaming hot coffee. "Breakfast."

Ever the morning person, she practically floated into the living room loaded with boxes and made herself at home, sitting on one labeled *books*. A stark contrast to last night's ensemble, Jayne's slacks and Egyptian cotton, horizontal-striped blouse kept her comfortable, yet still impeccable. "It's the most important meal of the day. Go ahead. Eat."

Too hungry to protest, Darrion pilfered what he assumed she bought for him – two chocolate doughnuts and two glazed. He spoke a quick blessing over them and ate standing up. Jayne rescued her cruller from the bag and delicately ate it, intermittently sipping coffee.

"Why don't you slow down before you choke?" she suggested, giggling at his voracity.

"I last ate lunch," he said, cheeks bulging. "...yesterday. I'm starving."

"I figured. It's the least I could do. That, and give you a ride to wherever you're going."

After his third doughnut, he paused to drink. "You remembered how I take it?"

"You don't fix coffee the same way for nine years and suddenly forget." She smirked. "I've got the car and I'm not expected back today, but we'd have to make 50 trips with all these boxes."

"Few guys from church," he mumbled. "They're going to store them for as long as I need."

"Good. Well, I packed myself a small tote, just in case you changed your mind...about me coming along. And this morning, I told Daddy the truth."

Darrion choked. "You did *what?*"

"First thing this morning, I sat him down and told him everything I'd done. And Daniel let me have it good for a bit. He's disappointed, but agrees that it's high time I got out from under his thumb and blazed my own trail instead of being a social butterfly type. I didn't go to college to plan tea parties and fundraisers and attend fancy balls. Mom wouldn't have wanted that for me."

Darrion took a seat on a box and silently nibbled away at the last glazed pastry.

"I've been thinking." She sidled up to Darrion and leaned on his shoulder. "We could go out west and start a new life past my father's influence, where nobody will know us or care what color you are. We could get remarried and have the little boy I always wanted, maybe a little girl too, and raise them with our *own* money. I can actually use my education and find some teaching work to help out. I'll adjust, just be patient with me. It's not easy." She looked into his eyes. "And I know you said you don't trust me, but you also said you'd forgiven me." Her hand found his. "I promise, I won't stray and I won't abandon you. Daddy won't interfere now. Let me love you again. We can't go back to the way things were, but we can start over, can't we?"

Without warning, Darrion stiffened and eased from her grasp. "We *can't*."

She nodded mechanically, the warmth in her voice suddenly iced over. "Fine."

"It's a quarter-after. The sheriff will be here at 10:00 and I gotta shower."

"Then shower." She pointed a finger in his chest. "But you're not leaving without giving me an explanation, even if the sheriff has to drag you out by your feet."

Darrion sucked his teeth. "It'll have to wait."

"Well then," she sighed, dusting crumbs from her lap. "Since I'm *waiting*, I can make myself useful and help load the lighter boxes when the boys get here then, can't I?"

After brushing his mouth and goatee clean with a napkin, he gathered some fresh clothes from a nearby table. "You'll stay until they get here?"

"Not leaving until I get answers."

Not long after Darrion vanished and the water started, Jayne began her search. She rummaged through checking account manifests, his wallet, and a pile of forlorn papers on the bedroom carpet for clues of a destination or possible significant other. *Nothing but trash.*

The pursuit did reveal the depths of his financial depression. She folded three hundred dollar bills into an unused section of his wallet and placed everything back the way she found them. Shortly thereafter, his friends arrived. Undaunted, they loaded all but his clothes and readied to depart before Darrion emerged with just five minutes to spare. With sunglasses donned, Jayne crossed her arms in earnest expectation.

"You want answers. Alright." His mouth suddenly dry, Darrion forced down the rest of his tepid coffee. "I *haven't* forgiven you – not for any of it. I need time away from you and this place to do that." As if it were a sandbag fortress, he knelt behind the rationale. "We had chances to make our marriage work and blew it. You wanted out, you got out. We'd be fools to do it again."

They remained in silence – so long, in fact, that Darrion considered just leaving.

Finally, Jayne inhaled. "Well," she muttered, lip trembling. "I guess that's it, then."

Darrion made tracks toward the front door. She gripped his left forearm. Pausing momentarily, he released suitcases from both hands. She readied herself for the forthcoming. Darrion clasped his right hand over hers, gently squeezed, and politely freed himself, leaving her.

The truck pulled away with Jayne's stationary form visible through the parted venetian blinds. Once the vehicle rounded the corner and the duplex shrank away from sight, Darrion opened his eyes. The pain in his gut ebbed away. Thankful that his driver respected the need for silence, he bowed and asked forgiveness. If he thought truth would have released Jayne, he'd have told her. Instead, he fed her the acceptable substitute. Considering what she'd put him through, not many would condemn him for nursing emotional wounds – including her. In the end, he wondered if he'd caused more damage than good by lying. Only time would tell.

Darrion waved to his departing acquaintances and purchased a one-way ticket to Beaufort, South Carolina, switching rails once in Richmond and again at a tiny hub in North Carolina. The latter was a straight shot. There, he planned to petition his great aunt to take him in for at least a couple nights so he could gain bearings.

After stowing his bags, he napped as best he could, given his seatmate with pork chop elbows sandwiched him close to the window. Between his fits of sleeplessness, she must have tired of the jostling and given her seat to an attractive young blonde whom he took for a student at the all-female state institution. They struck up casual conversation before it waned to discussions about politics, the weather forecast and trivial current events; none of which interested him. He drifted off once more and awoke next to a different passenger, who just happened to be holding his wallet. Darrion snatched it back and immediately signaled for a porter, but the woman tugged at his shirt sleeve.

"Easy," she said, nonchalantly. "I picked it up from the floor."

He searched it. The thief emptied it of all its money plus the transfer to the South Carolina rail. Darrion rustled through his pockets for cash and found only a few dollars, the transfer from Richmond to the North Carolina line and some old receipts. A quick scan of the female passengers produced several good-looking, college-age blonde girls, none of which he could have positively identified as the culprit.

"You mustn't ride the rails often. Everybody knows not to sleep."

"So now I'll be stranded in Zyonne. I was born there."

"Then look at it this way." Her smile flattened. "You probably still have your luggage. And I'm switching over to the Carolina rail, too, so you can sit next to someone who won't rob you. Think of it like a sort of homecoming. Maybe you can visit some family?"

"I was just *born* there. It's not home and I'm not looking to stay long."

He stared out the window and the passing scenery until it slowed to a singular landscape in Richmond. Indeed, his bags were intact, which brightened him up a little. When his traveling mate rose to disembark, her lack of stature amazed him by comparison. She barely reached the height of his breastbone, even with consideration to her high-heeled shoes. That, along with her teardrop-shaped eyes and the deep blackness of her locks, set her apart from the other females.

They boarded the next train together. Darrion appreciated the company, though she read intently from a handwritten journal for the first half-hour. He used his peripheral vision to get a glimpse, but before he determined anything conclusive, she moved it underneath her hand. "If you want to know what I'm reading, just ask. It's impolite to read over my shoulder."

"You're right, I'm sorry. Don't let me disturb you."

"You want to know?"

"No," he fibbed. "That's fine. Please continue."

Darrion immersed himself in distractive thoughts, but moments later the temptation to look lured him once more. A cursory glance and the way her finger traced the scripted lettering revealed an obvious detail – it was not written in English.

"Corinne October." She forced the right hand on his lap into a handshake. "Call me Violet. And you?"

He shook back. "Darrion. Sorry about that…"

"Yes, *October* is my legal last name." She tucked her left foot underneath her right leg and faced him. "I traveled abroad on an expedition last year and spent about six months there."

Darrion's eyes lit up. "That's interesting. I've never been out of the country. Where…"

"Don't interrupt me," she interjected. "Sorry. That was rude, but I hate being interrupted."

He waved it off. "Please continue."

"My organization did not send me to vacation." Violet sidled closer, her voice hushed almost to a whisper. "What do you know about *crucifixion*?"

"It's brutal," he spoke with interest, "but it hasn't been used since the Roman Empire."

"You won't read news reports about it, but yes, it *is*, in unmapped killing fields where it's all they do – even to adolescents. The soil stinks from the blood. Nothing grows there."

"Where?"

"They're left to die for what Americans consider misdemeanors. Most live through the nailing, but they starve, asphyxiate, bleed to death, or get eaten alive by scavengers, and no one cares. I had to do something. So, I started writing about what happened to them. Some were political prisoners guilty of ticking off the wrong person. Others could have stolen fruit."

The fact that she interviewed the dying without offering to help perplexed Darrion; so much so, that his brow furrowed enough for Violet to read his thoughts.

"*You don't do it.* Aiding the condemned carries a serious penalty, and that is not the time or place for a foreigner to make a point. What kind of help could I be to them if I hanged there too?"

He relented. "I suppose. But what could they possibly have to say?"

"Plenty, but nothing you'll ever read." Violet twisted the tresses at her right ear, revealing a jagged pink scar along the hairline. "Your money can be replaced, Darrion, but I lost six months of my life's work, plus three weeks in a hospital that I can't get back. This is all I have left."

She gave the worn leather notebook to Darrion, who flipped to the first page. His eyes bulged at the Aramaic prologue, which sounded like a fake religious axiom credited to an unlikely source. He chuckled and passed it back. "I can see why they didn't steal *this*."

"It's *real*. It's a replica of several manuscripts, but I copied it myself. Can you read it?"

"I aced Aramaic in college. I can read it, but you're insane if you think it's authentic."

"What makes it fake...because I'm a *woman*?" she bristled. "Resurrected Christ first appeared to a *woman* and the eleven did not believe her word, either...but she told the truth!"

"Then tell me why," he refuted, passionately, "why would someone, *anyone*, carry something this valuable and important on a train headed to the middle of nowhere?"

The argument had grown heated enough to attract the attention of the couple sitting in front of them. Violet noticed their irritation and tempered the volume of her rebuttal. "The Author of Creation descended to earth as a carpenter's son with a manger for a crib. Same reason."

"And for *what* reason was that?"

She stood up, ready to change seats. "Listen, believe what you want to believe, Darrion, but whether I tell you or not, it doesn't make the reality any less the truth, or easier to swallow."

"That's the story you're sticking with?"

She nodded.

"Then I'm ready to listen. Please stay."

Violet acquiesced and began by recounting memories of a dinner conversation.

TWO

FRIDAY AFTERNOON, JUNE 22, 1962

DARRION could not draw a positive bead on his traveling companion, as she played her conversation terse and emotionally close to the vest. Questions and interruptions harried Violet October, but not much else stirred the pot until she opened the journal and spoke of her research in an unnamed country. Her clues pointed to a Middle Eastern destination, but the tale twisted enough to cast reasonable doubt.

She lingered over the details of the long-ago meal – down to the type of Mediterranean fish and its complimenting sides, the character and aftertaste of the wine and the restaurant décor. Darrion followed her eyes, as they purposefully picked up these details from the pages, and he assumed she'd pieced together these particulars from eyewitness accounts and some personal experience. As it turned out, her penchant for mincing details was more than just eccentricity at work.

She looked him in the eye, then down at the scribbled notes. "Prior to the meal, I purchased my notebook and laid it next to me on the table. We ate and spoke openly without regard to our surroundings. Our carelessness helped produce what I am sharing with you. The authorities also believe it is where the assailants gauged their opportunity to attack.

"One of our partners on the project is a Messianic Jew and argued the existence of *Yeshua Hamashiach*. I chose to rebut – not because I disagree per se, but to expose the flimsiness and lack of extant text evidence in his case. Before I knew otherwise, this local had come over next to me, wrote the passage I showed you and sketched *this*..."

Violet flipped to a page depicting a crucifixion. Darrion looked beneath the picture, where Violet had scribbled a date two weeks after the dinner. *So, that's why she interviewed them.*

"Bringing attention to them was still my main focus and this was secondary. I discovered traitors are executed in a restricted area, so I slipped behind the lines and found the only person to be crucified on that same date. The others were already dead. He told me where to go. Instead of only copying it, as I was instructed, I removed the original."

"Then what happened?"

Violet cast him a cold glance before removing a fragile leaf from the rear of the notebook and placing it into his hand. Rather dry in texture, it bore what seemed to be an Arabic letter. When Darrion attempted to examine it closer, it disintegrated into dust between his fingers.

"Disobedience carries a *steep price*," said Violet, her voice echoing lament. "The parchment's degenerative process occurred quickly, but I did copy it first. My attack happened not long afterward. Apparently, whoever was seeking to purchase it was not amused by ambition, nor were they interested in a duplicate with potential flaws. What I copied is all that remains."

Darrion stifled his desire to pose the one question that niggled at the back of his brain. *She must still be of interest, if they let her live.*

"In the book of Acts, Luke mentions 'proofs' that Christ gave to the apostles of His resurrection and divinity over a 40-day period, but he did not elaborate beyond the general. Assuming you've read that, didn't you ever wonder what those 'proofs' might have been?"

He dismissed the notion. "Not really. He'd have given specifics, if they were needed."

"Suppose those proofs *were* chronicled and recorded as *another, lost testament?*"

"Lady," he said with contempt, "people have been claiming they found missing parts of the Bible since before the 1600's and none are valid. Say your story is true. How is this 'other testament' any different?"

Violet pursed her lips. "The author," she murmured. "Christ, *Himself.*"

To deny the logical nagging within him would betray his nature. He could not suspend enough disbelief in order to accept even the smallest grain of Violet's assertions. Skepticism crossed his face, making her more animated.

"The eleven thought Christ was a ghost when He first arose. Couldn't a proof of physical existence be *writing*? Think about it. Just a few years ago, the largest collection of Biblical documents from the first century church was discovered in the same area! Not many believed *that* was possible."

"But nobody claimed that they were handwritten by Christ! Look, even if it was, the original is destroyed, so how can you authenticate? Go public with this and you'll be called insane. They'll put you in one of those nuthouses or something."

"The Sanhedrin accused Jesus of the same thing." She set the strap of her handbag on her shoulder and stood. "Read it. Bring it back after you're done."

Violet entered the next car. Darrion committed himself to reading a page before putting it down. A page became ten, and then ten turned into 20. A half-hour later, he'd finished the text, feeling as if he'd dipped into a refreshing waterfall of spiritual understanding. He'd apologize and give the eccentric his honest opinion. *If Christ did not write an undiscovered Biblical testament, He certainly inspired its words.*

The locomotive lurched and pitched forward, like an ancient arthritic, picking up momentum through the mountainous clearing into a short straightaway to the next stop. Motion sickness had never afflicted Darrion before, but the sudden rocking threw his stomach for a loop. He eased back down in time to brace himself before the brakes hit, stopping the train a hundred yards from the platform. All looked around at one another, wondering what the problem was.

Fearing the worst, Darrion determined to search for Violet. En route, several uniformed men blocked passage to the next car. One in particular stopped to address individual concerns.

"Remain calm." One of the attendant's attempts to reassure lost its effectiveness beneath his own panic. "We apologize for the inconvenience, but we need you to quickly disembark and proceed to the platform from this point. Stay clear of the rear."

Darrion offered a weak excuse about his luggage being located in the next storage area and jostled past the attendant and ensuing crowd, where he assumed Violet would be. Inside the huddle near the rear-facing windows were whispers about a *body*.

He thrust his head at an awkward angle toward the window to get a view. In the distance, a gathering of men examined a shredded human mess. Quelling the urge to vomit, he tried not to assume anything. From what he could tell, it may have been Violet. He jammed the notebook deep into his slacks' pocket. *None of this makes sense.*

With bags in tow, Darrion departed the train, only to be shuttled to an area inside Zyonne's limits where authorities questioned each passenger. The interrogations, particularly his, were curiously cursory – as if the policemen were inept, or *did not want* to find out what happened to the poor soul. With no identification beyond hand-labeled personal belongings, they had very few leads. Darrion denied knowing the radical, save for small talk about the weather.

Through their questioning tactics and pieces of conversation whispered all too loudly, he cobbled together several facts: the victim had likely been knocked unconscious by the fall and dropped between the cars. No passenger could positively place the murderer, and Darrion's alibi had already been corroborated at the time the offense allegedly occurred. The investigators instructed him not to leave the area: a tiny hamlet of 2,000 or so people with a 14-man police force and enough traffic lights to count on one hand plus a thumb.

An officer ushered him to the station. A lifetime ago, he walked Zyonne's streets as a joyful youth, but in the hour since returning he felt dirty and ashamed. This place was hardly a home anymore, though the Nebo and Mitchell mountains and the Swannanoa Valley trail saluted him like long lost relatives. The mountain town was just a momentary pit stop en route to brighter pastures once his financial landscape improved a bit.

"Excuse me." A slender, pale brunette in pink and white jabbed him in the shoulder with a bony finger, breaking his thoughts. "Have you seen a bum around here?"

Darrion stared the flighty woman down. "What?"

"Scruffy looking guy, a foot taller than me, about two across, might have called out 'Betty Lou'...looks like he ain't showered in a day or so? And he..."

"As a matter of fact," Darrion interjected, "Dark brown hair?"

"Dirty blonde. Funny, I just searched the station top to bottom and he's not around."

"Check the men's restroom? He could be there."

"Thanks anyway." She walked away, heels clip-clopping with awkward, uncertain repetition. Darrion watched the unsteady porcelain legs wobble out of sight.

Betty Lou Everham propped herself against the building's frayed wooden post and waited. Jack Miles could very well be in the restroom, but she bided the time. Another few minutes without him could do no harm.

She nervously fished inside her beaten handbag for a Lucky Strike. Whenever the cheapskate left a pack at home, she helped herself to one or two – however many he'd be less likely to notice. With his next check still a few days away, he'd stretch out the pack until payday. Her stash down to a single smoke, she'd puff it a few times to take the edge off and extinguish it.

The putrid stench cooking in the subtle heat smelled like his brand: alcohol mixed with sweat pushing up through the pores. Even after he showered, the rural Georgian seemed to stink, as if it were natural. Jaw clenched, lips pursed, Betty Lou inhaled long, then rubbed out the cigarette's head on the pavement. Around that time, a pot-bellied, rugged standard of a man with wild gray around the temples exited the swinging restroom door. Satisfied with himself, Jack Miles Everham exhaled and scratched his armpit.

"Why am I here?" she sulked. These extra calls to duty were meant to police her activity. She loved him, or – if the past 15 years were any measure – watched love erode from commonplace to rarity. Years ago, he seemed to detect the sound of her brassiere hooks coming undone clear across the house. Now, a thousand hooks could unclip and he'd never notice.

"Hey." Jack Miles rounded the corner, shielded his cigarette from the temperamental wind and struck a match. "You ready?"

"Again, why'd you need *me* here so bad?" Betty Lou reluctantly limped beside him. It was a bad day for the leg.

"I just...got off the train, Betty Lou." He paused and puffed. "A woman died. Have some respect. B'sides, you ain't s'posed to fix yourself to start fussin' until at least after 4:00 and it ain't hardly half past 3:00."

"Well, guess I'm startin' early."

"Figures."

"Carry your bags?" she redirected. "That's why I'm here. Can't be 'cause you enjoy my company."

"Don't be such a crack-back fool." He fell quiet and puffed. "Be good for you to get out and around. It's been a month already."

Amazed that he remembered, Betty Lou played it cool. "S'pose so. Ain't been *that* long, though. Still smarts every now and again."

Jack Miles repositioned the bag slung about his meaty shoulder. A guilt trip and a wave-off of the true pain – if there were an effective way to drag out a mutually agreed upon abortion, she knew it. It was exactly the type of treatment he hoped to avoid by traveling.

Betty Lou gasped and tenderly touched the area between her belly and pelvis. Normally, she hid the more intense pain, but the sudden knifing below the belt caught her off-guard. "Little blood this morning," she grunted, "cramp or two, but ain't all that bad. Maybe you right 'bout gettin' out."

Eyes glued to the now moving locomotive, Jack Miles contemplated sparing Betty Lou the trouble and throwing himself beneath it. A minute or two more and he thought his revolted eardrums would burst open and bleed in protest. If that didn't stop her, then his brain would shut down, section-by-section.

Eighteen years ago, Betty Lou Graham, then a lithe vision of a girl, entranced him with a sweet southern twang and a subtle girlish figure. She hung out with his friends; locals she didn't know. He'd show up and they would flirt, natural at the beginning, later, more purposeful. Everything about her, from the perfumed scent emanating from her pressure points to the way she tossed her hair in a nervous moment – translated seduction. They wasted little time giving in.

Aware that her daughter's posture and walk had changed, Helen Graham demanded Jack Miles make her daughter an honest woman, unaware the girl had been secretly carrying his child for two full months. Though he had no interest in marriage, he waxed romantic and proposed on bended knee.

More confused than enthused, Betty Lou agreed. A month later, they tied the knot at the town courthouse before her belly began protruding, which turned out to be a blessing in disguise. The baby strangled itself dead on its umbilical cord, as if it knew the life it was destined for. Although the tie between them had been tragically severed, neither one had a clue on another direction to go. He was hard whiskey to her raw milk, burlap to napped leather. They stayed together, somewhat balancing out in similarities and differences, but both slaves to repetition.

"How was Richmond, Jack? Everything you expected?"

The sarcastic timbre of her voice bothered him something awful, as if she knew the old flame he intended to spend the night with during the trip had borne children and grown obese. He whipped the wheel toward the driveway and motored up to the house. "Whaddya care any?" he snapped. "Just a trip to see my favorite cousin."

"Don't..." Her mouth drew tight. "You got a swing-graveyard tonight. Go on in and get some shut-eye."

"Sure." Jack Miles jerked the luggage from the truck's backseat into his arms and left his wife to her own devices. By the time she tottered in the house, he'd stripped down and been in the bed for minutes. Undaunted, she proceeded to the kitchen and flicked on the radio when she heard the bedsprings violently shift.

"Turn that crap off, Betty Lou. I swear, I mean it this time!" Negro music drove Jack Miles nuts. There was something about the rhythmic singing, guitars and drum rhythms that fired up his nerves.

"Alright." Complaints this early were a bad sign. Disappointed, Betty Lou turned it off. Whenever she played Motown, he either dressed and left for the electric plant faster or, like today, told her to turn it off and took extra long leaving just to spite her.

"Wake me up *before* 6:00 this time, alright?"

"Yes, sir," she said with fake vigor. "Anything you say, sir."

"Had enough lip from you, Betty. Let me sleep now, you hear?"

For a former marine, he slept lightly. She shifted her weight onto the good leg and took a good long look at him. As a 16-year-old, she found the rugged look attractive, but the years had added a flabby beer gut and gray hair, overwhelming whatever appeal he'd managed to retain. *If only I'd not gotten pregnant...*

She limped into the living room, settled on the couch and dug into the book she'd checked out from the library. The main character was a rich, arrogant louse that carried on affairs with his children's former teacher under his wife's nose. She confronted him about it and, rather than curl up in shame, he shrugged his shoulders and admitted it. In the midst of reading about the mind-boggling romantic triangle, the clock struck 5:30. Betty Lou arose, and soreness traveled below her left knee, unprovoked. Each painful step felt like a rapid knife stabbing. Ten more paces and she'd be in the kitchen. Little by little, she approached Jack Miles who preened in the bathroom, a Lucky Strike burning on the sink edge.

"Thought you needed me to wake you up?" she grimaced.

"Oh, will ya stop it already, for God's sake," he said. "Can't hurt that much."

She continued into the kitchen. "Whaddya care any," she mocked. Her husband underestimated his ability to cause pain, which made him dangerous.

He puffed deeply and positioned the cigarette butt in his fingers. Two days worth of salt and pepper growth rounded his lips, covered his squared chin and chiseled jaw leading up to unkempt sideburns and tousled hair. Another day and he'd consider shaving it off. "Ready for my coffee."

Betty Lou initiated the routine by rinsing the filthy pot twice and filling it halfway with water. Not to be criticized or dissected, their schedule took on a life of its own, independent of her individual, day-to-day feelings. Varying it in any way meant change. His displeasure, in turn, resulted in verbal assault or violence. She tried to do so once years ago and he crushed her leg for it, then lied to the doctor and said that she'd been "hit by a car." Even after two surgeries, it never healed right.

Once the water settled, she inspected it for bubbles. It wasn't worth the slap she'd receive if he tasted soap.

Five rounded scoops of fresh grounds, the stronger the better, but better not waste it, then more would have to be bought next week and that meant less allowance to skim off the top. She opened the bag of white bread, stuck two slices in the wedge shaped, white toaster and set the lever on the second lowest notch. Too light and he'd cuss her; too dark and she'd have to toast more.

Jack Miles paced bare-chested to the bedroom. *He'll take ten minutes.* Betty Lou cursed. The coffee took just five minutes or so and the toasting cycle might last four tops. Lukewarm bread led to a lecture about forgetfulness and stupidity.

"Hurry up, Jack Miles. Your joe and sandwich's gonna get cold and it's a quarter 'til."

"Then put it in the oven," he yelled, "I'll come when I'm ready."

The toaster springs popped. It was Betty Lou's cue to shift weight from good leg to bad and back to good, remove the bread, and spread one-and-a-half full knife – lengths of mayonnaise across each. Halfway through stacking turkey and cheese, she called him again. "Jack!"

Weary from her nagging, he emerged into the kitchen, silent. The sandwich disappeared in swift motions from hand to mouth, ten chews tops and less than eight swallows. He chased it with the coffee Betty Lou emptied into a tall glass, hot to the touch.

"Still don't see how you drink it that fast. Look, try to have a good night." She tried not to smirk, while straightening his collar.

"Try to act harder like you ain't wanna see me go and I will."

"Wait! I need money. You'll forget by the time you get home. You ain't want me reminding you and we hardly ain't got no food left."

He used the dishtowel to wipe his lips clean and produced a wrinkled five dollar bill.

"For what?" He yanked the five back. "You spend too daggone much."

Strange, he never questioned her when she asked for money. "I need woman things, too," she fibbed. "And I need ten, not five."

Jack Miles dropped the bill onto the counter next to his plate and fished for another. "You always need *five*. What's changed?"

"It's different," she said. "Tomorrow, I guess I'll need more." After the necessities, she could pocket the change. True, she would need woman things, but those supplies could stretch until next week when she'd lobby Jack Miles again for money after payday. After a drunken night or two, he'd forget about this entire exchange.

"Make it last." He produced a few more bills before leaving.

Two steps into the 30 pace distance from her spot in the kitchen to the window adjacent to the front door, she gave up in agony. Trusting Jack Miles to head to the plant without turning back would have to be enough. Teary-eyed from the pain, she lifted the kitchen window.

Inside the drawer behind the useless knick-knacks, rubber bands, keys, paper scraps and blown-out bulbs lay her medicine wrapped in a worn gray dishtowel.

She eagerly grabbed the slender white contraband like it was a Christmas present, stuck it between her lips and leaned over the stove to light it. She'd be in another world soon. Long drags – deep, slow and therapeutic. She giggled, exhaled and fanned the pungent fumes outside. Slowly, the leg pain ebbed away.

Minutes passed. She laughed. Cried. Screamed. A puff or two remained. *Don't waste the buzz on bad things*, she thought. *Think happiness, good things. Make the pain go away.*

Nothing inanimate spoke up this morning to stoke her joy. She drew a blank and slumped over, frustrated. She snuffed the smoldering butt and tossed it into the weeds under the window.

Later, in the bedroom, she stared at her reflection in the wall-length mirror like some fantastic creation she'd never seen. After arranging her in-need-of-styling locks into pigtails, she pushed her nose skyward with her index fingers and snorted pig noises. She dug her thumbs into her cheek muscles, forcing them into a harlequin's smile. She tilted her head back and forth, puckered her lips and hummed a carousel tune. Jack Miles preferred women who did his bidding – – for money or at no charge, he didn't care. Wielding control over others amused him much like a circus clown.

She stopped, her freckled complexion settling back into place, and let her loosened robe drop to the ground. Diagonal from her pointed nose, definite lines confined her lips, similar to the ones etching themselves at the edges of her eyes. At 35, days out from 36, her body seemed to age harder by the day. She hobbled naked into the bathroom and ran the shower faucet hot. She lathered and rinsed, repeating the ritual in the shower until her skin assumed a pinkish tint and felt tender to the touch.

Suddenly, the bathroom door slammed shut. She froze, fearing her husband's return for a forgotten ID badge, or the pleasure of torturing her. Deep down inside, she knew one day that she'd have to stand and fight the abuse, but not like this. Nude and unarmed, he'd beat her to a pulp.

She yanked the white towel from the curtain rod, whipped it around her body and peeked out, fearing the worst. The strong air gusts from the kitchen window bore the blame. "God," she sighed, "that scared the country crap out of me!"

She set out her outfit for tomorrow; a pink and white concoction appeasing her desire for color, but promising to diminish her every petite curve. Then, she'd go out and finally spend money on something for herself.

THREE

JUNE 22, LATE FRIDAY AFTERNOON

STUCK with an abundance of time and the gravity of a murder heavy on his mind, Darrion determined to make the best of it. He stopped at a quaint luncheonette for a BLT with French fries and a cola. While the fries were good, the sandwich's bread wasn't lightly toasted, as he'd requested. It had a thick coating of mayonnaise on it, also against his wishes, which gave it a pasty flavor. Not that he ate much of it anyway, but the waitress would feel it in the tip.

Afterwards, he walked around the town's pristine promenade, sat down near the Founder's Fountain and admired the town's changes. In 25 years, development had shot up like weeds and exchanged its farm town cloak for concrete trappings. Here, ignoring his true Negro didn't pose an immediate threat, nor did it require adjustment. He'd venture to the white side of town and secure lodging for a few nights with his remaining funds and formulate a game plan.

He meandered in front of a trash can in the park and considered throwing out the notebook, but remembered the ultimate price she'd paid for obtaining it. Though he did not comprehend what she'd been through, he respected her and kept the treasure safe in its place for now.

As he continued milling around downtown, Zyonne unfurled in front of him with a landscape part memory and largely dream. In the corner distance was Wilson's Creek, which meandered two miles in front of the three-square-mile town and Mount Nebo. To the right, several three-story businesses huddled together at the town's edge. Behind him was the criminally-dark industrial district. These old friends stuck in his brain like pleasantly embedded splinters, but other mainstays – structures in the distance and street names tossed about in nearby conversations – felt as if he should remember them, but didn't. He turned around the block toward what looked like a tavern.

With a strut, Charlemagne Evans stamped her high ivory heels into the sidewalk, as if to punctuate importance and confidence into its texture. No wonder men stopped and stared at the blonde oozing bravado. Her presence *demanded it,* like a woman's should.

Unlike other women in the oldest profession, Charlie rarely proposed anything. *Business came to her naturally.* The two or three times she forwarded propositions, her skin invariably broke out in hives: a bad omen that required no interpretation.

From then on, she'd be suggestive to a solicitor perhaps. No commitment. But tonight, reneging was tempting. Four regulars passed and entered the Crooked Elbow Pub without word or glance. The last was a middle-aged, roly-poly joker who repeatedly asked for freebies. Before he propositioned her tonight, instead of telling him where to go and how fast to get there, she'd made up her mind to slaughter the aching emptiness inside of her with him.

When Charlie caught sight of the cheapskate approaching, she perked up, unfastened three buttons on her silken mauve blouse, and shuffled the things in her handbag. As he neared, she tossed her keys onto the ground and bent at the waist to pick them up, pausing long enough for her to have retrieved the set several times. The old boy rounded Charlie and pulled open the door to the bar. "Wait!" Her molasses-thick southern drawl oozed desperation. "John, you mind if I join you for a round?"

He saw through Charlie's feigned smile. "You turn me down four, five times a week. Why the change of heart now?"

"Girl ain't got the right to change her mind?" She acted offended and pressed a hand against his flabby chest. "Can't fault me for that, now can you?"

"Guess not."

"So?" She cuddled up closer. "Whaddya think?"

"No charge. Really?" John's expression flickered light.

"Sure. It's on me tonight, so to speak."

He nuzzled against her perfumed neck. "You think I can scratch your itch tonight?"

"Could think of nothing better." She beamed. "How 'bout it?"

"Scratch it yourself," he shot out venomously.

How dare he refuse me? She slammed the door fast enough to smack him hard in his wide butt, as he entered. He deserved it.

At first, no one would buy it. Now no one – not even *him* – would take it. She convinced herself that his rejection could be coaxed into a "yes," but doing so required far more effort than she was willing to exert. *Better to be alone.* Whatever he'd end up giving her might have been worse.

"Remember this day, Charlie." She moistened her ruby lips and slipped a cigarette between them. "He will never get another chance at you – ever. Every day, for the rest of your life, you will look better and better than you do today and he will regret turning you down."

Though she was raised to believe genteel southern men preferred their women smoke indoors, she continued to do so in full view. After the last puff, Charlie leaned against the wall and hiked up her skirt a half-inch or so to reveal edges of a garter belt. *For men, visual is key,* she thought. She refastened a blouse button. Showing too much meant there was less left underneath. But revealing a little heightened the mystery.

"Say Suga," she cooed at the previously-ignored man standing on the corner. "Got a lil' fire you think you can send my way?"

"Sorry Miss, don't smoke." He smiled pleasantly, oblivious.

"You look like you're lost." Charlie grabbed him lightly on the arm at the elbow and it stiffened like drying concrete.

"Ease up." She let go. "I swear I don't bite unless first asked."

"Nothing personal, I just rather...I don't like to be touched."

Too bad, Charlie thought. She had a knee-buckling weakness for tall men with deep voices. He towered at least a half-foot over her and his baritone oozed from his lips like warm syrup.

"My name is Charlie. And you are...new to Zyonne. Let me guess, a greenhorn tourist, first-timer, never been here before?"

"I was born here, but it's been a while since I've been back."

"Guess my intuition's a lil' rusty then. Well, welcome back."

"I need to get to a boarding house in Greater Zyonne. Do you know of one?"

She leaned close enough that wisps of perfume and strands of bleached hair blowing in the wind tickled his nose. "Do you have any money?" she whispered in his ear. "If so, then you can..."

His eyes bulged. "Listen, Miss, I'm flattered, but..."

"I'm sure you are, but don't bother," she retorted. "Take a taxi to the Fairgrounds, cross the tracks to the Negro side and hook over back up Superior. That Negro lady runs the best boarding house in town and takes everyone. Otherwise, you're looking at a bus to Miss Parsippany's. She's always in your business and salts down the food from what I've heard."

Superior struck a friendly nerve in his selective amnesia. "Where can I phone a cab?"

"Right here," she said, opening the door to the Crooked Elbow.

A gust of cigarette smoke mingled with alcohol greeted them. Inside the modest street-corner dive, a pudgy bartender with matted black hair and short sleeves dried the insides of a drinking mug.

Instantly, the newcomer caught the regulars off-guard. At the far end of the bar, Charlie's rejecter looked up and then quickly buried his eyes downward, aware that the attempt to draw attention had failed. Although she didn't touch the towering gentleman, Charlie shadowed his every move. *No doubt she found a taker, but far quicker than I anticipated.*

"Say, Roger," Charlie cooed. "He needs to use the phone. Fix me a dirty martini while you're at it, will ya?"

"I keep telling you this is a place of business, Charlemagne, not a phone booth." The bartender reached under the bar and produced a beige contraption. "Make it quick."

"Thanks, Roger." Charlie dialed the number. "You're a dream."

She relayed the necessary information in a flash; one passenger, the Crooked Elbow to the Fairgrounds – a complete waste of money he could have spent toward entertaining her for the evening.

"Ten minutes tops," the bombshell said, while sipping a cocktail. "Drink in the meantime? Roger, my gentleman friend here is thirsty."

Darrion lifted a hand in protest. "No, I'm fine. As a matter of fact, I'm going to wait outside. Thank you, Miss, for everything."

Trying not to appear rushed or uncomfortable, he gathered his bags and left Charlie lingering at the bar. The man who Charlie called "John" – whose real name was Larry – puffed his chest out and ordered a beer in victory. Charlie would spend the night alone after all.

Outside, Darrion passed a rock between his shoes for a while. Although his body ran on the warm side, he wanted to beat the setting sun. If things went well, she might offer him a home-cooked meal and firm mattress with pressed sheets. He'd figure things out from there – like how he'd disappear further south or out west.

Right after the number 12 bus left the bus stop, a white taxicab appeared behind it. Without hesitating, Darrion hoisted his luggage into the trunk and squeezed himself into the backseat.

"Got enough room there, Pal?" Hardly concerned with the response, the driver pulled off. Darrion could care. His erstwhile wife would have smacked him on the hand for being so passive, but why raise a fuss over a few inches and so short a drive?

"Drive through the Burroughs," he said slightly more aggressively. "I'm not in a rush."

"Burroughs burned down...what was it, ten, twelve years or so ago? You must not be from around here. Just visiting or something? You're going to Superior anyway, right? Fairgrounds as far as I go."

At the time the Burroughs was constructed on Zyonne's west side in the early 1940's, the town was hatefully segregated into two parts: Greater Zyonne to the whites, and East Zyonne to the Negroes. While the Negro side was larger, its houses were smaller. They were painted a horrid ebony with few windows, black or white doors, and they bore exhaust speckles from industrial plant exhaust blowing downwind. The affluent whites afforded themselves prototype suburban neighborhoods; large windows looking out into the street, plush emerald lawns, blacktop driveways and egg shell white frame or stucco paneling with shiny red or blue front doors.

The train tracks divided the portions into two. But the Burroughs drew the two groups together. Successful blacks cautiously approached the area and were accepted. The whites didn't seem to mind professional Negroes as much, like the pair of Negro brothers with a little resource who had the idea to capitalize on the experimental integration. They opened a business which flourished and was patronized by both races. Others followed with eateries, shops, grocery stores and clothing stores. That area; the rear of the Burroughs, became known as the Fairgrounds. Darrion experienced both as a child. They were places he looked forward to seeing. The way his mother talked about it, he imagined the place was like heaven.

"That used to be the best side of Zyonne," Darrion said. "I went there as a child."

"Not anymore. Condemned buildings, druggie bums, criminals – you name it. Five and Dime's the only thing left. You don't have the cash to get me to drive you there. We're going around. Look back if you want. There's nothing to see."

To the rich and well-off, it was *nothing*. To the have-nots, it became the hope to sing and tell legends about.

As the vehicle approached the Fairgrounds, it rumbled, almost as if it understood its precarious location and gradually increased its speed. In the dark, the gutted buildings, once imposing in structure and stature, now loomed as impressive, abstract-looking skeletons. On Myrtle and Superior, the car braked and Darrion settled the bill.

Exiting in the distance, he spotted a single light in the distance shining through a window on the house's far side.

He approached with caution, but the home grew recognizable as he moved closer. To his left was a wooden see-saw. Beyond that was a pole and tether for a dog and a water spigot with a hanging bucket. Over the years, the house's paint had rubbed off down to the wood. The prostitute directed him to the exact place where he'd spent the first years of his life. And, at eight o'clock at night, either he slept there or on the street. Miss Parsippany's was enough across town that he could not spare the cash for another cab, or make it there on foot at a decent hour.

His first knocks were rapid and tentative. This time of night, unwelcome strangers on this side of town usually met the business end of a firearm. He expected this rather than southern hospitality. While his fair skin bought him advantages and favor in most spots, he neglected them for this moment. *Perhaps the light is only a ruse to make others think that someone is home*? he thought. Smoke from the chimney and the light aroma of baking bread told him different, though. Its owner was home. Whatever the case, he hoped a mattress and clean linen lived there.

Against his better judgment, he obnoxiously clanged the brass knocker against the strike point – so much so that the commotion seemed to echo in the night. "Hello, anyone home? Hello?"

Shuffling feet followed by mumbling soon approached. A chain lock shifted and dropped and the deadbolt turned. "Yes?" A beautiful Negro woman a few shades darker than Darrion who appeared no older than 40 opened the door, a pan caught in her oven mitt. To the hungry traveler propping the screen door open, its contents smelled like cooling heaven.

"Miss, my name is Darrion James and..."

He quickly noticed the sundry facial resemblances between them, as did she. The pan plummeted to the floor and overturned, spilling golden brown Johnny Cake chunks across the hardwood. Before he conjured a response, Kelley James hurriedly stepped through the crumbs and embraced her only child. Though she had not lay eyes on him in some 25 years, his resemblance to his no-count father knifed her in the chest.

Darrion's heart skipped a beat. He dropped his bags, jacket and hat to pry away from the warm embrace – slowly at first, but then firm and sudden. His mother's sobs dampened his shirt on the left breast and her composure soon turned to bitterness. "Thought you ain't never comin' back."

Kelley's appearance and familiar alto restored the memory of his mother in his mind – from flawless sepia skin, elliptical eyes, lengthy lashes, hips native to Negro women, and deep chocolate locks. A few loose gray strands now graced the collar of her lavender and evergreen-flowered dress. Finally releasing him, she scooped up the mess barehanded. "Called my passuh an' told him I felt the Spirit movin' 'bout my son, but he ain't pay me no mind. E'erybody ignores me until I say somethin' gonna happen, then it happen an' they act surprise like I ain't say so jus' 'cause I ain't got much book knowledge." Kelley stood up, pan in hand. "Bet he'll believe it now wit' you starin' me in the face."

Darrion shook his head. Surely, his heart couldn't manufacture a trick this elaborate.

"C'mon in boy. You lettin' bugs in the house. From the looks of it, you ain't plannin' to go nowhere else anyways. You lucky I gotta bed ready wit' fresh sheets an' made up."

He followed Kelley through the foyer into the kitchen. Small familiarities like the dim azure wallpaper and brass chandelier sparked his childhood memories. Others, like the original woodwork and European-style buttresses, fascinated and intrigued him.

"Just fixed some coffee. Got mo' than enuff. Lay them bags down an' I'll get you some."

Darrion complied. A shot of caffeine and sugar may do something for his thought processes muddled by exhaustion. "I could use some after today, thank you."

The two proceeded in silence, alternately between sipping and eyes roaming elsewhere. His cup emptied first, which led him to an uncomfortable crisis; ask for a refill or find another method of avoidance. He fiddled with the glass face of his watch until Kelley, who recently ran dry herself, offered him the last of the pot with a generous slice of freshly-iced lemon pound cake. She then prepared more to drink. Even with purposeful movements, this took little time.

"Sounds like you had yourself quite a trip." The absence of color on Darrion's ring finger caught Kelley's eye. "So, you's married? Must got you a fine wife."

"If you consider 'fine' committing adultery, ruining my reputation, and divorcing me."

Kelley choked at the deadpan description of events. "You two have any..."

His face soured. "No, no, but she wanted them. It wasn't possible." His tone spoke of the impossibility of conception, as if it was physical. Kelley knew otherwise.

"Not having babies 'cause you color struck sound downright selfish, if you ask me."

A tense silence ensued. She placed the dishes in the sink and paused at the staircase at the rear of the kitchen. "Bed is upstairs, second door on the left," she recited, almost on cue. "Towel and washcloth on the bureau. Breakfast at 7:00 a.m. sharp. Minute later and the dog next door gets it. Room and board's $15 for the week. Expects it in the morning, no checks."

Darrion listened to his mother's staggered gait up the creaking stairs until it vanished behind a door he assumed was located down the hall from his. They would speak again soon.

After ascending to the second story himself and sitting for a moment, his exhaustion overtook him to the point he nearly felt faint. He stripped to his boxers and t-shirt, stretched out beneath the cover sheet and shut his eyes.

A rebel beam of auburn sunlight jabbing through the blinds and the aroma of cooked food snapped Darrion awake. His watch read 7:08, but he always set it five minutes fast to give himself a cushion, so he figured she'd just made breakfast. His mother thrived on threats in his early childhood but rarely carried them out. Without bothering to make himself presentable, he rambled downstairs. A nonplussed Kelley laid down her fork to gaze at the half-dressed, wild-looking man with two days worth of stubble, unkempt hair, and a look of earnest expectation.

"Mornin'." Her voice bubbled over with vitality. "How'd you sleep?"

Darrion waved off her greeting to look for the plate she must have set aside, but only drying pots and pans and a scent remained. *Perhaps she put it in the oven?*

"I knows you ain't been raised not to speak when spoken to. 'Good morning,' I say."

"Good morning," he forced out. "Good morning."

"How'd you sleep?"

"Well, thank you. I'm sorry for being rude." His apology was as heartfelt as possible for such an early hour. "I didn't miss breakfast, did I?"

She nodded. "Dog gotta eat, too. An' unlike you, *he* was on time."

"I was *three minutes late. Three minutes.*" His temper bubbled over. "I'm not just some boarder, I'm your *son!* Would it have killed you to put some foil over it and stick it in the oven?"

"*You* comes in here late at night; ain't no telephone call, ain't no explainin', jus' like a boarder." Kelley approached him. "Ain't say but five words since you got here, jus' like a boarder. Far as I'm concerned, a *boarder* – that's all you are. I birth you, but I 'ont knows you, an' until I do, Spot gets it when you *three minutes late.*"

"So," he said, tapping his foot against the tile. "I'd like to eat... Please."

Kelley sighed deeply, as his toothy ear-to-ear grin wore her down. "Fix yourself some coffee while you wait."

Shuffling happily over to the counter, he helped himself to a cup and enough milk and sugar to draw Kelley's attention. "Plain black is too strong," he mentioned. "I like it sweet and mellow."

"'T'ain't meant to be *sweet* an' *mellow*. Might as well jus' lick the suga' bowl."

Darrion's stomach growled on cue. "I'm hungry enough to do it, too."

"Still like eggs sunny?"

"Sunny side up is my favorite, yes," he confirmed.

"Salt poke or bacon? Got 'em both." She opened the refrigerator and started removing items. Darrion used to beg for pork as a child.

"Either or, but I'm partial to bacon this morning."

"'Biscuits and taters?"

"Now you're talking. Can I help?"

"Sure can. Help yourself to that seat and rest until I'm done."

Kelley selected two firewood cuts large enough to cook the food and vanquish the cool mountain chill for a while. After cleansing her hands in the sink, she opened the cedar cupboard and removed the sizable white, porcelain bowl with cryptic gold symbols painted around the lip.

She mixed the biscuit ingredients and transferred them to a wooden board for rolling and kneading. Once the dough had been thoroughly worked, she plucked it out a handful at a time and shaped it into twelve circles on a baking plate greased with lard. Before baking, Kelley pressed her thumb into the heart of each and dabbed margarine into the divot. Next, she rinsed the potatoes, cut and seasoned the slices and cooked them in a skillet on the burner adjacent to a flat pan crowded with thick bacon slabs. When the strips blackened at the edges, she replaced it with the eggs.

"I like to cook," he said, unceremoniously. "I do...*did* the cooking at home, most of it."

"So he *does* talk, after all." Kelley smirked and busied her eyes in the bubbling whites and yellow yokes.

"Eight years. We married right after I graduated college and settled down in the town Jayne's originally from – a cute little duplex apartment with a fireplace."

Kelley fixed his plate: three eggs, five bacon strips, a handful of fried potatoes and four hot biscuits. "Ain't much good I know of came from up north but education an' freedom."

Darrion gave pause at the generous amounts of food and his mother's insights. "You must have thought something good could come of it to ship me off up there."

Kelley stayed mum on the subject and set Darrion's plate before him. "Eat up. I 'on't fix breakfast twice for my health, you know."

"I really don't think I can eat all of this. I hope you didn't waste this much the first time."

"No." Kelley muttered a quick prayer of forgiveness. When Darrion finished and excused himself, she took his original plate, unwrapped its foil, and set it out for the neighbor's dog.

FOUR

SATURDAY MORNING, JUNE 23, 1962

BETTY Lou squirmed a bit entering the integrated Five and Dime. Numerous black faces, even the cheeky baby ones, inspired fear in paler patrons. It wasn't on purpose, though. Negroes more or less kept to themselves and ignored the outsiders. The whites, however, feared for their lives.

For one, Negro brothers Caleb and Joe Callahan owned the wholesale store built a hundred feet inside the western edge of the East Zyonne border. Though they opened the doors to both races, even after the Burroughs' demise, no one knew if the Negroes might turn on the whites. Second, besides the volatile mix and local crime on the building's surrounding streets, the local Klan promised misery to any of their kind patronizing the successful business. This threat kept most whites away, except the poor ones with no recourse – or the bold ones, like Rosalyn Franklin, the first white customer, and Betty Lou, a paycheck from destitute who practically put herself on display.

Sneaking around anywhere in a loud wardrobe with a halting gait was a lousy proposition, so she merely came across as a disabled white woman with no taste in clothing. Brown heads gravitated toward this site, but no one laughed. In a way, Betty Lou had become one of them. She visually examined the foreign skin texture and kinked hair of her observers – not anxiously, but curiously reverential. Inside, she wished a touch might transfer their mystery and transform her into something meaningful.

Just one woman stood between her and the makeup counter.

After a sizing up, the competitor posed no threat. Maybe mulatto, but she'd have to be blended with more than just Negro and white, with skin a degree or two lighter than butterscotch. *Cinnamon Sunshine* better suited those plump lips than *Pink Bubblegum*, the lipstick shade Betty Lou sought and the woman held.

"Excuse me." Betty Lou tapped the wooden storage bunker with chewed down fingernails. "You're gonna get *that* lipstick?"

Joséphine Courtiér jumped. She'd seen this odd woman before and wondered what drove her so scatterbrained. "Pardon?"

From the side, Joséphine's partially-revealed beauty was intimidating. From the front, fully unveiled, it absolutely petrified. Betty Lou admired the opaque garnet and golden butter scarf binding her crinkled ebony mane back into a bun, save a few strands lingering down the temples. Her haunting eyes; perfect taupe walnuts, sent ice shivers into Betty Lou's blood. Even the woman's humble black blouse and ruffled ankle-length wine gown failed to lessen her splendor.

"I asked if you're gonna buy that lipstick right there." Betty Lou smirked, believing she succeeded in her hunt after all. "That lipstick."

"Oh yes, yes I am." Joséphine gripped the tube tighter. *Why does this woman want Cinnamon Sunshine…a makeup color tailored to Negro skin?*

Surprised, Betty Lou backpedaled. *Maybe she wants her lips to look like a minstrel's?* "That's alright," she replied, shoulders sagging. "I'll look for another one. You have a nice day."

"Thanks, Cheri," said Joséphine. "I'm plotting one."

Named after a glamorous Negro jazz chanteuse but nicknamed "Jolene" for short, the one-quarter Lousiana Creole hated looking natural more than her country misnomer's cruel simplicity. With no makeup, she felt naked, but being called "Jolene" caused her to feel every bit the common housewife she believed Mark Williams wanted her, the future Mrs. Williams, to be. Even so, after a hard day's work, he deserved to look at more than a natural-lipped excuse for a real woman.

But at 50 cents, *Cinnamon Sunshine* cost a good 47 cents more than her frayed change purse held. These days, steady, halfway decent paying Negro work came hard, even at the town train station where Mark toiled as a railroad mechanic. The white conductors raved about how he rigged a train together, though they failed to see him paid for the work – even the overtime maintenance he performed last night untangling body parts from the machinery. One hundred dollars every two weeks hardly kept the ceiling from falling in.

Jolene resolved to steal the thing. She closed her palm and faked a coughing fit, then removed a hanky from her handbag with the hand clutching the lipstick and covered the tube with it. After a final hearty cough, she placed both handkerchief and lipstick in her purse.

Beside the makeup bunker a few feet away and still digging for *Pink Bubblegum*, Betty Lou witnessed the entire exchange and wished she'd thought to steal first. Stealing appealed to the ego, much more than begging Jack Miles for chump change every week.

"Stop," said Betty Lou, her wagging finger implicating the shop-lifter. "Stop her!"

Jolene whirled around, eyes wide.

"Stop! She's stealing! Somebody stop her!"

Head bowed, the petty thief advanced, followed by leering eyeballs and lusty whistles. Their imaginations stirred up within Jolene's consciousness, each seedy thought echoing in her mind. "Quit looking at me," she yelled at no one in particular. "Quit saying those things."

Bewildered, Betty Lou lowered her finger. This girl – bent over, hands over ears – had bigger problems than she'd thought.

"*You* de one dat wuz yellin' 'bout somebody stealin'?" Joe Callahan approached in a grease-stained apron wielding a baseball bat. "Well, wunt you?" He pointed at Jolene. "Wuz it, *huh*? If dat crazy gal stealin' *again*, I'll bend her 'cross muh knee and whippuh myself!"

Joe's question raised conflict within Betty Lou. "No, Sir," Betty Lou responded, eyes averted. "Guess I got it wrong."

"Den quit makin' such a ruckus. Cain't you see she ain't right in de head?"

Joe returned to the kitchen. Most folks misinterpreted his and Caleb's intentions in opening the door to whites. The move brought in money. But whites caused grief, same as Negroes.

Little by little, the voices decreased to whispers. Jolene straightened up and bolted for the exit, only to be turned around by a strong calloused grip she assumed belonged to a policeman.

"Hold up." Second generation Police Officer Geary Johnson tethered Jolene in place. "Now, settle down. You ain't goin' nowhere fast."

"Let me go," she said, yanking away. "Let me go. I'm innocent."

Betty Lou melted into a pool from a distance. Jack Miles' newly-separated stud of a best friend got her fires going – from his dirty blonde buzz shave, square, stubble-covered chin and aqua eyes down to raised neck muscles, powerful compact arms and barreled chest.

"Innocent of *what*? I ain't even charge you with nothin'. But, you know what? That's what they all say and I ain't accused you of nary a thing. Keep carryin' on." Something in the officer's voice suggested he delivered on his threats, but Jolene continued jerking just the same. "One ya'll niggers go get ole Joe right quick."

Wide-eyed with terror, no one moved. The worst kept secret in Zyonne was the identity of its Klansmen. Almost all the white civil servants in Black Mountain County had membership.

Betty Lou took it upon herself to slide from her position and fetch Joe. A half minute later, he shuffled out and approached the spot where Geary held Jolene.

"You know this woman?"

Joe eagerly nodded, head bowed. "Knows of 'er, yessuh."

"I ain't ask if you know *of* her, I asked if you *know* her. Answer me right now, hear?"

"Then y-yessuh, I know her suh. I knows 'er," he offered.

"What's her name?" Geary spoke as if Jolene didn't exist.

"Thank 'er name's Jolene, suh."

"*Joséphine*," she managed between gritted teeth.

"Don't sass gal. Ain't nobody ask you. Speak when you spoken to."

Hurl an insult at Jolene and she'd ignore it, except *that one*.

"Looks like Jolene here stole a lipstick, uncle, you know that?"

Joe glared back at Betty Lou. "No suh Boss. Ain't know that, Suh."

"Give it to him," he threatened, "or I'll search you 'til I find it."

Jolene reached into her handbag and produced it. Joe snatched the tube and held it up to her eye level. Betty Lou smiled from behind the makeup counter. It would be hers after all.

"Don't come back her no mo'. You ain't welcome."

"That's it? Don't ya'll want to press charges…have me take her in?"

Still motionless, the crowd of witnesses wished he wouldn't. No telling what deeds this man intended on if Joe said yes.

"Naw, she embarrass. Dat's enuff fuh me. Don't want no mo' trouble, Suh."

Frustrated, Geary loosened his grasp. He *wanted* trouble from the uppity nigger. *Gals like her need etiquette lessons on behavior; the kind of lesson I can teach.*

"C'mon." The officer reapplied a death grip and dragged his prisoner through the store doors. "We're goin' outside."

Away from the intrusive eyes, Jolene grew emboldened. "What do you want from me? Joe let me go, no charges. You heard him."

"Look here. You do what you told when you told to do it. Let's go."

"No."

A heavy, open-handed slap pounded Jolene's face numb. "Speak when you spoken to."

Hands clenched, she turned back and stared Geary down. Besides the power passed down through the bloodline, sharing lineage with a high voodoo priestess held its advantages. In Zyonne, the people lived unaware of anything unrelated to God. In Jolene's Lousiana hometown, no one took these things lightly. Offending a medium's children carried serious, sometimes humiliating and often deadly consequences, so Courtiérs rarely saw a harmful day.

"You are going to let me go."

"What?" Suddenly lightheaded, Geary stumbled a little. Jolene spoke several French phrases fast and softly. With a quick hand motion, she pulled a good luck juju from her handbag. A spell's effect depended on energy flow, but if she were to escape unharmed, it must favor her.

"What's your name?"

In a daze, his body responded with mild tremors. She waved a hand near his glazed-over eyes, testing the delirium. "I'm going to walk away. Any questions?"

There was no response.

Jolene circled behind Geary's back and trotted away, darting between alleyways until she was certain that no one had followed her.

Darrion's body jerked awake. He peeled off his soaked undershirt and pajama pants and circled the full-sized bed barefoot in sky blue boxers. He was trying to erase Violet's visage from his mind's eye, when Kelley suddenly appeared in the doorway wielding a fireplace poker.

"Lawd, you was screamin' somethin' awful. Scared me halfway stupid."

Darrion disappeared behind the closet door and dressed. "I'm sorry."

Kelley set the metal rod against the wall and rested on the bed, waiting until her son emerged wearing blue dungarees and a short-sleeved black V-neck shirt. "Bad dream?"

"You could say that." Darrion leaned against the wall. "I have a lot on my mind."

"Speak on it then, if you wantin' to. I'll listen."

"It's nothing, really," he said, hands on hips.

"*Nothin'* got you screamin' in your sleep like that? You's a lie!" Resolve overwhelmed the disappointment in his mother's heart. "Whatever 'tis, you'd feel better lettin' it out than weighin' yourself down. Believe me, I know a lil' somethin' 'bout that. If you dreamin' 'bout somethin', maybe your mind's tryin' to tell you to talk an' let it out."

"Look, I get it," Darrion said, a lump forming in his throat. "You're trying to help and I appreciate it, but I really don't want to *talk* about it."

His overemphasis on *talk* irked Kelley. "Must be Violet," she wondered aloud.

Alarmed, Darrion leaped to his suitcases and checked their contents, particularly the location of the notebook. "Where did you hear that *name*? Have you been going through my things?"

"No, but I'll 'mind you to watch that tone."

"How did you know about Violet then? Something you felt in the Spirit?" he mocked.

In a swift motion, Kelley slapped him so hard that his face felt as if a man had punched it. After reclaiming the poker, she started past him toward the open door.

"I know you grievin' an' in pain," she said, waving the poker toward him, "but you gonna be in a lot mo' pain if you talk to me out the side of your mouth like that again."

Darrion wet his lips. "I'm sorry for accusing you. But you're right, I..."

"I ain't finished sayin' my peace," she interjected. "You was yellin' 'Violet' in your sleep an' ain't nobody touch your things, but you gots me wonderin' why you came here in the first place after all this time. Fairly sure it ain't have nary a thing to do with your momma."

He confessed. "I was on my way to Beaufort to ask Auntie Martha if I could stay with her for a while, but I got robbed in Virginia."

Kelley stifled her emotional wounds. Her youngest sister died years ago and the family lost the homestead to a vicious flood not long afterward. "So, you thinkin' you stuck here?"

"Or at least until I get up enough to do otherwise." While he thought of it, Darrion counted out 15 dollars from his wallet and handed it over to Kelley.

"You needs another plan." She flipped through the folded bills. "She won't take you in."

Bewildered, Darrion took a double take. "Are you sure? She always liked me."

"She might now mind, but the hole they put her in ain't long enuff to fit you." Kelley snickered. "I see I ain't the only one you ain't keep in touch with. She's been dead ten years. I'm the only James left south of the Mason-Dixon. E'erybody else moved up north."

"Huh." Darrion nudged the raised head of a nail in the floorboard with his shoe's sole.

"What can you do besides insultin' people? Can't you preach? That's somethin'."

His options boiled down to the simple – there were *none*. "I don't know. Even if I did, I don't know where I'd go next or what I would do once I got there."

Kelley backed away. "When you figures it out," she said over her shoulder, "let me know and I'll make a call."

Later that evening close to five o' clock, Darrion reappeared in his mother's kitchen, cleanly-shaven and dressed appropriately for a meal. Hunched over the oven at the time, Kelley straightened up at the sight. "Got yourself a few minutes, if you needs to do somethin'."

"No, Ma'am, not this time." He pulled out the same chair he sat in for breakfast.

"Hmm." Kelley set a steaming casserole dish onto the counter. "You used to sit in that chair right next to the one you in, and dare anyone make you sit elsewhere when company came."

"I remember," he mused. "I think I put jelly on the seat once and Pastor sat in it. I still walk crooked every once in a while from that beating you gave me afterward."

"I ain't beat you like all *that*, but you ain't do it again."

"Whatever happened to Reverend Gordon?"

"Chile, he passed." She fixed Darrion's plate without regard to his preferences. "The one we got, we got him goin' on some 15 years now. We comin' up on revival in a few days. Service start at 6:30, but testimony service start at 6:00."

"Thank you." Again, the portions overwhelmed him, but the meatloaf, mashed potatoes, snap beans, corn on the cob and dinner rolls looked delectable. "Did you feed the dog already?"

Kelley started humming a nondescript tune and turned her back. After spooning out smaller amounts for herself, she joined him at the kitchen table. Darrion blessed the food and ate far quicker and with more voracity than Kelley, who seemed to indiscriminately pick at hers. Before long, all that remained on his plate was a half-eaten corn cob and a chew of a dinner roll.

"So, you been up in that room all day," she said, as he nibbled at the remaining kernels.

He took the bait. "I may need to stay here a little longer than I expected to at first."

"Already knew that," she muttered.

"And I'll need you to work with me on the rent front. I can pay you about one more week."

She nodded. "I figured as much."

"I don't know where I'm supposed to go next, but for right now, it's *here*." Darrion twirled designs in the mashed potato residue with his fork. "You spoke earlier of a phone call?"

"Passuh Whitehead. The revival at the church. Already talk to him. You're preachin' the Monday night service. They'll take up an' offerin' an' that'll help get you goin' a piece."

Darrion resigned himself to the possibility of taking the pulpit once more, as his alternatives presented themselves – there were *none*.

The retelling of the tale awakened the pudgy Polish child inside Geary. "There," he said, anesthetizing himself with the last of his fourth beer. The laughs ranged from mild giggle to the hysterical over the play-by-play commentary afforded by fellow police officer Jasper Gaston. "End of story. Are ya'll happy now?"

"So, I come around the corner and there he is," expounded Gaston, "standing in the middle of the sidewalk and swear if he ain't droolin' like he done seen Rita Hayworth in skivvies. Been that way for five minutes, I s'pose, maybe ten. Folks crowded around him, lookin' at him funny..."

"Wasn't even *five minutes*, wise guy." For the life of him, Geary couldn't find the humor in his blood sugar dropping so dangerously low. "If Betty Lou ain't give me a peppermint and juice, I'd *still* be standin' there. Gaston ain't givin' up food. I believe he'd starve his momma first."

"Peppermint and juice!" Jacob Watson, called "Kludd" by Klan position and the second biggest in stature of the three policemen in attendance, laughed riotously. "Betty Lou to the rescue! You sure that's the *only* thing she gave you, Chief?"

"Alright, boys, you play nice." Bobby Reifer, along with his long-time girlfriend-turned new wife Francine Reifer, or "Frankie," hosted the evening's poker game. As she passed, he smacked her on the behind. She stopped, mussed his blonde hair and kissed him on the lips.

"I don't get it," Geary interjected. "Ya'll known each other since the fifth-grade and act like you just met yesterday. I don't even think Hawk looks at Betty Lou anymore."

"Catch us in another 17 years like them and I might not look at Frankie, either," Reifer joked, drawing healthy laughter from his comrades. His wife crossed her arms.

"Yeah, well, try looking at me in the bedroom from the couch tonight."

When Frankie left the room, Reifer contemplated following her, but three months into their marriage and his best friends had already penned him as henpecked.

"Fold." He tossed the cards back at Kludd, who'd dealt.

"So Cykes, cards on a Saturday night? Figured you wouldn't want to give me your money again this week."

"We haven't done squat in a while, Jake, that's why. We need to do something *tonight*. That pretty nigger gal...it's time she learned herself some manners."

FIVE

SATURDAY NIGHT, JUNE 23, 1962

ACCORDING to Courtiér legend, someone in the bloodline was marked for death. Years ago, a witch doctor cursed Jolene's grandmother for jilting him. Ever since, it manifested with each distressed birth. Fourteen years ago, Jolene's distant cousin Dianna barely survived birthing triplets. Less than a day later, three relatives dropped dead of a massive stroke, heart attack and brain aneurysm.

Just today, Jolene's older sister Anna ended a three-day long labor. The boy, endowed with his mother's naturally crabby disposition, positioned himself rear first. Anna's high yellow husband, unaware he'd married into a family with such a powerful pox on it, ordered the flustered doctor to cut open Anna's stomach and pry the little demon out. Likewise, the approaching death to even the scales figured to be protracted and bloody.

It'd been many hours since the saints had delivered her from harm, but voodoo gods' emotions flipped from divine favor to insatiable wrath on a dime, regardless whether their worshippers were faithful or not. This, along with her sister's Caesarean section, perturbed Jolene. All day, she dressed in the right colors and spoke blessings when passing the statuette she hid when Mark came home. *Who does death intend to claim?*

Clad in a faded aqua nightgown with just underclothes beneath it, Jolene opened the evening *Zyonne Herald*, the sole luxury Mark afforded himself, and skimmed the obituaries, particularly that of a "Corinne Violet October." Tomorrow morning, she'd phone New Orleans and clear up whether or not there had been a death. No Courtiérs lived in Zyonne besides Jolene. *At least Mark's safe.*

"Evenin', Baby." An unexpected peck pressed against her lips.

Jolene yanked him by the dingy white tank top and prolonged the kiss. "*That's* 'good evening.' How'd you nap?"

The thick-shouldered chocolate man in striped boxer shorts winked. Indeed, he'd slept well. Jolene saw to his fatigue personally. "Now you know how I napped, woman, why you askin' me dumb questions?"

"Don't know. I guess I just don't be thinkin' sometimes, is all."

Puzzled, a thought struck him. "You thinkin' 'bout Anna and that mulehead chile comin' out backwards? You fixin' to die?"

Jolene teared up. "You don't understand, Mark. My cousin..."

"...had three babies and then three of your people died that day. Understand just fine, but ever think the Good Lord just called them home...that it was a *fluke?*"

"Families ain't have *flukes* for 50 years," she cried. "The family Bible got a death for every birth on the same day. I don't care what you say. *That ain't no fluke!*"

Mark kept silent over the irony of pagans recording deaths in a Christian text. "Sorry, Jo." He crossed his arms over her shoulders from behind and rested his chin on her head. "I know we fuss all the time 'cuz we different."

Jolene clutched his forearms and squeezed. "It's alright."

"Got sumthin' to tell you. Wanted to surprise you, but I ain't gotta shift 'til mornin', so I'm headin' back to bed. Think you maybe wanna help me nap?"

She curled her lips into a half-smile, pretending to feel better, and followed him into the bedroom. By the time she dragged to the top of the stairs, exhaustion swept over her. It had done the same to Mark. She heard him snoring minutes later clear down the hallway. Though he'd just awakened, he worked so hard he slept as if each time he laid down was his last. Jolene settled next to him and sprawled across his midsection, the fingers on her right hand dawdling in curled black hair tufts sprouting from his chest.

He awoke and inhaled. "Tickles."

"Sorry," she half apologized.

He grabbed her hand, kissed it, and set it back in place. He then repositioned his arm behind her back.

"Love you." Jolene adored how he locked her close in his arms.

"Me too." He pulled her close until her body met his posture. Somewhere between their rhythmic heart thumping and staggered breathing, the two fell asleep; Mark on his back and Jolene under his arm and draped over his body.

Later during the night, Jolene's heart quickened for no apparent reason. She squeezed from under Mark's heavy arm and sat up, listening. A crisp rustle of leaves and a series of *thunks* and *plops* ensued. Metal hammered against wood, liquid splashing and a *whoosh*! "Mark?"

Glass shattered. A hard, heavy object tumbled along the unstained wooden floor in the next room. Drunken angry shouts reached through the jagged windows and bent Jolene's ear. Several pokes to the gut stirred Mark, but he rolled over, growling. "Go back to sleep," he slurred. "Can't be snorin' that loud."

"Mark!" Her gentle whispers turned into desperate pleas, his slow responses increasing her anxiety. "Mark! Get up! Mark!"

"What? Huh?"

"Forget it." Jolene rolled out from her side of the bed, donned a tattered robe and scampered barefoot to the living room, almost tripping in the darkness. She smacked her toes against an unfamiliar object, cursed and bent to pick it up. It was a brick with a note tied to it. She strained to read its message in the faint moonlight shining through the house. *THIEF.*

Undaunted, Jolene approached the front window.

Mark opened his eyes. Even in slumber, where his concept of time unraveled, he knew his fianceé had left the bed and for some reason was taking way too long. "Baby?" He called again, louder this time. There was no answer. "Joséphine!" His shouting traveled throughout the small home.

He leaped to his feet and snatched the shotgun and ammunition from the broom closet. Whoever or whatever detained her, he intended to pump it full of shells and ask questions later. Mark treaded cautiously, loaded and cocked the shotgun. The broken glass crushed into powder beneath his calloused feet and the debris piercing his soles didn't hurt. "Who's there? What do you want?"

The closer he came, the more Jolene's trembling showed. He wished she'd duck down, slide over – anything – *just move away from the window!*

"Jo, move," he whispered. "Move!"

She heard him, but didn't listen. Any movement might incite them to strike, although that seemed their intent regardless.

Mark cracked the front door ajar and pulled his wife-to-be to the side. The burning crucifix planted four yards from the front porch took the chilled edge off the dusk air. Ten Klansmen in plain clothes and white sacks for masks surrounded this abomination in a half circle, their leader dangling a noose in his hands. It was the answer to both of Mark's questions.

"C'mon out. You or her...ain't make us no mind."

"You listen!" Mark's grip cut Jolene's circulation off. "Get dressed. Take the piece in the nightstand. It's got *two bullets*. Wait 'til they get real close and aim for their heads."

Jolene blinked, as if he spoke gibberish through the corner of his mouth.

"You hear, Joséphine?"

Somehow, he reached her. "No! Mark, I'm *not* leaving you!"

"You ain't gotta choice! Go!" He unhanded her. "Do it."

All of her brain's instincts screamed protest, but she nodded and did as he'd directed. The dungarees and blouse were both dirty but wearable. She slipped them on.

In the other room, Mark weighed his declining options. Ten white men, eight rounds, simple math. The ripe cherry pickup truck canceled out the decision to run and their firearms eliminated fighting fair. Plus, reason abandoned those living on basic instinct. He forced his mind down to that level. Cornered animals did one thing. He trained the barrel at a target and blasted.

Jolene's fumbling fingers stopped below her blouse collar button.

Pump. Another shell felled one more hood. *Two down.* Mark rolled away from the window, reloaded and faced the window again.

Frantic, she retrieved the revolver, popped the chamber and positioned it so a trigger pull would release one then the other.

Three blasts. Now four. Then retaliation before he could move. Mark dropped to a knee, bleeding profusely from the chest and neck.

Certain that her rescuer had already escaped, Jolene tucked the gun in the waistband of her dungarees and waited. Too much movement right away might attract more gunfire.

A last bullet ripped through the window curtain and shattered the hanging picture at the space between Mark and Jolene's smiling faces.

Silence.

Someone entered through the front door. She knew by the creaky hinge that Mark said he'd oil but never got around to. Footsteps clomped, then another set and some more. There were too many to count. A heavy weight dragged along the floor.

Is it safe to move? No way to tell. They likely spent all of their ammunition firing into an empty house. Still, running was risky. She waited until the thuds dissipated and then fearfully opened the door.

A swift blow floored her. Two Klansmen skulked in her direction; the one who struck Jolene was thicker than the other. "You right, Cykes," said the latter, unzipping his pants. "Neva seen a pretty nigga gal like this one befo'."

Too afraid to scream, Jolene whimpered like an injured animal fearing abuse. The smaller Klansmen clawed her blouse open and panted breath heavy on whiskey over her lips. Disgusted, she spit in his face. Too drunk to be offended, he laughed and returned the favor while undoing her dungarees and sliding them down her hips, which dropped the revolver into her waiting hand.

"Devlin, watch out!"

He turned around and Jolene seized the opportunity by kicking him in the exposed crotch. Devlin whinnied and fell backwards, creating enough room to raise the gun and fire at point blank range. She took aim and fired again. The second shot grazed Geary's head. He clutched his ear and backhanded Jolene flush on the jaw, sending her into a tailspin. Through blurred peripheral vision, she witnessed him reach under the mask and finger the blown-off skin.

A mad dash for the door earned another strike. This time, she received a heavy boot to the ribs as she crawled. Paralyzing pain jolted up along her left side, but Jolene continued kicking, clawing, scratching at her attacker until he fired his revolver. The bullet shattered the Florida water bottle she used for protection from danger. Jolene held her ringing head with one hand and her ribs with the other.

"That's right, gal," he said, undressing her. He'd have revenge after all. "Do what you told to do when you told to do it."

Jolene removed the mask and struck the face with a fist before she recognized it. Geary shook off the mild sting and his retribution jarred loose a couple of her bottom teeth. Head still ringing from the blow and gun blast, she fell limp underneath a smothering blackness. When things stilled a little, he forced his will and she screamed with each stab. A startled Geary stroked Jolene's hairline with his pistol barrel.

"Speak when you spoken to, remember?" A short time later, he pushed her away, donned his hood, lifted the window and exited. Jolene curled into the fetal position, shaking and hyperventilating. *Where is Mark? Why didn't he come save me? He promised to protect me.*

The night smelled of overcooked fruit and sweaty flesh. And Jolene, once peaceful after a night with Mark, feared moving. Every muscle and bone she owned felt torn apart or broken. Her throat burned and her mouth tasted like a cotton field in summer heat. Mark couldn't help her, so she would have to help him. She forced the numb limbs to raise a white dress with a blue orchid pattern overhead and encouraged the dead fingers to pull it down. She placed slippers on the wrong feet and stumbled outside, bleeding from the mouth and down the legs.

Fifty yards away, the pickup idled in the flaming trees. Mark couldn't stand on his own, so they propped him up with a noose dangling under his chin.

"No!" Jolene's voice failed to produce sound. "Mark!"

The truck's driver urged the vehicle forward a bit, but not enough for its cargo to hang.

"Keep going," they yelled, calling him all sorts of names.

He responded by pumping the gas a little too hard. Mark slid from the bed and the drop violently snapped his neck, making the Klansmen angrier since he hadn't suffered.

Even at that distance, she recognized Geary as the one showering the body liberally with clear liquid from a can. Jolene stumbled forward and fell face first. They laughed, not at her, but the strange fruit doused in gasoline. She clawed the dirt and inched herself forward, using the dead man as motivation.

"Alright, boys." Geary clamped a cigar in his jaws with matchbook in hand. "Time to put this one to bed." He lit the stogie, puffed four times, and held the cherry to Mark's pant leg just above the limp feet. While the flames consumed the body, the men dragged their dead, including Devlin, into the truck along with any condemning evidence.

Acrid clouds of smoke hung in the night sky above the scorched trees and choked the brightness out of the twinkling stars. The group piled into the truck as best it could and pulled away, leaving a smoking reminder to the Creole and other Negroes who dared disrespect a good, Christian police officer.

"Gaston!" Geary pointed in the distance among hoots and hollers. "Over there!"

Gaston grinned. So rarely did the Grand Cyclops of the Zyonne's local Klavern request something important of him. He clutched the wheel and pushed the engine toward the muddied mass lying prostrate a couple feet from the house.

"Gimme an arm!" A rifle jumped into Geary's hand. He aimed for Jolene's motionless head.

"Hey! I know you hear me, gal! Look at me!" Geary fired about two feet to her left, but Jolene didn't move. Another shot unloaded, much closer to her body, splattering leaves and grass. She remained unmoved. Frustrated, he cursed and aimed for her head. "Better not tell," he yelled, "else I'll be back and do you *worse*."

The threat fell on deaf ears. Without Mark, he might as well.

"Go!" Geary pounded the cab roof with the gun's butt.

Jolene's sullied head lifted with the truck's departure. She crawled over to the first apple tree Mark had planted years ago, the one tree the murderers didn't burn, and used it to prop herself up.

"Cykes, look!" One motioned to the ragged mess, now standing.

Geary scowled. "Gaston, pull around!"

Something snapped inside Jolene when the pickup did a U-turn.

The rapist aimed from the truck's cab roof and she stretched a halting hand toward him, unsure what she could do, but determined not to die shot like a rabid dog. Spontaneous fire burst from the packed bed. About half the living Klansmen jumped from the speeding truck afire, screaming and struggling to put it out while the others tried to snuff out the blaze.

Geary screamed. "Stop the truck now!"

Without weighing the consequences, Gaston mashed the brake, sending the swerving truck into a dizzying spin. It overturned and the kerosene spilled, setting off a small blast.

And she watched it take place. The Klansmen flapped around like wounded white doves desperate to take flight. Their automobile detonated into a yellowish-orange gulf, leaped 20 feet into the air and dropped.

Jolene pounded the dirt with her fists and screamed from inside, where it could be heard.

"Lord 'ave mercy!"

The sudden commotion woke Kelley. It wasn't the explosion. She barely heard that. It was her son stumbling around in the dark. Shoes clapping on the floor, toes stubbing against furniture, muffled cries of pain – – she wished the hardheaded mule would find the light switch. No doubt, he'd intended to go investigate.

"Be safe," she said, as her son shuffled outside.

Darrion used the momentum from the hill to push his stride. By the time he reached the street corner and hustled another block in the fire's direction, a dark Negro emerged from the shadows and bumped into him. "You heard what happened, Boss?"

Boss? Darrion used the last of his bleaching cream a day ago. "No. I'm going to look."

"Me, too. Name's Whitehead. You?"

"We should keep going. They probably need help."

The two jogged in relative silence. Darrion's feet smarted, but the cushioning in his tennis shoes and insatiable curiosity helped drive him.

Whitehead looked over at his partner, expecting an introduction. He didn't push the issue. Aligning himself with a white man could keep him safe, if the crowd was hostile. "Dang, look at that!"

From a distance, the orchard looked like flaming scarecrows with wild orange straw hair. To its right, a large fiery lump burned near mounds of humanity hunched over in some areas, writhing in others and screaming. Nearby, at the base of an unmolested apple tree, laid what Whitehead assumed was a Negro woman on her face.

"Oh, God," Whitehead said, shaking. He and Darrion rushed to her aid. Darrion turned Jolene over and assessed the damage. Busted lip, bruised cheek, scratches along the face...torn skin, missing hair...blood below the waist. He brushed away the mud from her face and let the back of her head rest against his hand.

"What've they done to her?"

Darrion looked up and hesitated. "She's been badly beaten."

"That ain't all, is it?"

"No. She needs help. Now."

Jolene's eyes bulged open and she gasped, clutching desperately to Darrion's arm. She cried out her fiancé's name in a hoarse screech. Whitehead jumped back and placed a hand on his heart. The girl looked half-crazy and her nails drew blood from Darrion's bicep.

"Sweet Jesus, have mercy on that heathen gal," Whitehead whispered.

"Go get help, Whitehead. Quick! I'll stay with her."

Whitehead tottered away in the opposite direction. Even if the stranger's intentions proved less than honorable, he could do no more to her than what had already been done. If left alone, she'd accomplish death by herself anyway.

Darrion rested his palm across Jolene's feverish forehead, looking around for anything to keep the night chill off her body. Finding just himself, he cradled her close to his chest and rocked until Whitehead returned with a woman twice his robust size.

"This here's 'Mamey' Davenport," he explained, out-of-breath. "She lives next to Jolene...and she raised a couple younguns, too."

Darrion looked up and then down.

"I gotcha." Mamey kneeled down and scooped Jolene up in her arms. After shifting her girth, she stood with a grunt. "Don't worry 'bout me. This chile ain't weigh that much wet."

The caravan of Darrion, Whitehead, and Mamey traveled with an unconscious Jolene back to Jolene's home.

"Worked out in the fields with my daddy sharecroppin'," Mamey testified, stopping to shift Jolene every ten steps or so. "Usedta carry tobacco, cotton, lumber. He ain't have no boy, so he made one outta me. This chile ain't no more than hundred pounds, plus 20 or so."

"Why don't *I* carry her Mamey?"

She shot Darrion a wary look. "That's a'ight. I got her. We almost there anyhow and I gotta wash and dress her and you ain't-doin'-that, is you? You volunteerin' for *that?*"

Whitehead snickered at Mamey's protective mother hen mentality. "He ain't gonna bite her, Freida. He's just tryin' to help out."

"Kind or not, Passuh, if you asks me, looks like his kind done helped out enough."

Darrion almost spoke up to correct her, but bit his tongue. "Anything else I can do?"

"Thanks, Boss," said Whitehead. "Mamey and I'll see her home."

Darrion stopped and waited until the trio entered the house from the back and the door slammed shut behind them. He then turned his attention to the recovery effort near the wreckage. About 20 yards away, a simmering chassis piece had welded itself to a victim's arm. Still with a cloth hood over his face, the man reached his free hand for Darrion.

"Help...me. Help me!"

As Darrion approached, the metal reignited and completely lit the man on fire. The flames seemed to rise, as he grew closer, consuming the live man within seconds. The extraordinary fire perked up wherever he set foot after that, even sparking in spots where it never burned, but not touching him. When he came too close, the flame retreated unless he approached someone, in which case it consumed its human kindling.

Gaston grunted and pulled. If he leaned back with all 295 pounds, he'd either free Geary from under the flaming capsized bed or tear the man's shoulder loose from its housing. Instead, he treaded foot-by-foot backwards, despite his own pain and the blood-curdling yells. The outside of Gaston's left arm was a bubbling bloody steak from the wrist up to the bicep. "Quit yellin', will ya? You sound like a little... girl!"

Geary cursed. "Get me out!"

"On three, move forward as much as you can. One...two...three."

Gaston shifted his leverage to pulling, while Geary did whatever possible. Halfway through the effort, Geary screamed and Gaston felt the unusual give in his pal's dislocated shoulder. Another pull would do it. He lumbered over the Grand Cyclops' midsection and dragged him along by the dungaree belt until his body cleared the wreckage and debris.

Gaston bent over and panted. "Geary?"

SIX

SUNDAY EVENING, JUNE 24, 1962

O**VERCAST** skies and faint mist cast a melancholy pall over the quarter-acre or so of scorched grass and metal wreckage. By late afternoon, all major vestiges of the damage were cleared, save the charred trees, floating flecks of wooden ash and the aroma of kerosene. No witnesses came forth, though throngs of the curious visited the scene all day like tourists, skulking the fringes of the blocked off areas and snapping photographs at the cleanup efforts.

Those involved also stayed mum, including Darrion, who lay in bed the balance of the day, only rising when necessary to use the restroom. Kelley left him alone, except to briefly knock at breakfast time and again for a late lunch when she'd returned from church. Both times, he failed to answer. Instead, he lazily traced the brown water stain on the ceiling with his eyes, intermittently dozing in and out of a light sleep. He briefly wondered how the argument between him and his associate, who believed God predestined everything, might go. The awkward relationship between him and the woman who gave him life entered his mind. He wondered how, or if, the two may ever truly connect. Violet and her mysterious notebook then crossed his thoughts. It remained in his blazer hanging up in the closet. *What should I do with it?*

He thought of Jayne's reluctance to answer late-hour phone calls. *Had she reconciled with Ben? Or did Daniel prohibit her from picking up?* His heart gradually ached with loneliness and for the first time in a while, Darrion desired to medicate his emotional wounds. But state law prohibited the sale of liquor on the Sabbath. Even the seedy Crooked Elbow would not serve him. He mused about the platonic company of another woman, but even if he knew of a woman, where could he spend time with the opposite sex with such little cash? *Certainly not my mother's house!*

Darrion descended the winding staircase with eyes desperate on using the telephone in the parlor, while Kelley got dressed for evening service. Determined not to communicate the current state of affairs through his tone, he set his finger on the rotary, dialed the operator and asked for the proper exchange, hanging up only when Kelly appeared before the call connected.

"Don't mind me none." She straightened her audacious sky blue hat. "Call's included in the rent. Not too many outta state ones, though, if that's what you fixin' to do."

He sighed. "I don't know what I'm doing calling her after all she's put me through."

"Ain't been gone but two days, so 'tain't exactly detective work. You miss her, *phone her.* Jus' do me a favor an' stay 'round 'til I get back, if you leavin'."

He gave his mother a tender look. "I wouldn't."

Kelley huffed. "Don't say what you *won't* do. Say what you *never* done. But if you change your mind 'bout revival service, address is on the countertop. The word Passuh's gonna bring...sho' gonna be somthin' to see an' you need the company. Dinner's warmin' in the oven."

"I don't get it. Something terrible happens in Zyonne and Negroes have *revival?*"

She tucked a large Bible underneath her armpit. "What you want us to do, *riot?* Tried that years ago, an' you see how the Burroughs turnt out. The law don't pay us no mind!"

"March then. Have a sit-in or protest. Do something other than rocking, moaning and praying in a pew! That doesn't seem to do much, either."

Kelley moved in closer with mannerisms more threatening than if she'd rushed him directly. "Look at *you*," she said, scanning him up and down. "Been Negro *two days* in all your adult life an' tellin' me how we oughta do things. All you lost is a *job*...ain't been beaten, chased by dogs, nothin'. *My* prayin' and moanin' kept you alive many a night, whether you knows it or not."

Darrion made motions to protest but his mouth wouldn't form intelligible words.

"Seems the more you talk," said Kelley en route to the front door, "the less I likes you."

For a small town flush with gossip, detailed reports of the explosion took longer than usual to reach the Everhams. At the news, Jack Miles paused in mid-meal ritual. "Geary," he said, food particles dropping from his mouth. "How bad is he?"

At the name, Betty Lou dropped the coffee pot onto the checkered black-and-white linoleum. If Jack Miles hadn't felt guilty last night for leaving Betty Lou alone, he would have been with Geary and the others.

"What?" His eyes bulged. "That's a lie."

Betty Lou examined his face for responses, while absent-mindedly cleaning up the glass.

Jack Miles waved his hand. "He's in General, right? I.C.U., Room 216. No visitors? They'll let me through, *trust me*." He hung up and dialed a number.

"What happened, Jack? Who you calling now?"

He ignored her. "Fred, I need to get off tonight." A trickle of humanity dripped in him. "Fred, please...yeah, I know, but we're like family. They'll let me...look, I'll do a mid-morning swing on top of my double. Give me a few hours so I can go..."

There was a pause. He dropped the phone on the hook. Humanity disappeared. Jack Miles chugged his coffee and swiped his hairy forearm across his lips. "Gotta go," he sniffled. "See ya."

"Bye." Betty Lou moved to touch his hand, but he stormed out before she could detect more vulnerability. She often wondered if emotion existed beneath the tattooed exterior.

Watching him drive away brought sadness. He did it the same way every day, around the trail divot, into the standing water pool, over the burrow of an elusive groundhog he promised to kill, then onto the street. A routine: like the eggs, toast and tepid coffee he chased them with, like getting up at 7:15, turning off the Motown by 7:20, and limping into the kitchen by 7:25. She'd fix breakfast by 7:30, watching him eat and leave by 7:40 and get doped up at 7:50.

Betty Lou showered, never bathed, and then selected an outfit from the closet flush with pink and white frilled patterned wares down to the intimates. She ate one customary meal a day, if that, lunch more often than not; a sandwich on white bread, glass of milk and a pastry or cookie. Radio until 12:00, television until 3:00, and cleaning the kitchen and bedroom next: the two rooms Jack Miles cared about and showed the most rampant disrespect for. After that, she cooked dinner — a simple meal twice every two weeks, which is about how often he ate at home. *Nothing, not even a bad news phone call interfered much.* Betty pondered these things while counting the 45 paces she limped from the porch to the bedroom for no other reason than it was 6:30 and she needed a change.

Mamey ran warm bath water, set the silent girl inside the bathtub and washed off the soil and blood. Jolene blinked when the washcloth touched a tender spot and every once in a while a renegade tear broke free and mingled with the water, which seemed to heat up the longer she sat in it. She patted off the poor thing, dressed her in the one clean nightgown she'd found and lay in the bed with her – taking up most of its space. She extended her meat hooks for arms around Jolene and tried to bring her soul back from wherever it had gone.

Now evening, Jolene drowned in her fond memories. Every February, Mark slaved away at double shifts for weeks to earn enough to buy his beloved a birthday present. At the first sign of the summer harvest, she'd pluck the best ripe apples and he'd can them, the one domestic skill he possessed. In early June, they went to the Zyonne Fair and splurged on pop and penny candy. They'd planned to go but did not make it this year. Christmas meant eggnog, a present and kisses under wild berries passing for mistletoe. Whatever the occasion, they were together. Jolene wailed his name over and over from her belly. "Mark!"

Mamey stirred from a heavy slumber. "Calm down, gal. It's alright."

"Mark!" She shed the meat hooks and crept to the floor. "Why?"

To a widow who endured miscarriages and helped deliver still-borns, human pain and discomfort were old friends. Mamey knew no amount of hugging, kissing, praying or words could salve the pain or silence Jolene, nor should it. This almost-widow had to grieve it out.

"Why?"

"Call on His name, honey." Mamey knelt beside her.

"Mark! Come back! I need you," she wept. "I need you so bad!"

"Jesus, help her, Lord."

The name bore a hole through Jolene. If Jesus was all Mark claimed, savior, healer, and protector, then *He* should have done something when *He* had the chance.

"Shut up," she said indignantly, her lips curled and eyes squinted fierce. "Shut up! Stop saying that name, *witch*." Without Mark, who needed *Jesus*? He never did anything, except function as the axis for her husband's prayers and receive a tenth from the nothing they had, along with all the credit when something finally went right in their lives. *But where is Jesus now?* He was on the wall, looking holy and white, praying with eyes lifted toward the sky – – like always. White folks didn't help Negroes do anything but stick their heads through slipknots.

Deep in prayer and tarrying, Mamey kept chanting. Jolene lunged, clasped her hands around the thick neck and squeezed all the "help me Jesus" out. Mamey's eyes widened and her head thrashed around in panic. Heavy-handed by nature, she chopped at Jolene's forearms with all her might, but to no avail. The women continued struggling until one of Mamey's powerful mitts pried Jolene's hand away, then the other.

She reared back with balled-up fists until Jolene's breathing slowed and her anger subsided. She stood, one massive foot at a time, and tottered around the bed on the way out, not even casting a glance in Jolene's direction.

"Got some...daggone nerve," she coughed, "Creole heathen."

Shortly after her comforter left, Jolene gathered her wits. Mark was dead and she'd been violated. She'd attacked her mother figure without a clue as to why, never mind the inferno in her gut when Mamey said *that name*.

Sweaty again, she dragged herself toward the bathroom and stopped at the hanging picture of white Jesus, which had slipped from its nail and fallen to the floor. Dismissing it, she continued dragging toward the commode, her reddened eyes dribbling wetness. A slight stabbing flared around her kidneys. She shifted positions on the seat for relief and it worsened.

Someone knocked at the front door. She grunted, muffling the sound with her hands, but to no avail. The fist tapped harder, then pounded, and its owner joined in a chorus calling out for a response. "Open up, it's the police!" The officer mispronounced her surname several times. "I know you're in there. Answer the door."

Maybe Mamey was right and she was a "Creole heathen," but Creole heathens needed peace and quiet, too. Pain made for a strong lesson in patience. She sat back and bore the throbbing, fixating on the draft wafting through the bullet holes in the wood until the ruckus stopped. Even the nosy suffered for only so long, it seemed.

After washing her hands, she fell back into her bed, burying her face into a feather pillow. For a moment, she hoped for sleep without a nightmare. Rest came in half-hour spurts, from which she'd awaken each time, terror stricken and damp. Mark had gone to whatever place people went when they died. Jolene had her suspicions about eternity, but believed his soul did live on in a good place, where peace, joy and happiness existed. She'd do whatever it took to go to that same place and meet him.

Higher Ground Baptist, the largest congregation on Zyonne's Negro side, filled up quickly during revival. Reverend Whitehead gave explicit instructions for the saints not to save seats, but they still set Bibles on the pews and stared down anyone who dared move them. The overflow packed into the back of the aisles and lined the walls.

When Kelley arrived, testimony service was ongoing and the sanctuary still had plenty of room. She placed a large Bible onto the pew behind the mother's row and managed to keep the space clear for a half-hour into service when a finely-dressed and nervous Darrion showed up.

"Glad you came," she spoke in a voice loud enough to hear over the music.

"It turns out the ability to insult people is hereditary," he chuckled. "I got the message."

"Good. You phone Jayne?"

Darrion pretended not to hear the question, still unsure whether he should be there.

Swaying to the call and response intrigued him. Southern Baptists were much different from holy white people. Stomping, clapping and tambourines acted as instruments. Their worship relied on a heavy diet of songs familiar to the congregation rather than book hymns.

In the middle of Reverend Whitehead's sermon about God's vengeance on murderers, Darrion's thoughts meandered back to the fire and its nature. Where he moved, it had moved. Where he went, it followed. The inferno moved as if it were being *controlled*.

"And God cursed Cain for murdering his brother," proclaimed Whitehead mid-breath, "and the Bible says the murderer shall be put to death!"

Behind flapping white fans were nods, "uh huhs" and "Amens."

"The avenger a blood...will put the murderer to death!"

"*Well*," came a response.

"Who, uh...is the avenger, uh...a blood?"

The masses remained silent through the dramatic pause.

"Je-sus!"

Mamey rocked in the pew to his far left. *No Jolene.* She was resting. When the calamity died down, Darrion figured to pay a visit just to check up on her. *Maybe tonight.*

Before he realized it, Whitehead had concluded his sermon, opened his arms and announced that "the doors of the church" were open. The 15-member female choir sang, "Blessed Assurance" during the altar call and the congregation rose, still fanning the humid air.

"You can still come. Come to Jesus right now."

Would Christ avenge the wronged before judgment day? Whitehead's sermon ultimately left that impression. Darrion disagreed. In the Old Testament, vengeance was quick and final. But in post-resurrection, God's mercy showed to all. The Father *could* pour His wrath out on those men, but He didn't guarantee it at an appointed time. Whitehead should not have played on their hopes, especially making a point of it before the offering plate was passed around.

After service, Whitehead approached Darrion and Kelley. "So, this is the son you've been talking about, Mother Kelley? Didn't notice at first, but I see the favor in your faces now. Was a mighty nice thing you did for Jolene that other night, son."

Darrion humbly bowed.

"This here my boy, *Darrion*," Kelley announced with pride, "He's stayin' wit' me at the house. He's a man of God, too."

"Really? You have a church?"

"Not anymore."

"You went to school then, huh? Fancy colleges up north acceptin' Negroes, I guess, high yeller ones at least?" Reverend Whitehead laid a powerful mitt on Darrion's neck. "Mother Kelley tells me you think something wrong with all us Negro folk gatherin' together for revival, clappin' and carryin' on like this."

Darrion cleared his throat. "A Negro man hangs and burns in his own orchard in front of his fianceé. The authorities do nothing and while we're in revival, *they're* still out there."

Kelley eyeballed him.

"Now, what would *you* have us do, *brother*? The police are for them Klan boys, so is the law. The mayor of Black Mountain County is a sheet-head, too."

"From the days of John the Baptist until now, the kingdom of heaven suffereth violence and men of violence take it by force."

Kelley feigned meditation on the statement.

"Saint Matthews, Chapter Eleven, verse twelve. So, you say *violence* is the answer?"

"Christ appointed twelve men as disciples. No one was closer to Jesus. Yet none of these men used a sword, spear or physical violence to advance the kingdom, but they did so by *force*.

"The Messiah's reign, the kingdom of Heaven, is a place where sin cannot be. If sin itself is to be done away with, the unrepentant sinner, *the old creation*, must also be done away with. In order for this to occur, the kingdom must advance *forcefully*. Satan will not leave willingly.

"*Violent* advance starts with *forceful* men and women of God. We have to claim what God wants for us by *force* – freedom and the ability to be safe again. We don't have to use violence to get it, but we also shouldn't have to die violent deaths, either."

Kelley patted a Bible against her chest. "Told you he can preach."

"Yes, he can," Whitehead admitted. "And he will – *tomorrow night*. I need a rest."

"Wait, Reverend…I'm not prepared."

Whitehead stroked his clean chubby chin. "You said we gotta be forceful, so slap a couple scriptures around what you just said and tell us *how*. Be here at six o'clock sharp. Vestments, if you got 'em. We'll expect you then."

Kelley squeezed Darrion's elbow joint, as they filed out. "What you thinkin' bout?"

Darrion kicked a stone on the gravel road. "I'm thinking about how you just set me up."

"Aw, hush. You'll be jus' fine. Jus' fine."

"Can I meet you back at the house? Will you be alright going home by yourself?"

"I been alright 20 some years by myself, ain't I? Where you goin' this late anyway?"

"Get some air, that's all."

"Don't be late. I mean it."

At the corner, Darrion hooked a left and continued until no one from the church could distinguish him from anyone else on the street. He then jaunted across a backyard and turned toward Jolene's.

"Excuse me, Mother Kelley, who was *that* you were talking to?" The accent identified the speaker to Kelley even before she turned around. Georgianna Milla was a dark half-Cuban, all curves with a curled raven mane tickling her shoulders.

"That tall gentleman over there, well, you can't see him anymore." She pointed where she last saw Darrion and flashed a disturbingly white smile. "Who is he?"

"What's it to you, Sister Mee-yah?"

Georgie rolled her eyes and held out a Bible. "Give this to him for me, please."

"It's mine, thank you." Kelley snatched it from her.

A misguided soul with wandering eyes approached the women. "G'night, Sister Mill-a. See ya home?"

Georgie ignored him. "You have a *son*? How long you been hidin' him in that big house of yours?"

Kelley sucked her teeth and craned her neck. "What I hides in my house is my...he's 32-years-old – 32. You ain't but 20. He's preachin' tomorrow night. That's all you need to know."

"Hmm." Georgie coyly wet her lips. "I'm 22, thank you. Do you think I could catch up with him?"

"Um, Sister Mill-a, sorry to interrupt, but can I walk ya home?"

"*Mee-yah*," she said tersely. Georgie whirled around to address him. "Sounds like a 'y', no l's. As you can see, I'm talking here and I'll be fine. *Goodnight*, brother and God bless you."

The parishioner left, muttering something under his breath. By the time she turned around, Mother Kelley had sneaked off somewhere.

Darrion checked all directions to ensure that no one else was around.

Near the next intersection, a branch snapped. *Could have been an animal*, he thought, *but such a loud break had to come from a heavy creature breaking it*. Someone trailed him. Wooden heels against the pavement clicked not too far behind. Darrion hustled into the woods, whipping his head around.

Who is it? His fingers tightened into a fist and sweat moistened his shirt under the arms and at the small of the back. Jolene's home stood in the distance with a light on in what he assumed must be the bedroom. The closer he came, the louder and closer the footsteps were, and they were now accompanied by multiple whispers.

"You don't belong here!"

"Who's there?" he asked with gritted teeth. "Show yourself!"

"We know who you are!"

"Identify yourselves."

"You remember us. And we remember you well."

Jesus, he prayed, closing his eyes. *Keep my mind.* The voices stopped. Darrion continued to Jolene's door and knocked. He counted a minute or two, and then knocked again. Once more, he waited. There was no answer. *Perhaps she left a light on for safety's sake?* It made sense given the other night. He circled the house and approached the back door, knocking. *What if Jolene is hurt or worse?*

Darrion sidled to the bedroom window, lifted his arms, clamped down on the windowsill and lifted himself up. There were scrambled sheets on the mattress and piled-up clothes, but no Jolene. When he descended onto the ground, a hand tapped his shoulder.

"You know Josephine Courtiér?" A white reporter with mussed hair and a stench wafting from his rumpled white shirt grabbed Darrion's shoulder. "Where is she?"

By instinct, Darrion shook loose and shoved the man away.

"What happened to Mark Williams' body?"

"I don't know anything."

"Look, I know you know and I'm not going away until you give me a quote I can use."

"I said I don't know anything." He shoved a finger into the man's face. "But you're going away. Leave her alone, and you touch me again and you'll regret it."

"Worthless nigger," he muttered.

Darrion yanked the man by the tie. "What did you call me?"

"You're yellow, but a *nigger*, no doubt, around the Fairgrounds alone at this time of night."

He backed up. "You're *wrong*. I'm as white as you."

"Keep telling yourself that, buddy."

Darrion released him and started back toward Kelley's home, wrestling with the new status.

SEVEN

MONDAY AFTERNOON, JUNE 25, 1962

ABOUT two o' clock, Kelley slid a newspaper underneath the door.

Darrion read the first page, which included a piece on the *Fairground murders*, but mentioned nothing about the victims' identity, except that they were upstanding citizens. It included very little about Mark Williams. Thumbing through the following pages of tedium, Darrion noticed a small obituary on Violet buried in the bottom-right corner of the fourth page.

Inheriting the deceased's flair for ambiguity, the passage simply read: *ZYONNE – Corinne Violet October, 38, died Friday, June 22. No visitation or funeral.* Much like their conversations, the lack of detail left him wanting. *No one survived her? Where was she from? How can I pay his respects?*

Dissatisfied, Darrion tore the small blurb from the paper and phoned the obit columnist for the name of the funeral home – which he dialed twice before getting an answer after a full minute of ringing.

"Collins Funeral," said the undertaker with a twinge of annoyance.

"Good afternoon, I'm calling about Corinne October and wanted to know, why isn't..."

"It's a murder case. I get it, but you news types don't listen. Cop came in, said he was her ex-husband, and told me to cremate. Had papers and everything. He piddled around 'til I finished and left with the ashes. Doesn't get any more interesting than that, big guy. Anything else?"

Ex-husband? "Don't you know anything else?" The line disconnected. As Darrion was not kin or a press member; an in-person visit might bear less fruit. The obit's lack of substance niggled at his brain enough to sway his focus from the sermon he was supposed to be writing.

Near three o' clock, Darrion immersed himself in the Word, but an hour later he still felt unprepared. He could not imitate the cadence of the traditional Southern Baptist preacher or crescendo his voice into "whoopin'," as he'd heard it called. The audience would expect its traditional fare and this minister could not deliver. If he refused to preach a message, he'd get no offering, which meant a longer stay in Zyonne. That would satisfy the smug Whitehead, who appeared put-off by his background – as if it was Darrion's choice to leave North Carolina.

He left the house without announcement, sans Bible, in the opposite direction of Higher Ground. The Negro children playing street stickball evoked childhood memories for him. As they rounded the makeshift bases, the little boys laughed and cheered with slender ebony legs caked with a mix of sweat, dust and grass stains. He journeyed down another street and witnessed a group of pig-tailed girls swinging a double-dutch jump rope, or hopping up and down numbered squares drawn on the sidewalk. Around the corner, an older gentleman's radio reported the Supreme Court banned prayer in public schools. Disturbed, he set his applejack hat low over his brow and chewed a toothpick.

At a corner store, Darrion purchased a soda pop. As he dropped the change in his pocket, he fingered a strange texture unlike the leather and cloth of his wallet. He removed the culprit – a folded-up piece if newspaper stuck in one of its rear compartments. Unfolding it revealed another mystery. The clipping was an article written about a five-man archaeology team whose members included a writer named Corinne October (née Schiffler). It was dated one year ago to the day.

Darrion squatted at the storefront, his back against the white stucco wall. *October,* he read while sipping, *a former copy girl and reporter for the Washington Post, said she joined the organization this January to truly change the world "instead of just writing about it." The decision to do so came on the heels of her mother Samuelle's passing on Christmas Day, 1960.*

My father, rest his soul, spent his life pressing his thumbprint into our souls. My mother loved escargot, porc, caviar—these things were not allowed under my father's roof for they violated Levitical law. "She was Jewish?" He set the bottle on the ground between his knees and continued. *After his passing, I learned to cook these things. I'd never seen her so happy to eat. On that day [speaking of her death], she told me, though she loved Aaron, he choked the purpose out of her life. I cremated her three days later and filed for divorce a day after that.*

He finished the drink and tossed away the bottle. When he returned home, he would place it inside Violet's notebook as the true obituary that never was.

Darrion's meandering brought him to a pool hall. Though the sunny skies proved an awkward backdrop for a nightspot, he entered regardless. He imagined every game paused, for the patrons stared at him like his head featured five eyes instead of two.

Without much fanfare, he sidled up to the bar area and ordered a bottled beer to appear casual. While he frequently drank from it to ease his discomfort, he ordered two more in quick succession. Halfway through the third, his legs loosened up a little and he settled on a stool at the back near an ultra-competitive game between two acquaintances.

"I hit this one and it's game." The thinner of the two bent over and slid the pool cue between his fingers. "Can't take yo' money back now!"

"Don't need to take nothin' back." His opponent, a gentleman in a sleeveless t-shirt and open striped shirt, stood akimbo, his pool cue resting beside him on the wall.

Though the cue ball hit the 8-ball soundly, it caromed off the pocket he called and settled perfectly in line with the back corner pocket. Too tipsy to resist, Darrion chuckled.

"Somethin' funny, Boss?"

"Sorry. It was an easy shot, or at least I thought. Well played."

Though inferior to Darrion's stature, the man rushed him anyway and was stopped only by his opponent, who interfered at the last second. "Ease back, Jim, he don't know better."

"Well, he better learn quick! Take the daggone shot."

As predicted, the ball dropped into that corner pocket he called and the winner collected his bills from the table, further infuriating "Jim," who thrust his cue against the floor. He looked up at Darrion, while arranging the balls. "You're next, Boss."

"No thanks. Besides, I won't play for money."

"Don't have to." He made a move on Darrion and grabbed the face of his watch. "You gonna play to keep this."

Darrion yanked his arm away and discovered that several men larger than him had blocked both the entrance and exit. He unstrapped the watch from his wrist and placed it on the table. "I win, I keep the watch *and* walk out of here."

"Cool." The hustler held up his hands in surrender and nodded to his minions, who backed off a little. "You the guest. You break."

He recovered the fallen pool cue, dusted its tip with chalk, lined up his shot and took it – knocking several balls out. Darrion moved around the table hitting shot after shot until he stood in front of "Jim," who distracted him enough to miss.

"You got on a roll there for a minute." The glint of the watch's face caught his eye. "Sho' will enjoy my new watch...least 'til I pawn it."

The hustler eliminated the remaining balls on the table until he reached the 8-ball. Darrion bowed his head, but was not praying so much as cursing himself for getting into this situation. He heard the balls clank together and one of them sunk into the netting; then, a collective groan. His head lifted. The 8-ball remained on the table.

Darrion grabbed his watch and moved through the sea of humanity, upset its hero missed a chip shot and gave the stranger a rare win by default. Desperate to avenge his honor, the loser spun him around at the door and punched Darrion, knocking him through the flimsy screen door and onto the porch. He regrouped in time enough to see the stranger unsheathe a switchblade. Darrion dodged all the blows but one, a slash across his midsection a hair's breadth too deep to call superficial.

Clutching his wound, he scrambled away at top speed to avoid a successful pursuit and capture. The wound burned a fiery path across Darrion's stomach, as he sprinted street-to-street, but he did not stop to rest until his mother's home was in the distance. At the sound of a passing car, he snapped to attention to make sure his attacker had not returned for more retribution. No, he'd extracted his pound of flesh and would still be canonized in pool hall lore as avenger of a loss, albeit a default.

Lungs burning and feet throbbing, he started up the length of the walkway. About the same time, he withdrew his wet right hand from his bloodied shirt and eased his left hand in its place. There was no sneaking back in and covering up what had happened. It was a quarter 'til six and his mother would be leaving for the service he was supposed to be preaching soon. He swallowed saliva in his mouth and hoped his breath did not smell like it tasted. Darrion neared the door on the brink of passing out when Kelley opened the door and helped him inside. "I'm sorry …" he panted, falling to his knees. "I'm … so… sorry."

"Lawd have mercy. What you done gotten yourself into?" Kelley set him against the foyer wall and proceeded to collect medical supplies and clean rags. "Swore to you, Lawd, wasn't gone do this no mo'… wasn't gone live this life an' here I am *doin' it again.*"

Darrion lifted the bottom of his shirt. The depth and ugliness of the wound took them both aback. Kelley swabbed around the wound with an alcohol-soaked rag. Its overflow dribbled into the open skin, causing Darrion to yell.

"C'mon now," she said, applying pressure to a clean rag over the area. "I ain't scream like that when I was havin' you and it took you a day to come out."

"I'm not as strong ... as you are," he responded through gritted teeth.

"Nonsense. You came from me. You at least as strong. *Stronger.* You ain't go lookin' for trouble, but trouble found you. Where you goin' gettin' cut in the middle of the day anyway, Crooked Elbow or the pool hall?"

He nodded at the latter.

Kelly instructed him how to hold the towel against his wound and fed him two aspirins. She unwrapped a wide piece of gauze and bandaging, and dressed the wound tightly. "Next time you wanna go, let me know. I'll cut you before you go, save you the trouble. It ain't too deep, but you gonna feel it for a while. Get some supper from the stove to soak up some of the booze in your gut. I'll tell Passuh Whitehead you ain't comin'."

He stood up slowly. "You said you swore you weren't going to do this again. Who else have you done this for?

"Who? You know good an' well who." She collected the supplies from the floor. "He loved his some beer and pool. One day, he got it in his mind to bet on one, an' the boy he set the wager with liable to cut you, win or not. When he stepped foot on this floor ... made him promise me never to set wagers again or play pool. You gone do the same, right now."

"Promise."

"Go on 'head, eat an' rest. I'll be here, if you needs anything."

Guilt-ridden, he followed the aromatic trail coming from the kitchen, stopping only to listen to his mother's telephone conversation.

"Passuh? Yes, this Mother Kelley ... No, Darrion ain't gonna be able to preach tonight... he's got a *bad stomach* ... uh huh ... so sorry. I'm gonna tend to him, you understand. Can he do it Friday?" She looked at Darrion, who waved and mouthed "no" to her vehemently. "Friday, it is. Uh huh. Alright, so long now."

Careful to temper his tone, he asked Kelley why she'd volunteered him.

"Don't know what you tryin' to do to yourself, or run away from," she muttered. "But it's time you did *somethin'*, even if you ain't quite sure it's right. God'll correct you."

Prior to the start of his regular overnight shift at Zyonne Power, Jack Miles stopped at the hospital, where his best friend and army buddy was in critical condition. He followed the signs to the area where he assumed Geary and the others were until a doctor stopped him.

"I'm sorry," said the man in a white coat and horn-rimmed spectacles, "but this area is restricted to immediate family members only. Who are you trying to see?"

"Geary Gwidon Johnson," he answered without delay, "and before you ask, I'm not legal next of kin. His father was shot 20 years ago and his mother is in a nuthouse. His wife divorced him. He's got no brothers or sisters. We were in the same platoon. I'm the best he's got."

The doctor personally ushered him to the help desk. "Miss, will you get Mister …"

"Everham, Jack Miles Everham."

"… Mr. Everham a visitor's pass?"

She obliged. Jack Miles followed the doctor to the portion of the wing to which he would be allowed access. Through a glass window, he saw an individual mummified in gauze around the face, chest, both arms and a leg. "Is that even him?"

"There are second – and third – degree burns over a large portion of Mr. Johnson's body. He's on medication to regulate the pain. He's scheduled for surgery in the morning to attempt to save some of the affected skin. I'm sorry, but this is the closest I can allow you to get to him. When his status changes, we'll move him and you can have a full visit."

Though the prognosis and Geary's appearance unsettled him, he knew at least *something* now. He shook the doctor's hand, thanked him, and returned to the truck. Driving to the plant meant little, if anything, now. Forget the others, his *best friend* would not be the same forever and he, the "Nighthawk," the man-at-arms of the Grand Cyclops, should have been there. If he had, perhaps he would be in that bed instead of Geary. On some level, he wanted that.

Jack Miles almost swerved off the road into the bridge support when someone honked their horn at him for riding over the double lines. He wanted to crash, to be free of thoughts about Geary and of Betty Lou, and how he messed up their marriage. It had never been good from the start, but while he felt he did not have to make it worse, he discovered an innate ability to do so.

He pressed the gas pedal harder, gunning the motor to nearly 70 miles per hour. The truck hopped over the imperfections in the road and raced down the street. He pushed it to the floor. The motor coughed and sputtered a bit before shutting off. Jack Miles cursed it and pulled to the side of the road. A hissing noise came from beneath the hood. In the effort to kill himself, he'd overheated the engine.

EIGHT

FRIDAY EVENING, JUNE 29, 1962

FOLLOWING testimony service, Whitehead relished the approaching moment where the high-yellow, bigheaded cat sitting beside him would fall. For that, he pitied him. But Darrion earned this tragic destiny for embarrassing him, throwing some Biblical nonsense up in his face.

"Like to thank the Lawd one mo' day," Kelley said, standing up. "An' saints, the devil was messin' wit me last night! Had me a dream. Ain't see nothin' but fire an' smoke. So, ya'll pray my strength in de Lawd an' I'll pray for ya'll."

Whitehead sighed, while tapping his foot. She'd once dreamed about a child's skeleton chasing him with a knife.

Georgie rose, curls draped low over a pearl white blouse. The all-female Higher Ground Choir, dressed alike in various shades of white tops and black skirts, followed suit. Georgie sang a dragging verse solo of *Sweet Hour of Prayer* and the church joined in on the chorus. Whitehead smirked, as Darrion fumbled through a hymn book. *He's in way over his head.*

Darrion gave up the effort and meditated. Prior to this, he'd excitedly described the message to a disinterested Whitehead. "There are three different kinds of words that God gives me," he'd said.

Whitehead stroked his chin and mechanically nodded.

"A teaching Word, meant to instruct; a shouting Word, meaning the people will get happy over it; and a cutting Word. The people won't like it tonight, but if the Word is comfortable, you're not growing."

Darrion readied himself for negative reactions. He'd have to prove himself worthy to preach. Service formalities flew by: testimony service, then the hymn, a deacon's prayer, and another selection led by Georgie, a scripture reading and finally the offering.

"Now saints," Reverend Whitehead said. "Give to God what you *can't* give 'cause Jesus gave what we *couldn't* give."

Darrion witnessed the people stingily passing the basket around, barely parting their fists enough to allow its few contents to drop. *No wonder.* Whitehead drove a charcoal 1962 Chevrolet sedan, which nobody in the congregation mentioned. Higher Ground commanded respect and dignity in the Negro community. The church's reputation evoked such reverence in the Black Mountains that aspiring politicians and civil rights activists visited the small town. Questions about Reverend Whitehead and his supposed licentious behaviors were erased. Kelley said he bought the car with his own savings, producing a bank slip to back up the claim.

"And now, it's time for the man of God to come forth."

Aware that Whitehead had eliminated threats or competition, Darrion figured he'd been invited to speak with the hope that he'd fail. Darrion faced up to the challenge, with head bowed, his sermon notes, and Violet's notebook in hand.

"On this last day of revival, Reverend Darrion James comes to us from New York and he's got a word from the Lord. Hear ye him."

Darrion noticed his introducer neglected to mention anything which might underscore his own abilities. He stood, greeted the pastor with a firm, sterile handshake and laid his belongings on the shellacked lectern. "Good evening, church."

Pleasantries, he assumed, *are an old Southern Baptist institution.* Last Sunday, Whitehead acknowledged, in order, his wife and six children, church officers, visiting preachers and their families, ushers, church mothers, associate pastors and ministers. Formalities like these were nothing he cared for. Delivering a cutting word was akin to amputating a gangrened limb and hesitation heightened the cutting intensity.

"Good evening. I greet you in the name of our Lord and Savior, Jesus Christ. If I may have your attention for just a little while, there's a Word from the Lord I've been sent here to deliver, different from anything you've ever heard before."

Whitehead's face fell at this young man's pomposity. *What does he know? Reverend Ralph Abernathy, himself, preached from this pulpit!*

"There are a number of scriptures I have tonight. Don't look them up, please. I need you to listen. If you spend time looking for what I'm reading, you'll just *hear* me."

"The Bible says," Reverend Whitehead loudly interrupted, "to be ye doers of the Word, but not *hearers* only. That's what the *Word* says, so *hearing* can't be all that bad."

"Three bones in your ear vibrate when sound hits. You have to *hear*. *Listening* means to gain understanding. 'Wisdom is the principal thing; with all thy getting, get an understanding.' This is what I believe Jesus *meant*."

He crossed his arms in temporary defeat. "Ain't what He said, though."

"How much are we willing to endure to get that for which we've been praying for? How far will we go? What will we give up? It's true that God will not put suffering on you that you cannot bear. But because He knows all things and He knew us before we were born, He also knows what we are able to bear and what we cannot. Throughout history, even now, Satan's plan has been to plant the idea in our mind that we are not able to bear the struggles and we wrestle with the idea that this too shall pass because of the enemy.

"The reason why the road seems so long and hard, why the lynching, burning, bombings, beatings, and Jim Crow continue… is because the glorious end has to seem impossible before your eyes because God works in the impossible, improbable and unlikely. In case you didn't notice: virgin girls do not have children, fishermen cannot walk on water, and carpenter's sons, ruler's daughters, and men dead for four days do not get up from the dead. Be honest with yourself and think to yourself that if you were Mary, Simon Peter, the centurion, or Lazarus' sisters, would you *believe it* or still *doubt?*"

Darrion paused long enough to observe the Word slicing into everyone's flesh, starting with him, down to the back pew and across the pulpit. Whitehead caressed his baby smooth chin and grunted.

"Peter doubted and he sank, the ruler doubted Jesus possessed the power to heal from a distance, and Mary thought Lazarus was long gone – so you are not alone. But bear witness to this fact, if nothing else: blessings, healings, and miracles; these things God wishes to give us and issue and perform in our lives are laid up beyond our idea of our limitations.

"We expect children to do something based on what we say. 'Go to bed.' The child asks 'Why?' You respond with, 'Because I said so.' 'Eat your vegetables.' 'Why?' 'Because I said so, boy, stop giving me lip and questioning me!' Why is it that the child gets rebuked for asking the parent for the reason why he or she is being commanded to do something? Why does the parent refuse to be questioned? Are parents above reproach?"

Darrion caught the approving eye of his mother from under her hat.

"It is because you, the parent, know what's best for the child. Regardless of whether or not your child understands the reason for the command, obedience to it results in good things. A well-rested, vegetable-eating child is a healthy child.

"God is calling for you, child, to believe in some things He, the parent, says because He said so. Do it because your obedience, plus His will, will bring the things you've been praying to pass, *if* you believe, go far enough and *if* you do not give up. 'And let us not be weary in well-doing: for in due season, we shall reap, if we faint not'."

Seemingly his sole supporter, Kelley clapped her white-gloved hands, but the remaining congregation members sided with Whitehead, who, arms still crossed, refused to concede defeat.

"In Romans Eight, the Bible reads as follows: 'The Spirit Himself beareth witness with our spirit, that we are children of God: and if children, then heirs; heirs of God, and joint-heirs with Christ; if so be that we suffer with Him, that we may be also glorified with Him.

"You are not human anymore than God the Father is human. You are an eternal spirit, like He is, but you are covered with skin, bones, muscles and flesh. When you die, your covering will decay into dust but your eternal spirit will live on in either heaven or hell.

"Both our spirits and the Holy Spirit agree that we are children of God, heirs of God and joint-heirs with Christ. Heirs inherit the estate once someone dies, so when Christ died, we became heirs to the Kingdom of God and Christ's glory when He rose, *if* we suffer with Him.

"Read the scripture. The suffering *precedes* the glory. Am I saying the water hosing, dog attacks, lynching, beatings, burnings, and bombings should go unnoticed? I am saying the suffering precedes the glory. Should we say nothing about it? The suffering precedes the glory. Christ suffered unto *death*. Are we better than Him?"

Whitehead scoffed at the attempted camaraderie. *We?* Darrion's last statement lost the audience. Shaking heads, bulged eyes and angry stares flooded the pulpit.

"That ain't what it means," Whitehead bellowed, standing up. The more he puffed up, the worse his diction became. "He's wrong. These things ain't comin' our way 'cause we're *Christians*. It's 'cause we're *Negroes*. And look at 'im. He ain't seen one water hose or dog in his day, have you?"

"Yeah!" A young man stood up. "Preach, Preachuh!"

"If this town got *one* white man with a soul for the Lawd," said Whitehead, edging toward Darrion, "then *he* surely ain't sufferin'. *He* ain't hangin' and burnin' from trees like us, but he's gonna hang and burn in hell like we ain't!"

The rabid applause mortified Darrion, who, despite his radical teachings, had rarely been confronted so openly before.

"God created man on the sixth day, both Negro and white. If Negroes were the only ones ever suffering that would mean God plays favorites in sparing the white man and He is no respecter of persons. So have you prepared *yourself*," he asked, pointing in Reverend Whitehead's chest, "to be judged for *your* wrongdoing? It is time for judgment to begin, and it starts here, in the house of the Lord, with the teachers of the Word *first*."

"How dare you?" Images of slain infants danced in his mind.

"Have you? Have you prepared these people for the judgment they will endure for tolerating ill behavior? The Bible says if we are aware that our brother is sinning and say nothing, then his blood is on our hands. But if we warn him, then his blood is on his own head."

Whitehead paused and backed up. The Word cut, indeed.

"Beware of His coming wrath, for repenting is not enough. Saying 'I'm sorry' is not enough. Making it disappear is not enough. You must repent and therefore bring forth fruit worthy of repentance. Say you're sorry, stop the behavior and push through."

Darrion's confronter unzipped his robe and shed it to the ground, held his hands up in surrender and exited the church in a t-shirt and slacks. The Higher Ground officers followed suit.

"For our wrestling is not against flesh and blood, but against the principalities, powers, the world-rulers of this darkness and the spiritual hosts of wickedness in the heavenly places. Your enemy is not the white man." He continued, despite the crowd trickling out through the squeaky back door, "but Satan and the spirits controlling the white man and using him for evil.

"If you ask God to pour His wrath out on white people, your prayers are misguided. God will lay a worse judgment on the unrepentant sinner, but a quicker judgment on *you*. Just like your bodies can be used for God, they can also be used by Satan."

People now filed out in loud groups, but Darrion's voice continued to fill the sanctuary long after the microphone had been unplugged.

"Jesus wrote a *Lost Testament,* and in it, says to us that evil spirits must live inside something, a person, like Judas Iscariot, or in some cases, an animal, like a pig or serpent. Animals do not possess the ability to reason, so they cannot refuse a spirit's entry into it.

"We, however, can resist them, if we belong to Christ. If not, they can inhabit us at will when we provide them a doorway through anything we do outside of the will of God. Once inside, more spirits are allowed entry until they are cast out or Satan uses you to do all he purposes to do with you and then destroys you and anyone else he can."

The door shut one last time. Everyone, including Kelley, was gone.

Jolene chomped on the sweet gum until it turned tart, then tossed it into the garbage can next to her bench. Three hours ago, this thruway flooded with parents dragging their children from store to store. Now, a quarter till ten, the sidewalks were deserted, save a few stragglers entering the Crooked Elbow behind her. She occupied herself in observing the different types; suits with loosened neckties snuck in for about a half hour and exited with a blonde or redhead woman wearing a conniving smirk. White winos stayed in long enough for the bartender to kick them out, two minutes tops.

In between sightseeing, Jolene sang with head bowed and fought tears. Mark worked until 10:00 p.m. on Thursdays and usually walked by this spot to see if his girl was waiting for him at the bus stop.

"Stop, Darlin'!" A blonde emerged from the bar, swatting her hand. "Charlie's just goin' out for a smoke, that's all. She'll be back."

She propped a delicate cigarette between her lips, struck a match and puffed until the stick's head glowed. She impatiently ripped the cigarette away and held it at her side, while blowing smoke rings and shifting her bra to point her breasts higher. The wispy ivory silk ruffled around Charlie's thick figure. Jolene looked back at the glamorous woman and assumed the body Charlie flaunted so liberally included a price tag. Expensive looking jewelry lined her wrists, neck and glittered at the ears. *Trinkets from suitors*, she assumed. The low cut blouse and clinging high hemmed skirt left little to the imagination.

"Problem, Doll?" Charlie caught Jolene staring.

"Huh? Sorry?"

"The *boys* have the staring problem, never the girls, so if if I nabbed your husband, I ain't force him to do nothin' he ain't want to do, promise you me."

"No, Cheri. No problems here. Just 'bout to leave myself."

"You have a good night, Doll. Be careful 'round these parts." Charlie looked down and took a drag. Jolene rose. She'd never seen anything happen on the thoroughfare other than a cursing wino in the gutter. Twelve years difference in their ages meant sometimes Mark protected the 23-three-year old more like a daughter than an intended bride.

A half block down, her pocketbook strap tensed. She winced. The strap cut down into her skin until the material snapped. She grabbed the bag in the air and pulled, screaming for help in the struggle to reclaim her belongings. The pocketbook opened and its contents spewed across the sidewalk. Charlie shuffled as fast as she could in her inch-and-a-half high heels, wielding a knife the length of her index finger. And Darrion, a quarter ways through the circuitous route home, circled the corner.

At a brief glance, the white mugger resembled her rapist; same skin tone, grayish teeth, and beady eyes. Where one succeeded stealing something from Jolene, she determined the other would not. She scratched and tore through his clothes and broke through the skin with her nails. She howled, kicked him in the groin, clasped her hands together and hammered his spine over and over again until he spit up blood and scampered away doubled over. Charlie removed her heels and chased him for another half block.

Darrion paused. Bent over the contents of her purse, Jolene went into hysterics. He approached, careful to maintain a presence in front of her at all times. After the other night and an aborted mugging, her psyche had to be delicately handled. "Jolene," he said in a voice above a whisper. "Let me help you."

The crying waned into a sniffle. Jolene's head raised and swiveled in his direction, a compact mirror and lipstick tube in hand. She dropped both and lunged for Darrion, but Charlie restrained her.

"Let me go!" Jolene saw a *man*. If it weren't for Charlie's weight advantage, she would have tackled Darrion and taken Charlie along for the ride.

"Just gone an' go, Suga," said Charlie, struggling to restrain Jolene without accidentally stabbing her. "Better that way. She'll be fine as wine in a few."

"Are you sure, Miss?" Darrion halfway trusted the knife-brandishing blonde. "I'm a minister. I've helped her out before."

"She don't need *prayer*, Darlin',' an' she sho' don't need no more men right now. Charlie'll see her home safe. Jus' gone an' go."

In times like these, where women fall victim to a violent crime, a female probably should deal with her. Darrion turned away, looking over his shoulder, convinced that Jolene still needed him – even if petitioning God was all he could do. As he walked on, he prayed for Jolene.

Charlie reinserted the knife into its sheath strapped to her inner thigh and stormed into the Crooked Elbow to say a quick goodnight. By the time she returned to an old customer who was confident that he'd spend the night with her again, she discovered four empty shot glasses and beer bottles littering his table. Evidently, his best friend had been in a terrible fire and would be hospitalized for a while.

"He won't be 100 percent again." Jack Miles slurred, while waving at the bartender, who eagerly sent him another beer and shot.

Charlie nonchalantly stood behind Jack Miles and passed her slender hand from his neck down to his chest and stroked it. "Come again?"

"Nothing." Jack Miles grabbed Charlie's fingers and held them.

She settled onto his lap. "Looks like you soakin' in your thoughts, handsome," she said, playing with his hair. "Don't let trouble worry you like that."

Charlie's name and loose reputation preceded her, but he played dumb anyway. "Say, what you say your name was again, gal?"

"Me? I didn't say. But tonight – consider me whatever you need."

Her smooth palms were velvet against his skin and the conversation even smoother. "I was saying things'll never be the same again."

"They ain't meant to be, Suga. Things ain't meant to be the same. You gotta change and keep changin' 'til you can't go no more. Life can be a beautiful thing, if you do it right."

"Well, if you're what I need tonight, when are we getting out of here?"

"Now." She left his lap and kissed him on the cheek near his lips.

"Now that's what I'm talkin' about."

"You missin' what I mean, Suga. Most nights, I'm a lover, sometimes a fighter, but tonight, I'm a doctor. Here's my prescription. Go home to your wife. I gotta girlfriend I need to see home. Last week t'was nice, but we'll catch up."

Jack Miles groaned. "Bring her along then."

"Not that kind of party, Hon."

"She don't understand me," he said, slapping Charlie's bottom. "But *you, you* understand how men work, so tell your friend later for her."

"Can't tonight. Make the ol' ball and chain understand you, John," she said. "I gotta feelin' she's gonna need you tonight. Gals need y'all, too."

"Name's *Jack*," he reminded her, "and she prolly won't even notice I'm gone... never does."

NINE

EARLY SATURDAY MORNING, JUNE 30, 1962

AT a quarter past midnight, Betty Lou flicked on the lights and parted the curtains.

She'd wasted hours primping – a knockout dress and 40 paces waiting for the slob. Last call was midnight, so in truth, her husband might drag in anytime during the seven hours between now and his morning shift. That "man without a father," a name she used when curse words were too good for him, forgot their 18th wedding anniversary.

After their thirteenth, the celebrations became fewer and further between. Five years ago, she spent the night getting her leg reset after "the fight." The next year brought a drunken Jack Miles home with a chocolate cake; his favorite and her allergy, and half of it hand-eaten at that. And on the following anniversary, she received a quarter empty bottle of booze. For the last three years, she received nothing, not even half attempts. Betty Lou hated herself for missing him. It had to be loneliness. It certainly wasn't love and intimacy.

Another 40 steps later, Betty Lou, settled on the unmade bed, face moist with loneliness and agony. With a dampened tissue wad in her left hand and a sleeping pill bottle in the right, she groaned. *Maybe her husband would change personalities, but not in this lifetime.* The first bitter dot dissolved and offended Betty Lou's tongue. She popped another without blinking, then another and another and another. She ran a hand underneath the bed, retrieved the three-year-old whiskey she sipped on occasion for girlish thrills and giggles, and pounded the bitterness away with chest-burning swigs. After a couple more pills, Betty Lou sucked out the bottle's last drops and stared through its clear glass into her distorted reflection in the bedroom's vanity mirror. The porcelain shell gazed back, with fading black lines trailing from lifeless hollow eyes, mimicking Betty Lou's movements down to the distorted depressed frown. "What...*chu*...lookin' at," she slurred. The whiskey bottle tumbled to the hardwood floor and broke into large fragments.

"Uh oh." She giggled and belched. "Jack...ain't gonna like that. Prolly ain't gonna like...this neither." She palmed the largest, heaviest broken bottle shard and chucked it at the vanity mirror, laughing as the looking glass cracked down the center. Her reflection rippled and distorted around the fissure that split it in half. The right side crooked into a faint discernible smile, and the left into a well established frown. Her body, once firm and desirable was now aged, sagged a bit and wrinkled.

Betty Lou reached out to steady her wavering image, but a large slice of the mirror loosened and plummeted to the ground. She scooted to the damaged site and touched the fragments with her finger pads until they bloodied, all the while wondering if the pieces could be reassembled again. *Perhaps things are better this way – broken beyond repair?*

With bloodied hand on hip, she slipped a Lucky Strike from Jack Miles' pack and smoked it slow, hoping for the end. Five cigarettes later, immersed in a tissue-thin smoke cloud above her head, Betty Lou coughed dramatically. If the pills and whiskey chaser didn't do her a favor and stop her heart, Jack Miles surely would when he finally made his way home.

Charlie walked with a strut, high heels stamping into the sidewalk with authority, punctuating importance and purpose into its texture.

No wonder every man alive stopped and stared at the blonde. Her body demanded attention wherever she went.

Jolene looked up and stepped softly, like Freedom Courtiér said dignified Creole women should walk. Stomping into the ground like a horse, she'd say, meant you failed to assume command of the area through your presence, style, beauty, manners and good graces. And Courtiér women oozed style, beauty, manners, and grace – always. Annie and Nona, Joséphine's older sisters, were clods, but the baby girl caught onto the etiquette lessons quite easily, much to Freedom's delight and her sisters' dismay. As the youngest, Joséphine already possessed light skin, long, smooth hair, instinctive elegance, and their father's eye.

"Suga? Darlin'? Hello, anybody home?" Charlie snapped two fingers and waved in Jolene's face. "Say somethin,' Gal. Dang! I left a good time for you."

Occupied with her own thoughts, Jolene missed whatever the white woman had said. If not for the attempted mugging, she would have told the girl to go somewhere with her intentions.

Charlie stopped and turned toward Jolene, extending a hand. "Given name's Charlemagne, Charlie for short. Nobody calls me Charlemagne 'cept people tryin' to sound smart. Momma loved history and folk said her tummy sat low, but out I come. And as you can see, I'm *far* from a man. And you are?"

No response.

"Right. Which way you goin'…west?"

Jolene's blank stare failed to unnerve Charlie, or silence her.

"C'mon then." Charlie advanced a couple feet to a wooden bench. "Sit. Rest yourself. A bus will come soon. Then you can go home."

Yes, if I'm lucky.

"I looked like you once, you know."

Negro, beaten and bruised? Heartbroken?

"This one fella, I reckon he wore a t-shirt and blue dungarees dang near e'eryday like James Dean and had his hair combed like him too.

Winked at Charlemagne one day and she rose up full of sap like a maple tree."

Jolene sniffed. *Nothing smells sweeter than tree sap.*

"She ain't know what she felt, but called it love 'cause it felt *good*. Gave him everything, but the boy still wanted more, so he took it – at the back of a burger joint on Main. Charlemagne had no money, and half a dress, and she looked a lot like you look right now."

The two did share a violation, but no one died in Charlie's version.

"A doctor, $60, and a rusty knife later, hereeee's Charlie!"

So someone did die. We're still different. "Why did you do it?"

"Well, well, well, the Gal *does* talk. Do what?"

Jolene repositioned closer to Charlie and nodded a knowing glance.

"*I* didn't do it. *Charlemagne* did it."

"Are you slow, Cheri? You're Charlemagne and Charlemagne is you."

"Wrong, I'm Charlie and Charlemagne is who I was."

"How can you stop being who you are?"

"Charlemagne's a name, a word, what they called me – not *who I am*. The way I see it, in the end, you become who you believe you are, even if it's the person someone tells you they think you're supposed to be. I never stopped being who I am, but I just started being who I'm supposed to be. Get it?"

The roundabout rhetoric stirred Jolene's consciousness into indulging. "So, why did *Charlemagne* do it then?"

"Bloomed before time, always looked older. When I was eight, I looked eleven. At eleven, I looked 15. And at 15, I looked 21. Eight, eleven, 15, and 21 is way too young to be a diaper changing milk carton with nipples."

"Understood," she said, trying to calm the animated woman.

Agitated by the memory, she continued. "Loved the kid. I think about him all the time. Death rips out your gut and lets it rot, if you let it. Then, there's this space you can't fill with nothin', not booze, no man layin' in your bed, money, dope, nothin' will do it. But my baby's gone. He ain't comin' back and I gotta move on."

"You sound like you tryin' to convince yourself."

"Some days I have to. Others, I don't. Look, enough memories." Charlie removed her left shoe and lifted the sole at the heel. Underneath were folded bills. "I always keep some loot around for emergencies and slow evenings. Let's go."

Mortified, Jolene refused to move. "We can't go to the same place."

"We're not. You have a home, right?"

"If you can call it that."

"Well, come on."

The 144 pulled up to the corner and stopped. Its door folded back and a blob of a man in a grimy navy jumpsuit greeted Charlie with a snuff stained grin. He tipped his hat and wet his lips.

"Goin' my way, Darlin'?" Charlie's flirting flattered him.

"Goin' wherever your way is, sweet thing." The driver's eyes x-rayed Charlie and then spotted Jolene. "But I ain't goin' hers."

"She's a friend, Darlin'. She jus' one of them Creole folks. And it's the law."

"Cre-*what*? She's a *nigger*. *No way*. Not on my bus. Don't care if it's the law or not. You see anybody around to arrest me, if I don't?"

Charlie boarded the bus like she intended to leave Jolene, who figured the white woman turned on her at last. Instead, she leaned over and whispered something into his ear. The driver chuckled and scribbled down something on a piece of paper that Charlie had handed him. A favor now exchanged for a favor later.

Although Jolene's figure was superior to Charlie's, the driver she called "John" ignored it as she boarded.

"What did you say to him, Cheri? How you know his name?"

The bus rattling along the divots in the road gave Charlie a second or two to refocus and ignore Jolene's question. Promising to touch the untouchable and sacrifice her body for almost nothing irked her nerves, although she never planned to follow through.

"Sherry? That's pretty what you call me. What's that mean?"

"Something like 'darlin'.' What did you say to him?"

Charlie's eyes rolled. "Don't worry 'bout it. You ain't walkin' home. That's all that matters."

Still, curiosity percolated inside Jolene. *What kind of sorted act changed John's mind into giving a Negro a ride for free?* Her young mind blushed with lurid possibilities.

"So, whereabouts you stay?"

"On the far west side."

That revelation alone shook Charlie. Most of the town's crime and murders took place on Zyonne's far west side. Common knowledge said that the extremely poor and destitute lived there. "Well," she swallowed, "this bus don't go to the far west side and I don't know no other buses go that way this time of night 'cause it's dangerous."

At last, the white woman revealed her true colors. Intimacy and friendliness aside, when it came to the nitty gritty, she stayed to Greater Zyonne; the white side, like everyone else.

"'Tis good, Cheri. I'll walk the rest, no worries."

"You believe in God?"

The question caught Jolene off-guard. "What you say?"

"Do you believe in *God*? She pointed up. "Big Guy in the sky?"

Both times, the name seared her chest like a hot iron. "*God*?"

"You gotta believe in something, if you stay over there."

Jolene crossed her arms and huffed. The more Charlie talked, the less she saw a kindred soul. Now, she sounded like the Bible bashers knocking down her door in the morning. "Who says I live alone?"

"You do. Ain't no Negro man in Zyonne that'll let his woman walk the far west side alone. She shifted sitting positions, removed the small blade from its concealed location and handed it to Jolene. "Here, you'll need this."

"No. I'll survive."

Charlie exhaled disappointment. The free ride hitched a right in the heart of the west side and stopped.

Betty Lou crumpled to the floor, her left leg awkwardly bent. The repaired bone refused to snap again in the same place that Jack Miles had broken it long ago.

They argued that night like never before. Betty Lou prepared herself for an anniversary evening of loving by using five week's allowance on a crimson V-neck evening dress with spaghetti straps and a lace back. It was the first time she'd worn such a vibrant and daring color in years. She looked like a *woman*.

Jack Miles burst through the door late, drunk and depressed. Fred had denied him the well-deserved raise he'd banked on, which meant the slinky showstopper slithering against his wife had to be returned.

"Nice. How much?" he asked, wetting his lips.

Betty Lou surveyed the obvious. "You're *drunk*. You've been at the Elbow all this time?"

"Answer me, Betty Louise! How much?"

"Twenty," she muttered, her hopes for an enchanted evening waning.

"Twenty bucks on a *dress*? You look like a whore," he slurred.

Betty Lou choked up. "Don't be such a mean cuss, Jack. You told me to go buy somethin' nice to wear for tonight – *remember*?"

"Well, you ain't *helpin'* me, Betty, so now you *hurtin'* me."

"But I can't work, Jack. We done talked 'bout this before. I don't know how to do nothin'!"

"You know how to spend my money, don'tcha? Don'tcha?"

She exploded. "Why are you treatin' me this way, huh? Why?"

"'Cause you're good for nothin', that's why! You ain't even good enough to give me a kid."

That accusation blasted her like a gunshot straight to the womb. "I hate you!"

Jack Miles smacked Betty Lou for the first time. Once she regained her balance, he slapped her again. Punches and kicks ensued. Although drunk, the former army boxer's strikes landed with alarming precision.

Betty Lou stopped fighting back and curled into a ball on the floor, screaming for him to stop. She blacked out and awoke in a hospital bed, feeling as if they'd amputated her heavily bandaged left leg. "High compound fracture of the tibia and shredded knee ligaments," they'd said, and if she walked on it again, more than likely she'd have a permanent and pronounced limp. A remarkable car accident, the doctor observed, as her husband did not have a scratch on him.

Jack Miles said nothing and drove them home.

Now, Betty Lou straightened out the leg. Satisfied, she closed her eyes.

Jack Miles snuck into the house, ashamed. He'd forgotten again. Although he remembered the significance of the date, *his* priorities came first. The living room was pitch black with shut curtains. "Betty Lou?" She always answered on the first call. She slept light too and his constant shifting at night kept her up, so when he called, she answered – the first time, always.

She could have taken a sleeping pill, but not this early. She'd stay awake long enough to assess his drunken state and piece together what had happened to him. *Maybe she's not home? But where could she go this late at night?* She never traveled further than the Five and Dime, never walked more than two blocks before turning around. Two hundred and fifty-five paces were her absolute limit on a perfect day. "Betty Louise?"

She broke the pattern. Jack Miles noticed the shift. He smelled cigarette smoke and burning food. After shutting the oven down and removing his charred meatloaf and vegetables, he glanced over his shoulder into the lighted bedroom, which was usually turned off at night. He came closer and paused. It was a red pump with a limp foot still in it.

He lumbered to the bedroom and cradled his wife, who was still wearing the dress he busted her up for buying. Around her were snuffed out butts, glass shards and a sleeping pill bottle; the same pills she swallowed to make sleeping in their bed tolerable. "I'm sorry," he rocked her back and forth. "So sorry."

Jack Miles pressed an index finger into Betty Lou's neck and found a slow and faint throb. He carried her outside and propped her body upright inside the truck, with his rolled up leather jacket as a makeshift pillow supporting his wife's head and neck.

The truck engine couldn't wheeze and turn over fast enough. He gunned it, careful to straddle the divot in the trail, the standing water pool and groundhog burrow. He steadied Betty Lou with his right hand and managed to drive and shift with the left. "Happy anniversary, Bets," he said in fake cheer.

She couldn't die. He refused to let it happen. "I'm drunk, had a few at the Elbow," he explained. "And I'm late. I know you wanted to do somethin' pretty special like you do." He did a pulse check. *Weak, but still beating.*

Thankfully, no one witnessed the truck's swerving around traffic and speeding through red lights. Although the ten minute trip to the emergency room took half the time, it felt like days. He parked sideways across two parking spots, scooped up his wife and shuttled her through the doors into the hospital. "Help!" he screamed without caring whom he disturbed. "Help me!"

An emergency nurse waved for a gurney. "What happened?"

"Sleeping pills," he said, laying Betty Lou down and producing the prescription bottle. "She took these and she won't wake up."

"Do you know how many? Sir, do you know how many?"

He failed to respond fast enough. The nurse and two doctors whisked her through double doors and out of sight.

"Ain't no pain in heaven. That's where I'm going, so don't be sad."

Eighteen years ago, Helen Graham's body began succumbing to cancer, first in the pancreas, then the back, hips, ribs, and lungs. The mind went last. When the illness started manipulating Helen's rational thoughts, her daughter struggled to maintain composure.

"Don't talk like that. You know how it upsets me." Betty Lou, a month past 18 and eight weeks pregnant, sobbed in spurts.

"Child, *time* ain't gentle," she coughed. "This life ain't been gentle to neither of us. But I gotta go. God is calling me home."

"*God?* What kind of *God* would let you go like this?"

"Everything has a purpose, Betty Louise, even death. I done lived my life. You'll have your time, too. Make your peace with the Lord before you go, so you don't die how you lived."

Comforted by the memory, Betty Lou lifted her lead eyelids in pain. Her head pounded, her body was sore from head to toe, and shooting sensations riddled her left arm and stomach. *This is obviously not heaven.*

Whiteness was surrounded by a rigid black border. The ceiling and walls were painted a spectral shade of white. Through blurred vision, she determined the firmness she lay on and its thick silver lines were a hospital bed. *Metal restraining bars.* Beside it stood an intravenous drip bag, which explained the discomfort in her left arm.

It still wasn't her time to go. Betty Louise Graham Everham turned her face to the wall and wept.

Zyonne's upper west side overflowed with large brick corpses, their glass eyes shattered, mortar bones broken and blackened by fire. At a distance, the abandoned buildings brought to mind abstract charcoal drawings with the jagged jutting out from the formerly smooth. As Charlie and Jolene walked its dimly-lit streets well past midnight, these beings looked imposing and intimidating. Charlie drew her knife, ready to strike at anything daring to leap into their path.

Jolene's stomach rumbled with irrepressible pain. She patted it down and composed herself. Getting home safe, and not eating, was first priority. Only Charlie had a weapon.

"I'm hungry too, Suga. That cheapskate John ain't buy me nothin'."

"John? You mean the bus driver?"

"No, Darlin', the guy at the bar. Ain't even offer me free peanuts."

"I thought the bus driver's name was John?"

"It is. All of 'em are John to me. No name, no connection, no feelings – no matter what we do, how we do it, where we go."

In that instant, Jolene felt sorry for her.

"This is Hoghoba Street, Suga. Let's turn here."

Jolene fought the urge to scream. Tall skeletons lining the sidewalk resembled the blackened remnants of the orchard. This neighborhood's former glory dripped from white fingers like Mark's blood.

"The good here packed up and left a long time ago."

Jolene sighed in assent. "How'd they let all this happen?"

"*They*? They who?"

"You," she responded without hesitation. "*Your people.*"

Charlie stopped. "Now jus' a minute, *Gal*. You don't know me, or nothin' 'bout me. I ain't do nothin' to no one!"

"But you *did*. Where were *you* when this happened?"

"Stayed my big ole Tennessee butt inside the house, that's what I did."

"Then you just as guilty as the ones who did it."

Though the rationale was flawed, Charlie understood. Poor Negroes and whites created it, crooked lawmen allowed it and the citizens kept quiet. Who cared if the epicenter of Negro wealth went up in flames?

"Ain't never say things was right," Charlie retorted. "They ain't right – ain't been right and might never be right. Negro, white – the world bruises everybody purple and you wanna black and blue somebody, so they purple too and e'erybody ain't wanna feel it."

"You're right," Jolene reluctantly admitted.

"I've been around. Experience makes you smart, or old and stupid. People do things, Joséphine, they think is right, so they keep doin' them and their kids do it and their kids kids do it until you gotta long line of people who think they doin' right while doin' wrong."

Freedom's color obsession surfaced in Jolene's mind. For her mother, courting Courtiérs meant passing the butter test. Otherwise, a gentleman caller never made it past the front porch, where Marc Joseph weighed his worthiness before allowing his daughters to even appear. Anna accepted this without protest, Nona, too, but Joséphine doubted, but to no avail. Neither Freedom nor Marc tolerated a child's challenge. On the bayou, finding such a boy was possible.

Zyonne, on the other hand, bred Negroes ranging from caramel to nut brown and chocolate, not a shade lighter. She succeeded in training herself to ignore Mark's tone, but when the Courtiér matriarch visited she departed days later, disgusted.

"Somewhere along the line of wrong, someone has to break the cycle." Charlie's words echoed in Jolene's ears. "Go against the grain."

"What's *grain*?"

"Natural way of doing things."

They walked for minutes without a word. Jolene broke the silence at the dead end of Hoghoba where it intersected at Sesame Drive. "I have to go home. I need rest."

Charlie's eyebrows raised. "You walkin' *alone*?"

"This is my street and I have to walk it alone."

"I'll bunk it on your sofa or somethin'. It ain't safe for you alone."

Jolene reverted to protective mode. "You don't know what happened."

"I read papers, seen the news. I know enough, Darlin'. Gotta pretty daggone good idea, that's why I'm sayin' somethin'."

"If I don't do it alone now, I never will again."

"Crazy." Charlie reached down to her thigh and extracted the knife. "Here. Take it."

"No. I'll be fine, trust me."

"Suit yourself. At least tell me your name, so if I see it in the obits, I'll know to feel bad."

"Joséphine Courtier." Jolene said, walking away. "I'll be seein' you."

Not too long passed before Charlie also disappeared in the shadows. Finding her in a few days should be no trouble. Flies migrate to sweetness and no place had more flies than the Crooked Elbow.

Getting to the far part of West Zyonne in the dark proved long and frightening – much more than Jolene had imagined. She jogged a little to make the time go faster but stopped soon afterward. The pressure on her already sore feet and ankles was overwhelming. *The house must be close now.*

A small street light 200 yards away flickered. Jolene sighed and pushed forward, trying to ignore the oversized vermin rummaging in the nearby garbage cans. If she needed protection, would whoever or whatever responsible for giving the fire against the Klansmen make it available? Jolene stared at the weed bushes at the roadside and concentrated. She thought harder, wished and hoped to set the landscaping ablaze, even said so out loud in English and Creole, but still nothing. *Maybe danger triggered the switch?* One thought consumed her. *If I could summon it at will, could I then shut it off?*

Time passed in indescribable blurs. Days of insomnia and lack of food caught up to Jolene and weighed her body down like lead. Faint and tired, she squatted cross-legged on the roadside and panted. "I sure need you now, baby. I need you, need you bad."

What you need me for? I'm here.

Jolene sullenly looked over. Mark's entire body glowed, but the ethereal form was transparent. *Am I dreaming?* "Make everything make sense again," she cried out.

Cain't do that, Jo. You know it.

"Then bring my heart back." Her fingers brushed his phantom lips, which puckered and released. She sensed nothing. "The whole world's taking what it wants from me!"

Jo.

"Why'd it happen? Explain it to me and then tell me what to do 'cause half of me died in that tree with you. Say the word and I'll do whatever you tell me."

Can't you smell it? Gotta get them apples down 'fore the birds get to 'em. You should bake them pies again this year.

"Pies?" she said under her breath, bewildered.

The trees can come back, if you believe they will.

"If I believe you comin' back, Cher, you gone come back, too? You ain't leavin' me tonight 'til I get some peace for my soul."

Be quiet an' lissen, woman.

Jolene self-consciously closed her mouth.

Ain't nuthin' gone grow overnight. Takes time. Peace's like the tide comin' in at night. Somethin' bigger then you gets pullin' at you an' after while, the waves get bigger an' bigger an' then just flows and washes o'er you an' almost knocks you o'er. Mark's ebony skin shone richly like polished metal. *Love ain't grow o'ernight neither. Starts small an' when you give it what it needs, it grow like trees. Trees an' love ain't die. They jus' get taken away time an' again. They grow back, sometimes bigger an' stronger then the first. Ain't your fault. T'was just my time to go.*

"Will it be my time soon?" she interrupted. "To go?"

Don't know, Doll. Mark looked down silent, the sun rising in the distance. *All depends on you. You cain't hurry it. It jus' happens when it does an' you ain't gone die 'fore it is.*

"Will it?" Jolene pecked for specifics. Mark's spirit dimmed in the approaching sunrise. "Mark! Don't leave me! Mark!"

His spirit fled. Inside, Jolene experienced a slight pulling.

TEN

SATURDAY MID-MORNING, JUNE 30, 1962

"**M**ORNIN', is Reverend James home, Mother Kelley?" Georgie flashed a winsome smile, her light cotton blend blue-and-white patterned dress reaching an inch below the kneecap.

"What you bring this for?" Irritated by the girl's persistent knocking, she reluctantly accepted the casserole dish. "I cooks jus' fine. An' where's the rest of your clothes?"

She smirked. "Summer dresses are supposed to be a bit short. And I know you cook real fine, but these are *mariquitas* I fixed to cheer him up. Can I see him before the church meeting?"

Kelley reluctantly accepted the platter. "*Marry-what?* What you wanna see him 'fore?"

"No offense, Ma'am, but it's personal. Can I see him please?"

Personal? "Don't know if he 'ceptin' company, but I'll tell him." She headed up the stairs, mumbling. "Jus' ain't right to be callin' on a man, if you ask me my mind."

Darrion stretched facedown across the bed. Whitehead had embarrassed him before every upstanding Negro in town. Tomorrow morning, Darrion expected him to whoop himself into a tizzy over this victory up until the next revival.

"Giddup boy," said Kelley, "an' get dressed. You've got company."

He turned his head to the wall. "Company? Nobody even knows me here but you."

"That Georgie girl got somethin' for you. I ain't touchin' it. Be best served if you didn't either. Might've put somethin' in it."

"The choir director? What does she want?"

"Lawd if I know. Put on a shirt or your robe or somethin' an' find out. She's in the parlor. I expect her to leave 'fore I do, so don't make me late."

Minutes later, Darrion appeared in the parlor wearing a short-sleeved canary dress shirt with two buttons undone, taupe slacks with a subtle grey pinstripe and coffee cross stitch, and polished cordovan wingtips.

"Please, sit." Georgie patted a spot next to her. Darrion distanced himself further down the couch's cream cushion than she wanted. "Where's Mother Kelley?" She sounded a little anxious.

"In the kitchen."

"Lord, if I make Mother Kelley late for her meeting..." Georgie turned toward Darrion, moved closer, wrapped her soft, warm hands around his and whispered. "Meet me this afternoon."

Inspired by the killer combination of walnut-shaped onyx eyes, pout pink lips and an unforgettable smile, Darrion blurted out a quick, "Okay."

"Great." Georgie's face lit up. "Two o'clock then?"

"Where?"

"Meuller's Lake, on the east bank. You know it?"

"Very well."

"And don't tell *anyone*." She stood up and patted him on the shoulder. "There's something important we need to talk about."

He said goodbye and watched Georgie stroll happily down the porch steps into the street, her hips swaying beneath the breezy fabric. He wished to experience a woman's embrace again. *She'd feel slender around the waist and limbs*, he imagined, *baby soft mahogany skin, like black coffee intertwined with swirls of heavy cream. Is that what she wants?*

Darrion bided the time in between by listening to the radio and flipping through Violet's notebook, almost feeling as if he'd invaded her private thoughts by doing so. Quite a few of its entries included portions about her last husband, "Johnson," whose personal habits she detested. The two had an appointment for Saturday a week ago – a day following her death. He dozed off for some time and awoke hours later refreshed, but almost late for his rendezvous.

As he arrived at the meeting point a half hour later, enveloped in summer heat and pointless reverie, he failed to notice Georgie had been beckoning him for quite some time.

"Hi!" Georgie waved emphatically from a distance, unsure what to call him. *Reverend James* sounded too formal and *Darrion* too casual. "Did you hear me? Of course you didn't. That would be awfully rude of you…to ignore me."

"Hey there." He gestured back. "No, I didn't hear you."

"It's alright," she said, planting an awkward kiss on his cheek. "Reverend Whitehead kept us late. He went on and on. Isn't it beautiful out today?"

"I've never seen anything more gorgeous."

"With all the industrial smoke, you can't see it well in the city. When the sky looks this pretty, like over there…" Georgie pointed out an ocean blue crag in the distance surrounded by white film at the crest. "Zyonne feels like the center of the world." She hummed a delicate tune and started walking along the east bank with Darrion beside her.

"Who taught you how to sing like you do?"

"I always *could* do it. Nobody really taught me, but I didn't know I could sing until I tried. I write songs, too, but Reverend Whitehead won't let us sing them."

"Why not?"

"Some folks just stuck in their ways, I guess."

After a period of protracted silence, Darrion stopped. "So, what's this all about?"

"Quite a stir you caused in revival."

He exhaled, figuring it would be mentioned sooner or later. "You don't say."

"All of us ain't leave because of what you were saying. Some of us left because Reverend Whitehead expected us to leave. That's why I left, you know. He baptized me and my sister."

"Because he *expected* you to follow him?"

"You ain't the first one to be walked out on…prolly not the last."

He was familiar with church politics. "What are you getting at?"

"After service, a big group came together outside and asked him questions about your sermon; questions he couldn't answer. He called you a phony, said the reason you didn't preach Monday was because you got cut over a bet."

Darrion bit his lip at the truth. "I was cut at the pool hall, but I wasn't gambling."

Her eyebrows arched. "What business does a pastor have in a pool hall?"

"I was trying to blow off some steam, and I'm nobody's pastor."

"Well, he also said you were a heathen fool and anyone who listened to you would go to hell and that's when your mother slapped him."

"Sorry I missed it," he deadpanned. "And I was mad that she left, too."

"That's when I knew I had to see you. I never heard a sermon like yours before and, I don't know, there's just something about the words you spoke that made all the sense in the world to me. Something down deep in me won't leave it alone. I have to have more."

"More?"

The sensual way his lips curled flustered her. "N-not just me, y-you know. There are others. 'Bout 30 of us." Thirty people represented a third of the Higher Ground congregation, enough to be noticed missing.

Darrion swallowed. "Spell it out. What are you asking me to do?"

"Teach us."

"No, I can't. Not anymore."

Her voice raised in pitch. "Why not?"

"Preaching, teaching – it's a calling, God has to call you to it. You have to know it down inside your spirit. I don't know much of anything there right now."

"Reverend Whitehead's been doin' wrong a long time, so it's not like we haven't thought about leaving before. We just didn't have another option until now. Tell me God's not calling you to do this. Look me in the eye and tell me that with a straight face that all this happened for nothing."

Darrion stood toe-to-toe with Georgie and complied. He couldn't lie to those eyes.

Georgie coyly kissed him on the cheek before leaving. "Think about it."

Bone weary and red-eyed, Jack Miles pulled his chair up to his sleeping wife's bedside. "See, here's the thing. You have to live." He gripped her hand and, remembering her condition, loosened its grip. "I done a lotta bad things, Betts, and you have to forgive me." He said, clearing his throat. "Forgive me for what I done did to you. Can't die 'fore you do, you hear me?

"I guess I owe you the truth, why I done some of these things." The confessional flowed from his lips. "I ain't know why I done things sometimes, tell you the God honest truth. It's kinda like, deep down, I know what I'm supposed to do." He cradled her limp hand. "But I don't do it and I'm killing you."

Betty Lou's eyes tightened and her lips pursed. Still faking sleep, she wanted to roll away from Jack Miles and reclaim her hand.

"I don't deserve you, Betts, never did. If you can hear me, I want to try and make you happy, you know…be a good man to you."

Wild tears dropped down Betty Lou's face at the cruel joke.

He dotted the tears with a tissue. "My momma used to say she knew it was Tuesday when daddy came home from bowlin' and beat her around. He said 'sorry' and made nice until next Tuesday night until bowlin'. He blacked her eyes couple times, broke her arm once. One Tuesday, he came home and she had left." He sniffed. "I'll never forget it. Look. Wake up and tell me you gonna be okay. Doctor said ain't no way to tell 'til you wake up."

Betty Lou continued breathing steadily, unmoving, eyes closed. *Is he being persistent just to absolve his sins?*

"I want to give this marriage thing a shot. You know…start over. Just don't leave me. I don't think I could handle it."

And if she stayed, Betty Lou wondered how long it would take for Jack Miles to remember to tell her what day of the week it was, any reason not to take him back with open arms.

"Gimme one more chance. Jus' one more. I'll prove it an' show you the kinda good man I can be. Please? Jus' gimme one more chance."

In 18 years, Jack Miles cried exactly three times in front of his wife; the first at their wedding, the second, in the emergency room after "the accident" when he thought the police would arrest him, and now, kneeling by her bedside, his damp face buried in her stomach. Her defenses shattered, she reached down and stroked his hair. He composed himself and looked a red-eyed Betty Lou in the eyes. "You heard me?"

She nodded, her voice coarse and ragged. "Every…word."

"Then why ain't you say somethin'?"

"Pourin' out your heart to someone ain't somethin' to interrupt."

"So, how 'bout it? You forgive me?"

"Promise to tell me the straight truth. Always. No more lies."

"Betty, truth ain't always pink and pretty like you want it to be."

"I don't care about that. You promise me, *right here, right now*."

"Ain't never been honest, bet I lied comin' outta my momma's tummy."

"Promise me, please."

Jack Miles bore down and told a boldfaced lie. Betty Lou considered the shoddy performance and breathed a fairly convincing sigh of relief. At least he tried to make her believe his sincerity this time. She preferred the pretty pink lie to apathy.

"So? I *promised*," he said like a child expecting reward. "Well?"

They kissed – a long, soft caress full on the lips. She savored its sweetness and intended to store it as long as time allowed it to remain color fresh. "Alright," she whispered hopelessly. "Alright. I forgive you."

The cacophony of hospital noise irritated Geary beyond his singed nerve endings. He heard squeaking wheels belonging to a particular cart that made rounds the same time each afternoon. He tired of listening to his own breathing. Each time he slept, a brown bird outside the window insisted on chirping him awake. He promised himself he'd shoot the first brown bird he saw after being discharged, which he hoped would come in the next few weeks.

Soon, "Nurse Boring" entered the isolated room, replacing the looker on the morning shift who rarely came to attend to him unless there was a problem. While she cleansed his wounds and checked his vitals, the woman, who never saw an attractive day in her life, told Jack Benny jokes in a way that made Geary detest his favorite show. Though she rarely spoke, he sensed terribly bad breath behind the coffee-stained teeth and browned gums.

So, he did as the doctor said and "concentrated on healing." He did this by focusing on positive moments. Closing his eyes, he recalled the *baranina, kielbasa,* potato and cheese *pierogies,* beef sirloin and veal – traditional fare that his immigrant mother Joanna cooked him and his father with a side of fresh bread every day. Those were the good days before the Depression, when Christian Johnson plucked his son's rosy cheeks after a hard day of tailoring and gave no thought to the corpulence. After all, the boy rode a bike. He'd eventually thin out.

After the market crashed in his seventh year, they ate an abundance of watered-down soup in those times and were lucky to get a crust of old bread. Geary did what he could to contribute to the household as a youth, as he noticed the toll it took on his unemployed father. He enjoyed working, like his father before him, and it was during this period that Geary became athletic.

Christian lost the shop, and two years later, he turned to law enforcement. The day he was sworn in, Joanna got a photo taken of her two boys together. That picture still sat on his nightstand, next to another taken years later when Geary's number came up in the '42 draft. Then, while he and Jack Miles fought for freedom on the shores of El Alamein, a Negro thief shot his proud father in the chest. Geary did not find out until returning home the following year.

Prior to that time, as well as his mother's subsequent committal to a mental institution, Geary had no problem with Negroes. In fact, during their tour, Geary became involved with an African woman, unbeknownst to the rest of the platoon – Jack Miles included. She had the most delectable accent. The mere thought of her brought a crooked smile to his face. As they courted, she spoke of a time where races would not think ill of each other but would get along. Geary never thought it was possible, especially in America.

He enjoyed the relationship until Jack Miles found out and encouraged him to take her by force, not knowing they had already made love. The elder soldier made the rookie his pet project, educating him daily on the virtues of imposing will upon a weaker specimen. He offered to demonstrate on a local, but Geary declined. One night, he picked a fight with the African, escalating it to a crisis highlighted by the pinning of her to the floor and making her obey. Afterward, she did not speak, though Geary knew he'd killed something inside her. Through tears, she looked at her lover like a wounded animal at its predator – the same way that Creole girl had.

But Jolene was no stranger to him. They first met on the station platform last fall, as she said goodbye to her boyfriend. That burly Negro Mark Williams looked way too old for her, and he was sure there was at least 20 years between them. Geary pictured himself in his place, kissing Jolene passionately, wrapping his arms around her waist just above her prominent bottom. He positioned himself in her way so that when she waved at Mark, still continuing backwards, she bumped into Geary.

"Pay attention," he warned. She gave him a look and apologized.

Geary followed her to her home without reservation. When avoiding detection by automobile became impossible, he ventured into the orchard by foot. Around 8:00 p.m., she disrobed in her bedroom and got into the bathtub. The sightline through their wispy curtains allowed Geary to see basic shadows, but what he could distinguish he *liked*. She would never have him, at least willingly, and the town would never accept it. But as God was his witness, they had not seen the last of each other.

He remembered his ex-wife *Schiffler*, the microscopic beauty mark dotted on her left cheek, the arch of her eyebrows, the fine tan of her lithe limbs, the feel of her well-moisturized skin. In his mind's eye, he buried his face in her black hair, inhaling the honey-scented shampoo and personal sprays she used along the hot points of the neck and behind the ears. The aroma mixture drove him wild, but she managed to temper his excitement to a low, idling rumble. She occasionally allowed the beast room to roam, but would not let it take control. That mastery attracted him more. She claimed an "epiphany" and left him. The two never crossed paths again, save for formal paperwork, where the "Johnson" got replaced by the poetic surname "October."

Darrion peeled the foil from the top of the small platter and sniffed. The *mariquitas* looked like thin, wavy bananas and smelled like nothing he'd ever sampled before. As he wolfed one down, the combination of salt and slightly bitter citrus flavors threw his tongue into a sensory frenzy. Others quickly followed until he'd eaten the last of the portion Georgie afforded him.

"Slow down 'fore you choke," Kelley said from behind, startling him. "C'mon an' help me bust suds. Can't pay me, might as well earn your keep startin' now."

He did so somewhat morosely, assuming a position at the sink while his mother dried. Dinner was quite delicious: a bottom roast, medium well, seasoned mashed potatoes, fresh peas, corn, and buttered yeast rolls, but some of the drippings and leftover fat strands burned into a crust on the roasting pan were difficult to remove.

"Jus' let it soak," said Kelley, noticing the overly tense forearm muscles below his rolled-up sleeves. "I'll get it in the mornin'."

"That's okay," he said, scouring it with steel wool. "Thanks. I've almost got it all."

Kelley placed a damp hand on his. "Go on an' speak your peace 'bout what's eatin' you."

"You left," he blurted out, withdrawing his hand. "The *one time* in my life where I needed your support the most, when I *expected* your support – since you're the one that pushed me into preaching service in the first place – and you left. I want to know why."

Kelley shook her head. Her son's tone spoke more than his words. "No. *That* ain't it. That ain't all you mad about. Your daddy died an' ain't set you straight 'bout why you left. That's what you really wanna know, so I'll tell you.

"Your daddy," she mused pleasantly, "did somethin' ain't no Negro ever done in this town. He built this house wit' his own two hands. But he wanted more than I could give him. He start talkin' one day 'bout how 'better opportunities' were up north and how it would be 'a better life'."

The explanation caught Darrion off-guard. "You let him *talk* you into taking me away?"

"Was he wrong? Up 'til a couple months ago, ain't you live the life he talked about?"

"No," he said, storming off upstairs. "Not without you, it wasn't."

Kelley leaned against the sink and let him go. The pressure in her chest evolved into a seizure. Her lungs suddenly froze. Knuckles white from clutching the counter's molding, she resisted panic. A few seconds later, she relaxed and took short breaths while opening the wooden drawer to her left. Inside it, she removed a small pill container and a half-empty bottle of syrup. She took a pill and a teaspoon of the liquid, intending to tell Darrion the truth, but at another time.

ELEVEN

SUNDAY AFTERNOON, JULY 1, 1962

No words passed between mother and son following the previous night's confrontation. Darrion did not leave his room until after 9:00 a.m., when he knew Kelley was definitely gone. He emerged from the room in his pajama bottoms and walked freely. Curious, he entered his old room. The walls had been painted a flat eggshell white, but he noticed its original faint blue in small flecks near the baseboards. Along the doorframe were several notches no higher than a few feet, which is where his father routinely checked his height.

Inside the closet were a rusted old music stand and a page of sheet music. They must have belonged to a former boarder, as he did not take up an instrument until his teenage years. On the top shelf was a composition notebook with a thick coating of dust on it. Its inside cover bore the initials *C.V.S.* in flowery lettering. He relaxed a little, thinking that in an outrageous coincidence it might have belonged to *Corinne Violet Schiffler.*

He returned to his new room. There were other assemblies in town where he could have attended morning service, but in a small town, news traveled fast. With his complexion and dialect, it would not take long to be picked out. He dug out his Bible from its place in his suitcase and got into the Word for a few hours, allowing it to spiritually refresh him. Violet's notebook was still in his suit pocket untouched since the day he'd hid it there. He wondered what to do with it.

A short time later, Darrion ate breakfast downstairs. The morning sun shone so brightly through the kitchen window that he closed the curtains. Noticing a half open drawer near the sink, he opened it to see what the obstruction was and saw Kelley's prescriptions. He'd inquire about them later.

As he chewed, a mood of desperation suddenly swept over him. He was *alone* in a spacious, empty house. He missed Jayne. *Was she home?* It was after eleven o' clock, so the answer could be *no*. It could be *yes*. Darrion went to the phone. It rang once before connecting.

"Hello?" Jayne's voice exuded pleasantness.

Her voice made his heart jump. Darrion wished he could reach out and touch her. *Jayne?* He could not bring himself to audibly respond. *Suppose she rejects me, or worse?*

"Hello? Who is this?"

Jayne, it's me. I'm so lonely here. I do forgive you. Can I come home?

"Darrion?" Her voice trembled with emotion. "Is it you? Where are you?"

In Zyonne. I'm stranded at my mother's house. Can you wire me some money?

"I miss you so much. I've been thinking about you and waiting for your call."

I miss you too. I've been calling on and off for the past week, but you haven't been there.

"Where are you? Just tell me wherever you are and I'll send you a wire. Just come home."

Someone knocked at the door. As if he'd committed sin, he hung up and stepped to the front door. Darrion left the matching top to his pajama bottoms there just in case, but did not expect company. He opened the door without thinking. Georgie stared at his bare musculature and the hideous red scar across his stomach before catching herself and covering her eyes.

"Good morning," Georgie said with a smile. "Do you have...something to put on?"

"Sorry!" He quickly dressed behind the door. "Come in. What are you doing here?"

"Same as you, I guess. Playing hooky. I told Reverend Whitehead I had a throat cold."

He laughed at the fake congestion she put on to pronounce *throat cold*. She held a cumbersome picnic basket. "What do you have there, Yogi?"

"A little lunch. It's my way of saying I'm sorry for walking out on you. Plus, I thought I could show you around, since you're new here, sort of. Go get dressed, Boo Boo."

"Ten minutes?"

"Sure. Hurry up before the iced tea gets all hot."

Darrion rocketed upstairs. Georgie wandered into the parlor, but not too far in case Kelley returned unexpected. On the end table was a picture of Kelley as a young woman, which Georgie admired as there were ways she favored her in the face and body. In the china cabinet was a picture of Kelley with a fair-skinned, curly-haired boy. After looking around, she opened the drawers beneath the cabinet and found a photo album. Too afraid to turn through the whole thing, she picked a page in the middle and found a picture of who she assumed was Darrion's father. Though he was handsome, he appeared white. From the stories she'd heard, he'd taken Darrion north with him and left his wife alone in Zyonne to rot.

"Ready?" Darrion descended the stairs slowly enough for Georgie to replace the album and move to a less-suspicious location in the room.

"Sure. Let's go." Sensing his eyes following her, she swished her hips a little extra in approaching the porch steps. While the light cotton dress allowed her skin the ability to breathe in humid air, the fabric was soft to the touch and slithered about her body's features. "Can I have your hand?"

Mesmerized by her movements, Darrion snapped back to attention. "Sure." He offered his right hand, which she used for balance going down the stairs and held at the bottom. He self-consciously let hers go. "Where are we going, the promenade?"

"No...someplace a little less...public."

While they walked to a secluded section of the town park, Georgie peppered him with questions – first, the general. *How do you like the weather here? What's it like being back? What have you done since you've been here?* Then came the more invasive and specific inquiries. *Where did you live up north? Are you still married? How long have you been divorced?* Darrion avoided the probing questions with "I'd rather not talk about it right now, if you don't mind." Georgie responded with an uncomfortable silence.

They arrived at the destination, both weary of small talk. Georgie unpacked fried chicken and biscuits wrapped in wax paper, mustard potato salad, collard greens and two mason jars of iced tea. She fixed him a plate, then her own. Darrion said grace and they ate, he more ravenously than she. He spotted Georgie's chicken leg and wing, spoonful of potato salad and greens. *Is this a date?* As she finished his portions long before she did hers, he asked for extras. He'd have eaten everything if he thought it would prevent her from asking him more questions.

"Do you find me attractive?" she shot out.

Darrion almost choked. "Excuse me?"

This time, she looked him directly in the eye. "You know, do you find me...good looking?" Her suddenly demure demeanor was a pleasant shift from the aggressiveness.

"Georgie, you know you're a good looking girl." Her smile down-turned, as the lilt in the phrase indicated he was not finished. "You don't need me to tell you that, but I'm at least ten years older than you..."

"Just *ten*," she interrupted, "I turned 22 just this March."

"... newly-divorced, and jobless. You wouldn't want to bring me home to your mother."

"My parents died before we left Cuba," she murmured. "My sister Livvie was at service and, from what she saw, she likes you. Even Raul likes you. So do I."

"I don't think I'm ready for a relationship right now."

She wiped off her hand with a napkin and extended it. "Can I be your attractive *friend*?"

He smiled. "Sure. I could always use an attractive friend."

In silence, the two ate miniature peach cobblers for dessert, until Georgie suddenly perked up. "So," she said while taking a sip of tea, "have you given any thought to my other proposal?"

Astounded by her tendency to flit from subject to subject with aplomb, Darrion admonished her. "Georgianna, it hasn't even been 24 hours."

"I know that, it's just...if something is meant to be, don't you usually know it pretty quickly? And yesterday, you didn't come out and say yes, but you didn't say no, either."

"Give me more details. What are we talking about here?"

She sidled up to him. "One night this coming week, we'll all get together and have a Bible study that you'll lead. See how you like it. If you don't, fine, walk away, no hurt feelings. But if you *do*, well, we'll see where it goes from there."

Intrigued, he pressed further. "Goes from there?"

"Zyonne has no shortage of Negro churches. I'm sure you know that. So, if this is not what God has called you to do, no big deal. But one thing I'm sure of – he *did not* call you to be newly-divorced, jobless, living in your mother's house and not doing a thing with your life."

Darrion thought about it for a minute. "I'll *try* it." From that point, he loosened up a bit. Georgie was a nice girl and definitely attractive. He sneaked looks at her as she packed away the plastic containers and tossed away the trash in a nearby refuse can. He pretended to busy himself when her eyes were within sight.

"Let me walk you home, *friend*," he offered. "I'll even carry the basket."

"Nice offer. But you forgot the *attractive* part, unless, of course, you don't think it's true?"

"No. I mean, *yes*." He fumbled his mason jar, nearly spilling the leftover drops onto her.

"Thanks." She smiled, flirtatiously. "Carry the basket, huh? It's a lot lighter now."

The two joked much of the walk back until Georgie struck a somber note by talking about her parents. "I miss him, my *papi*, you know. He died when I was eight."

"I had so many questions to ask mine," Darrion said. "I never got the chance before his accident. He avoided them most of the time."

"Like what?"

"I was about six years old and I came in from playing outside because it was getting late. When I got there, he sent me upstairs to my room. He and my mother had fought so badly that night. I don't remember what they said as much I remember *how* they yelled at each other. I shut the door and put a pillow over my head. I still heard them. I'll never forget it.

"My dad came into my room, got me off the bed and started packing my clothes into any bag he could find. I hadn't bathed or eaten. My mother was crying and she yelled at him from their room. I started crying too. The next thing I know, I'm on a bus north with him, and all he said was 'We're headed to a better place, with more opportunities.' I never saw her again until now."

"Gosh." The confession caught Georgie off-guard. "Mother Kelley won't talk about it?"

"Not until last night. Sorry to tell you all this; I've had it locked up inside me for a long time."

"That's okay." She had no idea the depths to which her new friend had experienced hurt. Georgie offered him her left hand, which he accepted.

"I've been divorced for a few months now," he sighed. "My ex-wife came to me the day I left and asked me to take her back. I phoned her this morning just before you came."

"Oh." Georgie felt like dropping his hand, but didn't. "So, you're not over her?"

"She really did a number on me. I thought you should know, since you asked."

"Sure," she responded with a hint of disappointment. "That's what friends are for." For a while, Georgie did not say a word. "Any plans for the Fourth?"

"Not that I know of. What are you doing?"

"Raul likes to cookout, so I'm sure he'll be putting everything but our dessert on the grill. Some of it'll be Cuban. I didn't make us any for lunch because I wasn't sure you'd like it."

"I liked what you made me."

"The *mariquitas*? Good, so you'll come then? Afterwards, we can watch the fireworks they set off in the park. There's a real good view from this area."

"Sounds like a plan." He looked around. "Where do you live? We're getting close to my mother's house."

"Just down the street from ya'll, but you don't have to walk me home. It's out of your way. I'll take a rain check, though."

She walked with him, hand-in-hand, all the way up to the porch, where they parted. As Georgie rounded the corner and waved, he spied on her again, convinced this observation was to ensure her safety and not in admiration. When she disappeared from sight, he entered the house prepared to answer to the woman standing at the kitchen window.

"So," she said without facing him, "how was the service at Bedside Baptist this morning?"

"I spent some time in study," he said, innocently, "and then I had lunch with a friend."

"That same friend that ain't hardly dressed, in my backyard, walkin' 'round my garden?"

"Same one, yes."

"That girl's tryin' to trap you."

"You can relax. We're just friends. Besides, I know if she does anything, you'll put her in her place. She told me that you slapped Reverend Whitehead, defending me."

"Friends, huh? That's how it starts."

"I was wondering if you wouldn't mind letting me hold a Bible study here this week."

Her head nodded. "Bible study, you say?"

"About 30 people or so, for about an hour or so. Would you mind?"

Kelley subdued a heavy cough inside her chest by drinking water. She was running out of medicine and needed a significant amount of money for more. "Takin' up an' offerin'?"

"A freewill, of course, and I didn't forget. You'll have your money soon."

"Then have your Bible study," she grunted. "Thursday night, 'round seven's good."

"Thank you, Momma." He rushed forward and embraced his mother around the waist. She allowed him to hold her as long as he was willing and wondered if calling her *Momma* was as awkward to say as it was to hear. Darrion rushed upstairs and took the notebook belonging to *C.V.S.* from the top shelf of the closet in his old room. Freeing Violet's notebook from his coat pocket, he sat at the edge of his bed and started translating.

TWELVE

THURSDAY EVENING, JULY 5, 1962

A SHIVER ran down Jolene's back. She felt indebted to Charlie for seeing her halfway home, but involuntarily cooking supper at a strange white woman's home forced the already small appetite crawling from her belly further away.

During a telephone call, Charlie asked about Creole cuisine and seconds later strongly hinted that she'd never eaten it before. At that point, only borderline spoiled roast beef and two buns remained in Jolene's refrigerator, perfect for a last meal of skimpy Po' Boy sandwiches.

"Why ain't you eatin' Doll," asked Charlie with a full mouth.

"Not real hungry."

"You ain't get *that* figure by not eatin'."

Jolene blushed and fidgeted. "You always talk like that?"

"Relax. I don't like you. You just real pretty."

"Been told so my whole life. Makes me wish a brain counted for something around here."

"It do," Charlie said, chewing, "but if we got looks, gotta use 'em to get what we want."

"I got a brain."

"Yeah, you do, but as long as you got *those*, they ain't much interested in it."

Jolene crossed her arms over her breasts. "Says you."

"Well, what you doin' for money these days, thinkin' hard?"

The white woman pulled no punches. "None of your business."

"If you want some of *my* business, let Charlie know."

Selling her body to anyone with a dollar bill disgusted Jolene, but she fixed her lips into a half-smile and said a polite, "No, thank you. I'm fine."

"Oh." She put her sandwich down. "I ain't no street walker, Joséphine."

"What you call it then?"

"Doin' a *favor*, that's all. You doin' me a favor now with this food and I ain't on my back, am I? Same thing. Most times, me and my Johns – we just talk. Other times, we don't."

"So, what do they do for you?"

"A drink here and there, a lil' present. One lets me borrow a car every now and then. You'd be surprised what a lonely man'll give a woman just for company. Anyway, I'm talkin' 'bout sumthin' a lil' different. You ever read your horoscope in the papers?"

"My what?"

"Wait here." She tossed her napkin onto the table and flew into another room. Jolene looked around for a weapon. The blunt knife she used to cut the sandwiches would have to do. Charlie returned with a folded up newspaper in hand and sat down. "When's your birthday?"

"What?"

"Birthday, you know, that one day where you get older once a year?"

"February 22nd."

"You're an Aquarius!" She popped open the paper. "You're generous and flexible and you like things that run against tradition. You love pictures and can be shallow at times."

The newspaper read like Jolene's life story. "Tell me more."

"How many sisters do you have, one…two? Two, I bet."

"Annie and Nona."

"They poked fun at you, huh?"

Jolene swallowed and shifted weight.

"You're the youngest, right? They teased you."

Anna and Nona used to chase and tackle Joséphine, pin her down, rub mud into her face and then heckle their mud-masked little sister with ugly names. She'd cry and run to Freedom, who reminded her that she was an acceptable shade, unlike them.

"How do you know?" Jolene asked in a hurt voice.

"This is my *real* business. I tell you about your life. Do you know what a housewife will pay to hear something good headed towards her borin' life? Most of those gals' husbands don't pay them no mind and jus' give 'em money to spend."

"But how did you know about *me*?"

"I didn't. *You* told me. I know the qualities of the signs by dates, an' I go to the girl in the market, ask 'em questions 'til I get their birthday. I tell 'em it's a gift. Then I say stuff 'til I get a reaction out of 'em, like you wit' your sisters. You real kinda quiet and shy, so you ain't the oldest and every baby gets picked on. It's easy! I make the connection and you tell me everything I need to know."

"Ain't right stirrin' up and troublin' folks past like that."

"We talk an' they offer me a few bucks for my troubles. Then they become regulars. Regular clients equal regular money. You want in? Or would you rather starve and be honest?"

"Why *me*?"

"I ain't gotta problem wit' your people, but they got problems wit' me. They'll listen to you. You make the money, an' when you build up, I get a small cut – like a fee or somethin'."

Jolene buried her eyes in the food on her plate. With piling bills and her rations all out, she'd even considered doing what she imagined Charlie was proposing a minute ago.

"It ain't like you gotta world of options. When it comes down to it, you gotta do what you gotta do to get by. Ain't nobody gonna do nuthin' for you now but *you* and that's the truth. You gonna let bums in the alley eat better than you? 'Cause they are right now." She paused. "Look, I like you, Gal, but don't get no ideas. I just think you a great young Negro with a good head on her shoulders and you gotta bad break. I'm sorry about him. But you gotta live, one way or another, plug up all these holes you got inside, and do something. You gotta better way to do it? Show me and I'll do it tomorrow."

Jolene's alternatives were few. She finished sopping up the juice on the plate with sandwich bread. Freedom taught her never to make big decisions on an empty stomach.

"And so saints, you *must* change. There's no other way."

Sixty brown faces leaned in.

"For if we believe what the apostle John writes is truth and Jesus, who is with God and is God, is also the Word made flesh...and the Word is changing, then you, like the Word, also have to change.

"But is the Word changing? You have heard it said God does not change. This is true. He is the same yesterday, today and tomorrow. Since Jesus is the Son of God and is the Living Word, then the Word of God does not change, either.

"So what changes then? This message is new to you, but not to God. So, God is who He always was, but your understanding of Him and His Word is what *is* changing."

Georgie stood in the parlor behind the man she hoped would one day become her *man*. Through her urging, he grew facial hair extending into a thin beard connected to his sideburns and his complexion, once sifted white sand, had tanned thanks to the southern sun. If it was possible for the preacher to become more handsome, he'd achieved it with ease.

Although they had chatted over the telephone the past couple days and had casual get-togethers; ice cream on Monday at the promenade, morning coffee Tuesday, and nothing Wednesday (he had to work), Darrion never seemed relaxed around her. *He's still pining for Jayne, or something, so much that a romantic relationship with him will certainly fail.*

And Kelley grew increasingly curt with her presence. If Georgie called, Kelley opened the door and went about her business. If they crossed paths, it happened by accident.

"This *lost testament*," he continued, "is not an addition to the Word of God. Your Bible is complete without it, so it's not a deletion, nor does it correct what has already been written. It's just a tool to further shape your understanding of who God is.

"We don't know for certain who He is, but when we gain any kind of greater understanding of Him or His ways we get confused. He'll do something in our lives using a different method than before and it seems like He's changing. Not so. Remember, He-does-not-change.

"God has millions of ways to bring blessings to His people. We cannot get locked into our multi-talented God doing something just one way. Otherwise, our lives will grow stale with the expectation for Him to do something using a method He intended for one use only.

"Look at the text. In verse six, God instructs Moses to strike the rock to provide water for the Israelites. This is method number one. Later, in 20, Verse Eight, God instructs Moses to *speak* to the rock. This is method number two. Moses trusted God's provision only through method number one and couldn't make the switch later to method number two. He missed out on the blessing of a lifetime."

Outfitted in a floor-length black skirt, sky blue blouse and a matching satin ribbon around her ponytail, Georgie opened a nearby bay window to cool off. But the five dozen sweaty bodies crammed into the room nullified the small breeze.

"How many of you are stuck in your ways and refuse to change? You do the same things every day the same way, in the same places at the same times – never any variation. If something moves in to disrupt your everyday routine, you cuss it out in Jesus' name.

"The devil is a thief who comes to steal, kill and destroy. Thieves study patterns of behavior and the easiest people to steal from are the predictable ones who never do anything different. So, the devil disrupts your routine, steals your joy and destroys your peace.

"God never meant for you to stay the same. If He did, He wouldn't have created you with flaws. Human perfection didn't exist until Jesus. God created man in His image. The sixth day creation is a three-dimensional image of God. What you see in the mirror is a two-dimensional image. It's not your complete being. It can be much *like* you, but it cannot be you.

"You are God's three-dimensional reflection. When He looks at you, He should see a spiritual image like Himself. And if you are in His image, you have to come to a greater understanding of yourself, so you can achieve the purpose He designed for you before the world was formed."

"I know what you're thinking. I've thought it before, too. *Can you tell me who I am for real? What is it that I'm supposed to be doing? How do I know what I'm doing is the right thing?* Raise your hand, if you've ever wanted to know the answers to these questions."

Georgie's hand lifted first, setting off a hesitant wave around the room. Even Kelley, who glowered at the young woman fawning over her son, put up her hand.

"You know who you are. You just don't *know* that you know. Achieving purpose means mind, body and spirit must be in agreement in all that they do. Your spirit and mind will always fight one another because your spirit is from God and your mind is sinful. If your mind wins the battle, you will never discover who you are or achieve your purpose because your mind controls your body. The spirit urges but the mind must agree for the body to react. This battle is what Paul meant when he said the flesh lusteth against the spirit and the spirit against the flesh. If the spirit wins, the flesh does not get to sin."

"Uh huh, *lust*," said Kelley, fanning her hand in Georgie's direction. "Lust, lust, lust."

"Pray and honestly seek God and ask Him to reveal who you are. Like Jacob, stop believing in what people say you are because of your family name and ask the Lord to tell you who you are. Stop asking other folks. Then, like Israel, your responsibilities and your purpose on this earth will become as clear as glass. God bless you. Let us pray."

Kelley led a short prayer and Darrion delivered the benediction. No sooner than the word "Amen" left his lips did Georgie glue herself to his side, greeting whom he greeted and shaking hands with the wives. "God bless you, brother, sister," she'd say or "I'll be praying for you, mother." They seemed to generally accept her as Darrion's appendage, albeit temporary. And, while he despised traditional amenities, Georgie *adored* them. He did not rebuke her. Unlike Kelley, he did not see the harm.

"T'was some word you preached, Darrion." As the crowd cleared, Georgie lifted a crumb-littered cake plate with the intent to take it to the kitchen. Kelley snatched it away.

"That's alright. Ain't need no help. Thank you much."

"Momma..." Darrion said, as Kelley fled into the kitchen. "I'm sorry."

"She doesn't like me."

"I don't understand why."

"Women are territorial, Darrion. You haven't been hers for 20 years."

"So what?"

Georgie enveloped Darrion in her arms and rested against his chest. "You're such a *man*."

He stiffened up at first and then hesitantly embraced her. "I've been called worse."

"*So.*" She pulled back and looked at him. "Do *you* like me?"

He planted a patronizing peck on her forehead. "I'm starting to."

"Then that's all that matters. I'm cashing in my rain check from Sunday. Walk me home?"

"Sure."

They used the well-lit streets, which doubled the distance to Georgie's house, but neither minded. He enjoyed the company and mutual flirting back and forth. She was attractive to him, more so than he'd let on at first. He toyed with the idea of a casual relationship but did not want to lead her on. So, he refused to hold hands, which worked until she grabbed his under the auspices of "feeling more safe."

"Your beard looks great. I forgot to tell you that after service."

"Thanks." He stroked his chops. "I'm getting used to it. I haven't grown one like it in quite a while."

"I like it, too," she said, beaming. "So, we've talked every day this week…"

"Yes," he said, as they slowed in front of Raul and Livia's house.

"Do you feel any better about the Bible study now?"

"Bigger crowd than I expected, but that's a good thing. And the freewill offering will help my mother. She's been struggling. She won't talk about it, but I'm sure it's been hard."

"I know she's had boarders in and out, but the last regular I remember was some short white woman who stayed there during her divorce. Don't remember her name. Mother Kelley's was the last place he'd look for her." She slowed near the concrete steps to the house. "This is me. I'd better go before they start watching."

"Thank you," he said with solemnity. "You helped bring me back from a dangerous place."

Georgie stood on tip-toes and planted a firm peck against Darrion's lips. He did not pull back immediately, nor respond to the soft expression. Georgie withdrew, mortified. "I'm so sorry. I didn't mean to…"

Darrion silenced her with a kiss of his own, passionate in its own right. His arms confidently enveloped Georgie and she returned the affection.

Inside, Livia and Raul parted the Venetian blinds and smiled.

THIRTEEN

TUESDAY EVENING, AUGUST 14, 1962

FORTY days ago, Jolene had weighed dishonest business against cut-off notices. She gambled with the former. Then, after dinner, Charlie spearheaded the transformation, tossing hanger after hanger onto the robust king-sized bed. Her charge voted each outfit down. Charlie's waist measured an inch larger but she lacked the Negro woman's curves. That could be ignored, except around the hips. But the bodices clung to Jolene's upper body like a second skin.

"Pick *somethin'* girl. Dang! We ain't got all night!"

Jolene held up a demure pearl silk button-down chemise. "This."

"Try it on."

Charlie watched Jolene shed her own blouse and change into the selection, fastening it up to the top button. As with the other outfits, the material pulled snugly around the bust.

"And this. This will do." An eggshell white skirt hit the bed. "I wonder how I'd look in these." They were warm colors; flesh pink, raspberry, pewter, chartreuse, and tangerine followed.

"You a *beautiful* woman," said a mesmerized Charlie.

Annoyed, Jolene continued ignoring her. "Can I try these on?"

"I'm talkin' to you. You don't think you beautiful?"

"Charlemagne, enough."

"Just a simple question. You *don't*, do you?"

Jolene looked around the room, in the open closet, on the bed, anywhere but right into Charlie's ice blues. "A flower ain't up and call itself a flower. Somebody calls it a name and then it is what it is."

"Gosh, Darlin'." Charlie put an arm around Jolene, who moved on the other side of the room.

"Freedom told me to think for myself," she said above a whisper, head bowed and eyes misting. "She told me I had a good head."

"Ain't Mark ever tell you that you was beautiful?"

"He ain't have to." Jolene repeated it like she'd trained herself to do so.

"Who says?"

"He worked all the time for me. He kept the house going. He kept *me* going. Ain't *that* beautiful? Why he gotta tell me what I look like? I got a mirror. I don't need nobody to call me this and that." Jolene found her reflection and examined it. The eyes glistened and danced in their sockets. Her cheekbones resurrected a smile. She unbuttoned the blouse to its second button, then the third. Shocked at the revealed cleavage, Jolene buttoned up. Then, she undid them. She let her hair down and clothed herself in silk and cotton rainbows. She giggled and covered her mouth, happy and unable to control the laughter.

Now, weeks later, Joséphine was turning the suburbs bordering Zyonne upside down with pinpoint accurate prophesies. Charlie eased her in at first. She performed a few times and Jolene witnessed it from a distance. First, there was an "accidental" bump, then an apology followed by an introduction. Her infamous, man-devouring ways forced her to use the ridiculous alias "Marie Bloomfield." She despised confrontations, especially with jealous wives.

Jolene laughed each time she heard the surname. It was so prim and proper for a carnal girl who admittedly had trouble staying out of bed.

The first name gave a clue into the woman's personality. "Marie" adjusted the first questions to cater to it. From there came the astrology; zodiac signs, new, half and full moons, star constellations, alignments and other things that confused Jolene. The one thing she remembered about the science was that everything revolved around the birthday. "Marie" intertwined that information and produced a fairly accurate analysis. If the woman said nothing at all after that, then she likely had herself another paying client – which were plentiful as of late.

Once her own success began, Joséphine thought to sock away about a third of her client fees for a rainy day and use the rest to pay her bills. An adjusted diet helped Charlie's clothes a little in the trouble spots and eliminated the need for a new wardrobe.

Tonight, the pair dared to venture inside the suburban Zyonne lines. Joséphine spotted a surefire target in the market in aisle one near the window, a sorry looking white woman with a disheveled pecan wig.

"You a sharpshoota now," said Charlie. "Follow your mark."

Betty Lou self-consciously adjusted the wig on her head and advanced down the market's baked goods aisle. She tossed two loaves of bread atop the preserves, butter, rice, pasta, beans, and tomato sauce – staple foods, set to last at least a week and prevent Jack Miles from complaining about how much daggone groceries cost these days.

Seems like yesterday we agreed to change and work on the marriage. Both were reneged, one after the other. Betty Lou cracked first. Jack Miles let her sleep the first few days home. She woke up around noon each day – no toast to make, no coffee to brew, not even a dirty dish or cup from breakfast. He'd already gone to work, so she couldn't watch him depart. There was no reefer left and she promised herself not to score any more. Without him bothering her one way or another, she didn't know right from left.

Her husband kept his promise, but everything seemed so *perfect*, unreal and scripted. *How can I enjoy it when deep down, I know someday it's gonna disappear?* This man wasn't the *real* Jack Miles! Betty Lou wondered what his motives were, so she gave him everything she thought he'd want. The next day, he bought her a day's salary worth of mixed carnations. None were pink or white.

That became something to pick on him about. He didn't know her taste. She pestered him for money, picked a fight for no good reason, and watched his frustrated face redden like a cherry. Then she downplayed his improving bedroom tendencies. That counted as the final straw. Fed up, he reverted back to his old ways, which Betty Lou hated but found consistently believable.

The staggered *clip-clopping* of Betty Lou's heel clicking against the floor aggravated her ears, so she compensated to silence it. Instead, the *clip* grew softer on the right leg, which pronounced the left leg's *clop*. Annoyed, she let the issue ride and walked normally.

"Can we hurry along a bit?" Lately, some of Jack Miles' reemerged rudeness rubbed off on Betty Lou. "Ain't got all day."

"Right. Sorry, Ma'am." The ruddy and freckled boy hesitated in bagging her groceries because he spotted a smoking hot blonde outside.

"*Miss,* not *Ma'am.* I ain't old enough to be called Ma'am."

"Yes, Ma'am…I mean *Miss*."

"How old you think I am?"

A number of eyes behind her urged the boy to say something, anything to get her to move on, so he waxed hyperbolic. "Twenty-five."

Betty Lou pinched his cheek. "Why, you're not far off!" Someone behind her snickered.

"Have a good night, *Miss*," he said. Betty Lou hugged the bag and exited the store strutting, too distracted to see the shadows shift.

"Excuse me, don't I know you?"

"Geez!" Startled, Betty Lou dropped the paper bag onto the ground. "You scared me. You always approach folks like that?"

"Sorry, Cheri. Here, let me help you."

Joséphine gathered her pristine gold-and-plum skirt at the hem and bent to assist the white woman in gathering the items. Nothing had broken, but the impatient woman shooed her away. "Name's Joséphine. Joséphine Courtier."

"Betty Lou Everham." The two shook hands. There was a connection.

"Can I ask you something, Betty Lou…something simple?"

"Sure, if you can you talk while you walk."

Pebbles and stones noisily cushioned their soles. Charlie watched the duo from behind a vehicle a few yards away.

"Why wouldn't you let me help you out?"

"I'm just particular 'bout my things, is all."

"Bull."

"Pardon me?" She sounded offended.

"You a Taurus, a *bull*. You must've been born in April or May."

"May 16th." Betty Lou saw Charlie in the distance and grew suspicious. "I gotta go."

Betty Lou scampered away. Joséphine turned to Charlie, hands outstretched as if to say *now what*? Charlie jabbed an index finger in the air toward Betty Lou and mouthed *follow the mark*.

Joséphine obeyed. "Wait, hold on. Wait. I can help you."

"Right." She stopped. "Help me do *what*? What do you want?"

"You're a Taurus. That's a fixed earth sign."

"What kinda nonsense you talkin' 'bout?"

"It means you fixed. You don't like change too tough. You determined and you like your things. You supposed to be *patient,* too. Your sun must be Capricorn then."

"My son gotta be a cappa who?"

"Try to follow along. Look." Joséphine pointed to the mountainous horizon. "The stars. They connect and paint pictures."

"Pictures? Stars make pictures?"

"You draw a line and connect them, like a puzzle. Your sun is the picture the stars formed over there on May 16th. Your sun gotta be Capricorn, so the picture gotta be a goat."

The conversation mystified Betty Lou. "Tell me more."

"You like your things, steady as a spring rain. And you're patient, so much you'd wait for the earth to rotate twice. But that also means you do the same ole things, even if you ain't like 'em just 'cause you ain't want 'em to shake up any."

The bag stuffed with edible routine suddenly felt heavier.

"You tend to like Capricorns and Scorpios."

"My husband was born on Valentine's Day," she said eagerly. "Tell me 'bout him. Can you tell me something?"

"He born at day or night?"

"'Bout midnight or so, I think."

Joséphine's eyes fluttered a second in thought. "He's a Capricorn, that's for sure. But his sun might be Scorpio, a scorpion. Ya'll two together like oil and water, I bet?"

"You ain't said nothin' but a word."

Now came the hook. "I gotta run, Miss. Nice talkin' to you."

Betty Lou's mouth drooped. "No, please. Wait. Tell me some more."

"Can't. Time is money, Cheri, and I got someone waiting."

"Let *her* wait." Betty Lou set the grocery bag beside her feet and fished out all the grocery change. "I got a couple dollars left, I think. One…two…and some nickels. Here. This enough?"

"'Bout my fee, I s'pose." Joséphine received the bounty. "Give me your hands."

Betty Lou thrust her palms toward Joséphine, who stared at them beneath the poor outside lighting.

"You real sensitive and you picture the world perfect. You trust everyone you meet, but you ain't real controlling. Responsible, most of the time, but you get lonely and sometimes you do things that ain't right 'cause of it. You worry a lot about things, things you can't don'thing about. And one more thing."

"What's that?"

"You ain't get angry real quick, do you?"

"No, not really."

"Well, when you do, hope I ain't there to see it."

The knot in Darrion's stomach failed to budge. The muscles around his shoulder blades bundled and tensed. Georgie loomed over his shoulder and poked him in the side.

They were waiting, the 90 or so people packed into the house, crowding on the porch, or listening intently through open windows. They'd come to regard him with great respect and admiration.

Kelley refreshed his water glass, and he forced the liquid down in slow, even swallows. There was no avoiding it now. Georgie piped up and crooned a familiar hymn to buy him time. The already worn voices joined along. This particular hymn had five verses, but Georgie intended to sing just three. After two songs, five more verses in 80 degree-plus heat might incite rioting.

More so from anxiety, Darrion perspired profusely, soaking his jersey blue short-sleeved shirt beneath the armpits and along the lower back. His fingerprints moistened the pages of the completed translation at the edges. He came to formally call it "The Lost Testament." "If you have your Bibles, please turn to the book of Genesis Two. We will start here with our foundational text, starting at verse 20."

After reading the verses, he closed his leather-bound Bible. "These texts give us the backdrop for the first marriage."

"What's wrong wit' Passa?" A church mother whispered in Kelley's ear. "He awright?"

"That *girl's* what's wrong with him. Been calling on him every day, jus' 'bout." Kelley whispered such a way so Georgie perceived the voice, but couldn't understand it.

Darrion's eyes flashed up to Georgie, who gave him a look of encouragement.

"Think she done put some kinda evil rut on 'im?" asked the church mother.

"Chile, hush, that's some foolishness."

"By the way, Adam," he managed, "he, he'd to name all the animals, every living thing. This lets us know from this process that the first man is intelligent and not a Neanderthal like historians and scientists would have you believe. But, as good as the sixth day creation is, Adam is missing something important."

The Lost Testament fell from his hands onto the hardwood floor. He turned for his water glass but fumbled it to the floor. The glass shattered in quarters. Kelley collected the shards and scooted to the kitchen.

"Darrion," said Georgie in an admonishing tone. "What's wrong?"

"Nothing's wrong," he snapped back. "I'm fine."

For all Kelley's morality, she still had superstitions. Whenever too many things dropped on the floor, like tonight, with the drinking glass and the book, turn a wary eye.

Darrion snatched the notebook from Georgie, who mumbled something in Spanish, sat down and abruptly crossed her legs.

"In the Lost Testament, Jesus tells us in order to understand God's original intentions concerning marriage or anything else spiritual, you must take each piece of meat one at a time. Understand each part of it and connect it to the whole picture. Like puzzle pieces, His Word fits together piece-by-piece to give you a detailed snapshot of His divine perfect will.

"If you stop at verse 26 of Genesis Chapter One and insert Chapter Two, verses 21 to 25, and then continue with verse 27 of Chapter One until the end, you get the events in order.

"First, the man, whom God calls Adam, is formed from dust and the Lord's own breath. I want to get on with the lesson, but just imagine how precious God thinks you are to *breathe* life into you. When you feel ugly, depressed, beaten down – just remember that.

"Adam is commissioned by God to name every living creature on the sixth day. He completes this work alone, but even then, God recognizes that Adam has a great need going unfulfilled. All of creation was considered good by God, but Adam's loneliness wasn't good. I believe Adam felt spiritually spent; not because he didn't rest or had to perform unusually hard work, but that he'd to do it *alone*.

"God causes the man to go to sleep and removes part of him; the rib, part of the bone structure designed to protect the fragile organs. The Lord then forms a female from the rib and brings her to him. Adam calls this creation woman. Then Moses, who authored Genesis by the Holy Ghost, adds for this reason that a man will leave his parents and be united to his wife, and they will become one flesh.

"According to the Lost Testament, both men and women were created as intellectual beings that need God, are called to work for God and have a desire to be loved. Look at the text. God's presence meets Adam, fulfilling the first need. In verse five, we see Adam's work is to tend the garden; work is the second need. His aloneness in verse 18 led to the creation of a help meet in verse 22 to meet the third need. Look at those verses and tell me what the Lord shows you."

"Didn't Adam love Eve?" Georgie's voice cracked.

"It is never written in Scripture whether he did or not. From the text, it seems like the marriage was more functional than anything else, but I'm sure he felt *something*."

"I ain't dusted in a good day," Kelley interjected, handing a handkerchief to Georgie, "an' there's all kinds a dust 'round an' I reckon you got some in your eye."

Georgie dabbed her cheek dry. "Ma'am?"

"Course Adam loved Eve. God put 'em together an' b'sides, the Lawd took her from *his* body. They belong to each other. Ain't e'erything wrote down in books, you know. Some of the Bible you gotta feel. God never once told nobody in the Bible that He love 'em, but He do."

Darrion lowered his head. *Georgie was asking about them.*

"The man's there to protect the home," Kelley said. "The woman protects the man's heart."

"She's right." Darrion agreed. "Adam did love Eve, Georgianna."

"But he never *said* it."

"Sometimes, people don't say I love you. They pay the bills and put dinner on the table. Not everybody says it the same way. Adam's love for the woman could have been shown when he ate the fruit she offered him from the forbidden tree. The Word of God says he was with the woman when the serpent deceived her and yet, after she disobeyed, he also disobeyed.

"Disobedience is by no means a good thing, but can I suggest to you that Adam loved his wife so much that he disobeyed God to be with her? Someone will say no because it's too radical. But if the Word says a married man seeks his wife's pleasure first before the Lord's, is it that difficult to believe a man would ignore God's command to please his wife?"

"You g'head an' preach that thing," said a married man, whose wife smacked him on the hand.

"In the New Testament and Lost Testament, the relationship between Jesus Christ and the church is symbolically described as a husband/wife union. Christ is the groom; believers, all of us, the living church, are the bride. Men should want a spotless woman. Women should want a spotless man. When Jesus, the husband, returns, He wants a spotless church to wed."

Various negative reactions surfaced, from hissing and head shaking to whispers, mumbling, grumbling and complaining.

"He cain't mean *dat*?"

"Cain't mean *whut*? Woman, *you* ain't spotless."

"You married me and *you* ain't spotless, Lenairus, so shuddup."

"Who in here spotless? *E'erybody* done done some spottin' in here."

"This," he interrupted, "is why God reserves intimate relations for the marriage bed and why He requires you have no other God before Him. Being intimate with someone is a sacred act. Just like you shouldn't allow any warm body that wants to climb under your sheets, our Father does not allow every warm body into the intimacy of His Spirit. As a man, you should want your own wife in your bed. Women should want their own husbands. Our Father wants you, but you must be spotless.

"If you have intimate relations before marriage, you are no longer spotless. If you spend more time in the bar than in the church, that barstool is your god. You are no longer spotless. If that black-and-white picture box has your attention more than the Word, a bundle of wires and knobs is your god. Church, you don't have to take off your clothes to be an adulterer. You can do it by looking too hard or too long at someone or something that ain't yours and you can't have. The only thing able to cleanse you and make you spotless again is the blood of Christ.

"It seems God has a sense of humor. Bloodstains on your white clothes are almost impossible to get clean, but the blood of Christ will cleanse you white from sin. Let us pray."

Georgie closed her eyes, allowing her thoughts to overrun Darrion's voice. She had a question and gotten it answered in unacceptable fashion. Spending every waking moment with Darrion led to *this*? *No, he owes me an explanation.* Following the benediction and the exit of the last parishioner, Georgie sat down on the couch, her fingers twisting the curls at her temple.

He knew *that* look on a woman, though he'd not seen it on Georgie before. Careful not to upset her further, he sat a considerable length away. Her eyes fluttered, so he moved a bit closer, unsure whether or not that was what she wanted. Sensing the tension between the two, Kelley excused herself to the kitchen, which was still within earshot.

"So, *that's* why you were all thumbs tonight…because of *yesterday*?"

Darrion sighed. "It's been a little over a month."

"And I keep telling you time has nothing to do with how I feel and it shouldn't with you. Where's it written that it's supposed to take a certain amount of time to fall in love?"

"I'm fond of you, *you know that*."

"Do you still love Jayne? What is it about me that you can't love *me*?" she asked with her voice at a whisper. "I told you that I wanted to make love, but *you're* the one saying no."

"*That's not it*," he whispered fervently. "Let me walk you home."

The two argued back and forth the entire way. For Georgie's every emotional point, Darrion had a cogent and logical counterpoint. Instead of agreeing to disagree, they traded blows until they tired themselves and the hour got unreasonably late to be outside.

"Come inside," she said. Her tone lacked any hint of warmth. "It's not safe to be out now."

Darrion looked at her incredulously. "I'm going home. I'll phone you when I get there." Like before, he stuck to the lit areas and walked swiftly. Very few people were outside, save for the random floating cigarette cherry on an unlit porch or crowd of shadows surrounding a radio. He remembered the sting of the knife slashing across his body and started a light jog. A few blocks away, he trotted into a flat out sprint, as the sound of footsteps approached. Closer and closer they came and Darrion dared not look back. Breathless, he burst through the unlocked back door of Kelley's home and locked it behind him, setting his mother affright.

"Boy!" She slapped him with a dishtowel several times and clutched her chest. "Almost scared me half to death. What you runnin' from?"

He flicked on the back porch light, expecting to see a lynch mob… Klansmen, anything but wavering weeds and the neighbor's dog relieving himself in a compost heap. "I don't…know."

FOURTEEN

TUESDAY EVENING, AUGUST 21, 1962

"TAKE my hands, Cheri, and try to relax."

Georgie entrusted them to the woman seated across from her. A week into the breakup, she regretted telling Darrion the courtship never had a chance because he longed for Jayne.

"Stop shaking. I can't concentrate."

Georgie steadied the trembling fingers. "Sorry."

Now, Bible study was about just *Bible*. Georgie packed away the high-hemmed skirts. No batted eyelashes, extra lipstick, or purposed accidental touching. She wept over that alone. And she tried everything she could think of to reverse the separation, but Darrion tasted freedom and seemed drunk from it.

Much to Kelley's delight, he even stopped taking Georgie's calls. In turn, she faked a cold to get out of Bible study tonight. One of the choir girls, who everybody said had a tendency to backslide, told her about two women who read fortunes around Greater Zyonne and that they might be able to help her relationship with Darrion.

Right before she intended to find out, someone called for her at the front door. She slipped out of her stockings, unzipped her powder blue skirt, shed the white lacy blouse, mummified herself in a forest green robe up to the neck and shuffled to the door. She smelled the person long before she identified them. "Mother Kelley!" Shock, disappointment, fear, and a fair amount of disgust regarding the aroma crossed Georgie's face.

"Sound like your throat work jus' fine to me." Kelley, who didn't look well herself, tottered into the parlor.

"It comes and goes." She faked a scratchy voice and coughed from the pungent fumes. "What is that horrible *smell*?"

"Poultice. Ain't you had one before?" She handed Georgie the offending paper bag. "Wrap it 'round your neck and sleep with it. Wake up tomorrow and you'll be right as rain."

"Thank you."

"Girl, what you plannin' on doin' tonight?" Kelley spotted the discarded clothes on a chair in the parlor.

"Nothing, Mother Kelley. Nothing to worry about."

"Oh, I ain't worry 'bout *you*. I'm worried for whoever it is you gonna use them wears on. Hope he know it comin'. Look like trouble, if you ask me."

"Mother Kelley, please."

"Naw, *you* listen to *me*. I know you takin' a likin' to my son. But you gotta let the boy have time to breathe. *Slow down*. He ain't goin' nowhere. Neither are you. *Wait*. Figure it this way. He like you, I know that an' so do you."

Georgie nodded.

"But if you suppose to be with 'im, it ain't matter how long it takes. It still gonna happen. No matter what you try, you can't rush somethin' good 'cause it ain't that good if it gotta be rushed along. Take your time."

Georgie lowered her eyes. "Thank you, Mother Kelley."

"Now, gimme that poultice back so I can give it to Mother Dorothy."

"Mother Dorothy?"

"Unless you need it?"

"Even if my throat was sore, I'd rather heal by myself than put that on my body.

"Thought so. Open up the windows for ten minutes or so; the smell'l go away. And Georgianna?"

It marked the first time Kelley called Georgie something other than "you" or "gal."

"Ma'am?"

"Be careful 'bout what you doin'."

She shut the door behind Kelley, backed against it and thought a few seconds. The old woman made a good point. Darrion had been through a lot and probably just needed a friend. She missed him. If she waited like Kelley suggested, she might be able to build a stronger friendship, which might evolve into a more solid relationship.

On the other hand, this fortune-telling woman's abilities stoked her curiosity. That girl said it worked for her and it must have. Georgie always saw the couple together, smooching, holding hands, hugging. She wanted that. For all her advice, Mother Kelley never touched anybody or anything remotely resembling a man. *Besides, looking for help isn't a crime.*

"Quiet your mind and relax. You're thinkin' 'bout too much."

The violet-draped room surrounded by curious objects fascinated her. Flasks of unlabeled liquids, small, white-faced doll heads with stitched features, and a petrified alligator head lined the cherry ledge above the fireplace. Georgie assumed the bottled kaleidoscopes in the china cabinet were potions and elixirs. The candles centered on the table, the one light source in the room, smelled funny. Something about the atmosphere unsettled her spirit.

Joséphine squeezed the girl's chewed-down fingernails. Trying to consult on behalf of someone with a mind cluttered with thoughts felt like crossing a busy highway without being struck by a speeding car. "Miss."

"Huh?"

"*Relax.*"

Close your eyes, thought Georgie. *Pretend you're praying.*

"Now you're ready. Let's begin."

Suddenly, the room temperature perked up, enough that Georgie's forehead became moist. She thought to dab the sweat away, but the fortuneteller's grasp secured her hands.

"He will never love you the way you want him to. No one will ever love you like that."

Georgie chewed the words and digested them. "I don't believe you."

"Believe whatever you want to believe."

She squeezed out a tear and blinked the others away.

"After you give him what you think he wants, he *will* leave you."

"Why?"

"You don't have what it takes to keep a man satisfied."

Georgie's mind flipped through her sorted histories with men. No one, from first crush to first love, remained long in her life. No amount of cooking, sex, or obedience had changed that. "So, tell me how then," she said, bleary-eyed. "How do I get Darrion James to love me back?"

"Get him away from *that book*. It's controlling him like a god."

"What book, the Lost Testament?"

"Yes."

"And what else?"

"Do that first. The rest will take care of itself."

So much time had passed between the last committed crime and the next important call that the Zyonne Police Department literally fell asleep on the job. After all, one could only play so many games of poker, chess, checkers, and watch so much television.

Police Chief David Riggins, a stern, stout, graying man in his mid-50's, used to insist that the men remain active at their posts. Now, he'd eased up and allowed his officers to snooze on the cell cots, so long as no one snored.

There, in the station offices, the Ku Klux Klan division, or "Klavern," worked underground. Geary, "Exalted Cyclops"; its highest officer, or "Kludd"; the group's chaplain, handled all incoming emergency calls. Anything Klavern related, they passed off to Riggins as something insignificant – a prank call or something. Riggins would sigh and blow it off. Then Geary or Kludd would nod to one another, down the line to Reifer and Gaston, who phoned Jack Miles, the "Grand Nighthawk," or sergeant-at-arms.

The communication was short, brief, passed along verbally as "a problem" with an address, time, and estimated body count for munitions' sake. Big problems meant a "hot" night with firebombs all around. They would go out on "patrol" and be the first assailants.

Everyone on duty that afternoon was knocked out on the cell cots in t-shirts and uniform slacks. Marinating in his own sweat, Riggins nodded off at his desk, shirt open and chest dribbling streams of sweat.

The phone rang. Riggins snorted and jumped. Kludd stirred. Already awakened by pain from his scabs, Geary clambered up. Reifer and Gaston continued their staggered snoring.

"Psst, Cykes. *Cykes.*"

"Yeah?" Geary answered.

"Gotta feelin' 'bout this one…like this one's somethin'."

"On it." He limped to the closest phone. "Chief, I got it."

"Good." Riggins slumped in his chair and resumed sleeping.

"Police."

"Got me a problem, Son."

The caller spoke the language, but strangely muffled. "Come again, Cousin?"

"I said," he coughed. "Got me a *problem.*"

"Alright." Geary awaited the details. "What can we do?"

"The James' home. You know it? House on the hill at Superior?"

I remember that house. "Yeah."

"'Bout eight o' clock. A hundred…niggers'll be there 'round."

Annoyed by the breach in protocol, Geary broke it himself. "Hey, who *is* this anyway?"

"Frank." He fumbled with the fake name. "Frank Abraham."

"Kin to *Nate* Abraham?" Geary whispered. The late Nate Abraham, a retired policeman, started the Klavern tradition where leaders selected their successors. Geary followed Abraham as Exalted Cyclops.

"Second cousins."

"Done." Geary grinned across the room at Kludd. Arms crossed and leaning against the detention center wall, he smiled back.

After the policeman disconnected, a balled-up handkerchief and telephone receiver dropped from Whitehead's hand.

It's over. No turning back. He betrayed a brother-in-Christ, a co-laborer in God's kingdom; someone so anointed by God that he felt compelled to put a permanent end to the man's life and ministry.

Whitehead opened his top drawer and removed the loaded revolver.

Higher Ground now struggled to fill three pews on a good Sunday and without big tithes and offerings coming in anymore, the facility could barely operate. He'd fix this problem the one way he knew – quick erasure. It worked in the case of his young lover's child and would have to work for James.

He popped the gun chamber open and removed all but one bullet.

The insurance policy will cover Julie and the children for a while, he thought. *She can sell the house and the car and move in with relatives after that. Six children are too many for one family. The twins should stay together. The rest will have to be split apart.* He placed the barrel at his temple and closed his eyes.

"John?" Julie knocked, twisted the locked knob, and called his name over and over again in a silky voice until it thumped in his brain.

"Yes?"

"Can I come in?"

His peripheral vision studied the long black rod against his head. "I'm not decent."

"We have six children, Negro. I don't have time for this. Pick up some eggs, milk, and bread on your way home? My purse is plum empty and the children ate sandwiches for breakfast. Don't worry. The grocery store is open for another half-hour. And John?"

"Yes?"

"You are such a good man. Hurry home. The children need you. And I love you so much. I'll see you later."

He waited until Julie's heels clicked out of earshot. Whitehead set the pistol down and sobbed miserably over what he'd done; the property sure to be destroyed, the blood he'd bear on his head. *If I hurry, I still have enough time to be a good man.*

Darrion's tongue used to salivate with a taste for baked honey glazed ham, candied sweet potatoes, mustard greens, and buttery yeast rolls. The olfactory essences swirled in his imagination, while he snacked on cold ham sandwiched between two room temperature rolls for the second night. Kelley had fallen ill with a wicked cough about two weeks ago; a malady she charged to the changing atmosphere, except, it never went away. His mother never complained and refused to do anything for it but prayer, rest, cough syrup and pills. Kelley kept her regular schedule and cooked every day until last Sunday, when she refused to leave her bedroom while he preached Sunday service downstairs in the parlor.

Darrion claimed his cooking expertise revolved around simple dishes, which the church mother's said wouldn't do. Georgie wanted to jump into action, but such a thing no longer fit her station. So, in three hours flat, four mothers whipped up the feast he now dreamed about, plus homemade chicken soup for Kelley. But by Tuesday night, he'd tired himself out with those leftovers.

After plunking three ice chunks in a glass, he filled it with lemonade. Halfway through the glass, Kelley appeared in the kitchen. With her ever-graying hair sprawling loose from its clip, cheeks and eyes puffed red, and thinning figure, she appeared to have aged 15 years since the last time Darrion had seen her.

"Miracle you got somethin' to eat in this house without me."

"Momma, you shouldn't be out of bed."

"I knows a thing or two 'bout my own body," she coughed. "I'ma heat up some tea. Join me?"

"No, thank you. Can I tell you a story, Momma?"

"Love one." Kelley set the fire to high.

"Elijah prayed and God didn't send rain for three years."

She filled the kettle a thumb segment high and positioned it on the burner. "I know that story."

"After Elijah confronted the prophets of Baal and Ahab, he spoke about hearing the sound of rain coming. He prayed for it. Elijah's servant had to go up seven times to look for the rain and the seventh time, he saw a cloud coming, small as a man's fist."

"Sound like a sermon to me. Where's my story?"

"When the Pharisees and Sadducees tempted Jesus to show them a sign from heaven, Jesus responded by asking them a question. How can they tell what the weather is going to be by the way the sun looks, but not discern signs from heaven? The Lost Testament gives this explanation: He compares the two, the foretelling of a certain weather pattern and the recognition of a spiritual sign in parable-like fashion.

"The sun," he continued, "looking the way it did signaled to them the forthcoming weather. God gives us signs from heaven and it as easy to discern those signs as it is to predict the weather by what we see the sun doing. Determining what is a sign from heaven is a matter of seeing with our spirits what we don't see with natural eyes."

"So, what is it you sayin'?"

"At that time, it meant the men were too spiritually blind to see God's ultimate sign from heaven – the Messiah, right in front of them."

"An' now?"

"I'm saying that's not a cold, Momma. I've seen the signs. You've got pleurisy."

Kelley fixed herself some tea and again offered him the same. Darrion held up his hand. "No, thank you, Ma'am."

"Please," she said in a small voice. "Have a lil' tea with your old Momma. Ain't askin' you for to do me nothin' but that."

To oblige her, he relented and sipped from the cup she offered.

"Ain't been scared but two times in my life. Your daddy took you from here; I ain't know what he'd gone on an' done. He *left* me for some visitin' white woman he met downtown. I promised myself I'd never tell you, but thought it's 'bout time you needs to know." Kelley's mouth puckered at the cup's edge, enough to allow a little tea to seep in. Darrion slid his hand over hers and squeezed warmth back into the wrinkled hand. Her now-plentiful wrinkles connected for a subdued smile.

"Boy, you give me joy unspeakable." Kelley tapped her chest. "Make my heart proud to seen what you done grown into."

"Listen, I won't preach tonight. Let me make a few calls to the mothers."

Kelley sipped again. This time, she drank the remainder of its contents, set the cup on its saucer and slid it between Darrion's empty jar and his teacup, which he had yet to dress. "Other time I been scared when I found out I got this condition," she said somberly. "But it ain't clearin' up in one night. You teach Bible study tonight. I'll be fine. I'll go to the doctor soon."

"Promise me?"

She rose from the kitchen chair straight as a lynchpin, and hobbled up the winding staircase and down the hall into her bedroom without answering Darrion. There, on her frayed mattress, Kelley laid in the fetal position, eyes closed, praying for another way out. She'd seen the cloud inside. Rain was soon to come.

FIFTEEN

TUESDAY NIGHT, AUGUST 21, 1962

A HEAVY downpour forced the Bible study attendants from Kelley's porch inside. The home strained and stretched to accommodate almost 200 people in its every nook and cranny. Without the extra space available outside, it seemed so congested that everyone had to breathe in perfect unison or give up respiration at all.

The early birds crammed into the parlor, sitting or standing until it filled. They then spilled over onto the foyer and the adjacent hallway. With no more room in those places, they pressed into the dining room or lined the wall between the butler's pantry and china cabinet.

Much to Kelley's chagrin, the latecomers and stragglers squatted in the sewing room among the machine and materials, or entered the house through the rear and stood in the kitchen.

At its fullest during all the times he'd held Bible study, the house suddenly felt stark empty to Darrion. Kelley wasn't fussing about the mess she'd have to clean up later. Worry darkened his face. Not long ago, he'd opened her window to allow her to smell the falling rain. She'd smacked her lips a little to catch the dewy taste in the air. Before he reached downstairs, Kelley had wheezed herself asleep.

"She'll be fine." Georgie rested a soft hand on Darrion's shoulder. "It's just a cold."

"It's something more serious," he admitted. "But she's going to the doctor first thing tomorrow. I don't care if I have to carry her on my back to get her there."

"Not many men button their cuffs with their hearts like you do sometimes. You have a big heart. It's why your hands are so warm all the time." Georgie slyly fondled the back of Darrion's right hand and turned it over to examine it, like the Creole instructed. She fingered the lifeline, a certain crease in the palm between his pinky and thumb. His had been cut in half by a healed-over scar. "What happened here?"

"Thank you." Darrion self-consciously reclaimed the hand.

"You're not as alone here as you think. You're alone because you want to be, or you think you have to be."

He redirected. "I should start. Thanks for the talk."

"Just think about what I said."

"I will. I promise." He squirmed through the crowd over to his customary small circle of space in the parlor. There, in their midst, he realized that the search for a suitable, affordable space had to prove fruitful and fast. He'd be forced to petition the people for regular offerings, something he despised.

"I know we usually start with some hymns, but tonight the Lord impressed upon my spirit the importance of this message and you must receive it as quickly as I can preach it.

"If you have your Bibles, please turn to Hebrews, Four. We will start our reading at verse twelve, which reads: 'For the word of God is quick and powerful, and sharper than any two edged sword, piercing even to the dividing asunder of soul and spirit, and of the joints and marrow, and is a discerner of the thoughts and intents of the heart'."

"Let us pray." Heads bowed in sequence. "Father, may your Holy Ghost guide and direct my tongue. Teach us, O Lord, precept upon precept, so that we may not stray from your laws. Examine our hearts and minds, remove any impurities and keep us focused on Christ. In the name of Jesus, we pray. Amen."

"Amen."

"We want to talk tonight about moving beyond our comfort zones. Moving means advancing from one place into a certain direction. Comfort is a word used to describe something that feels good or calming. There's no pressure in comfort. Everything is okay.

"So, to move beyond your comfort zone means to leave the place or the mentality you have that has felt so good and calming to you for so long that you have no desire to leave. There's not supposed to be pressure in the comfort zone, but I'm here to tell you tonight that the Lord of Hosts is pressuring us while we're in our comfort zones to *move out and move up.*"

The dead silence pleased Darrion. Cutting was going on.

"The text tells us the qualities of God's Word. It is quick and powerful like a double-edged sword. It cuts, dividing marrow from bone, spirit from soul, the God in you from the 'you' in you, and judges why you do all the things you do.

"Let me explain: Say you go to a certain church in town and all you hear from the Word are things that sound good and calming. God is good and His mercy endures forever and His Word does promise good things. *But*, His Word is designed to show you who you are.

"The Word does this by cutting away everything you use to cover up your faults to expose your heart's motives. Cutting *hurts*. Hearing God's Word isn't supposed to feel good all the time!

"Read the Scriptures. Every Old Testament prophet was unpopular because the false prophets prophesied peace and the true prophets foretold of war, bondage, discomfort and suffering. Even Jesus told us we would have trouble. But, by the grace of God, as He overcame these things on the cross, so will we."

Four firebombs with extra long fuses, two half-full kerosene tanks, ten baseball bats and five crowbars – it was a "hot" night indeed. Geary went overboard in preparation and admittedly so. Their blood pumped in excitement; one hundred Negroes at once in the biggest

Negro home in Zyonne. Destroying it effectively required more effort than their past few excursions, but it warranted the work.

Jack Miles egged his leader on once he discovered it was where Geary's ex-wife hid during their separation. But Geary had known this ever since she left but did not act because he did not *want* to. All he wanted was *acceptance*, which Schiffler couldn't do.

"Alright guys." Still difficult to understand, especially in an open field, Geary spoke with slow intent. "We take two trucks, seven in mine, eight in Hawk's. No plates, speed down, lights off when we get there. Approach slow. Park where I stop. Reifer, Kludd, Harrison and Borden set the bombs after me. Steimler will gas it. Get close 'cause of the rain. Watch my signal. If Riggins is gettin' wise, he might get people here quicker than we think. Ready?"

"What do we want?" Kludd shouted.

"White power!" they cheered back.

"When do we want it?"

"Now!"

"What's the solution?" Geary bellowed.

"White revolution!"

The Klansmen donned their hoods and scrambled into the truck beds.

"God needs to cut us open because we've become a fake people."

The silence evolved into short gasps for air and painful grimacing.

"Like a scab, we cover up our hurts and pains, hoping no more pain will come. We act like everything inside is punch and cake, when in reality we want to scream our heads off and take somebody out for hurting us. We want everything God promises us – freedom from this separate bondage – but we don't want to do anything to make it happen besides sitting on our behinds, singing and praying for a better day.

"Well, tonight, we're talking about moving beyond comfort zones. Understand that, like an aisle in a market, there are only so many blessings that you can receive in the comfort zone. If you want baby food, applesauce and juice, then stay in the comfort zone, baby. But if you want steak, macaroni and cheese, and cornbread, child of God, I'm telling you tonight to get uncomfortable, get bad, get restless, get up, get out, and go get it!"

Inside the house's crowded confines, the applause tore through the air like a thunderclap.

Two pickup trucks hopped the sidewalk and parked beside one another on the sloping embankment beside the house's west side. The beds emptied, with hoods, robes, and munitions.

Geary pointed to the house's side, back porch corner, and its east side. Reifer, Harrison, Kludd and Borden shielded the wicks to the bottled explosives from the breeze. Geary and Steimler rounded the outside and deluged the house's walls with kerosene. The others assumed their posts at the assigned positions or exits.

Once the rain dissipated, Steimler met Geary at the front. They lit the wicks.

Whitehead chugged around the corner like a runaway truck. He counted it a blessing that the bus driver had a little religion and stopped for the well-known Negro reverend.

Once he boarded, the driver went into full confession mode, explaining why he hadn't been to church in years and detailed an explicit catalog of his past sins. Patient as a fisherman, but frantic because there were lives on borrowed time, his passenger urged him to continue talking and to *drive*.

Eventually, Whitehead ended up praying with the driver for salvation. He felt so grateful that he offered to stray from his route and take the pastor anywhere he wanted to go in Zyonne for the fare he'd already paid – until the reverend mentioned the destination. The driver backed off. "No offense," he said, "but I'll go no further than the Fairgrounds."

Now motoring closer to the house, he gripped the pistol in his right front jacket pocket and nearly fired it from nervousness. In the poor lighting, he swore he saw at least 13 man-sized shadows. *Too late.* Exhausted and spent, he huffed on, pistol in hand.

"Move, people of God! Move past your insecurities and fears. Fear is nothing but a tool Satan uses to convince you that you are not capable of doing whatever it is that God has already enabled you to do. If you want something to change, step out and do something about it.

"That seamstress Rosa Parks did something about it and she wasn't even trying to make a statement. Her feet hurt. When you move outside of your comfort zone and journey into God's will, even the little things you do have a ripple effect on the world. Like a pebble in the ocean, little pebbles make waves just like the rocks do.

"Move, people of God! Move! Move! Move!"

"Move!" A chant started. The people pumped their fists with fervor. Then, with a *whoosh*, the front porch burst in flames. Panicking elbows, fists, and forearms flailed with abandon, pushing and shoving to gain position away from the heat. In the center of the mayhem, Darrion fought to keep himself from being crushed. "Everyone, listen!" he screamed. "The doors and windows are blocked. Use the door in the kitchen to get into the basement!"

The cement cellar wouldn't fit everyone. If the Klansmen found the outside entrance or the ground floor collapsed into the basement's drop ceiling, they were all dead. But all obeyed. As the crowd thinned out, Darrion shot up the staircase and bounded down the hall to Kelley's room. "Momma!" He juggled the antique iron doorknob. It was locked. He rammed his shoulder into the bedroom door until the jamb gave way and the door slammed into the wall.

Kelley was kneeling at the foot of her bed, her hands clasped together, head bowed. She was sculpture still and not wheezing anymore.

"Momma," he said softly. "Are you alright?"

"She's gone." Whitehead's strong hand gripped his shoulder.

"No. No, she's not. Not yet." Darrion extended the Lost Testament toward her. "Momma, get up!"

"Brother James." He shed a tear.

"Get up, Momma," he screamed, shaking and waving the book like a wand. "Get up! In the name of Jesus, I say! Get up!"

Whitehead gripped Darrion in a tight hug.

"No, no, no," he sobbed, screaming. "Momma! Momma! Get up. Get up!"

"We have to go, son," he said firmly. "*Now.*"

The pair rounded the flaming wreckage into the cellar. Somehow, the people had found enough space to fit. Georgie did a quick search for Darrion and found a slobbering mess trying to compose itself behind Whitehead.

"I'm going out first." The pastor pulled out his firearm and assumed command. "Run as fast as you can, as far as you can. Don't stop."

Whitehead opened the basement doors and hopped out, brandishing his pistol. *It's clear sailing!* He waved his hand and a few men sprang out, bracing themselves for a fight. Then the women hurried out, too jittery to do anything but shake in terror or sprint away.

Geary looked around. "Where *are* they? They can't be inside!"

"Don't see how, Cykes," said Harrison. "Place's goin' up so daggone high, bet you can see it from the top o' Black Mountain."

"Fan out," Geary instructed. "Surround the house and find 'em. That many niggers jus' don't disappear into thin air."

A third of the people had escaped when Gaston strayed off to pass water in the bushes and saw Negroes running for their lives down the soggy embankment.

"Here," he yelled, pointing toward the escapees. "Over here!"

Determined to defend the people whichever way possible, Whitehead aimed for the approaching masked group and popped off all six shots, hitting nothing but air. He tossed the pistol and stood his ground, fists up, ready for self-sacrifice.

Borden smashed a right cross into the pastor's jaw. With one quick motion, Whitehead's bloodied face snapped back and he lunged forward into the off-balance Borden, sending them both into the mud. Harrison and Gaston joined Reifer in stomping on the man, who rolled off Borden and tried to shield himself from the crushing swings.

Georgie, who escaped in the largest middle wave, tried waiting for Darrion, but didn't see him. The last she remembered, he was still in the cellar. A woman grabbed her hand, told her to run, save her own hide and, whatever she did, don't turn back.

And what about Mother Kelley? Or Darrion? "Darrion!" Georgie kicked away her heeled shoes and dashed back, lungs aching with cramps.

Meanwhile, the surrounding Negro neighbors crowded inside their respective homes and gave silent pause to recognize the demise of the audacious house on the highest hill in Zyonne. For most, the home functioned as a beacon; a ray of hope that one day, all Negroes could own a home so large and prosperous. Others hated the eyesore structure and, likewise, envied it for what it was; a rose in the sidewalk. Those would say Kelley James joined herself to a half-white man, and now, the Lord rewarded her treachery to the race by allowing the abomination to burn down.

The house, now glorified aglow in yellowish-orange destruction from frame to roof, exhaled a groaning from its flaming innards and exploded glass fragments and an acrid smoke puff into the sky. It sagged, snapped and bent beneath its own weight, collapsing in three separate obnoxious symphonies. At that exact moment, the skies cracked open and poured forth rain.

SIXTEEN

EARLY WEDNESDAY MORNING, AUGUST 22, 1962

BETTY Lou eased the covers above her head. The grandfather clock showed 2:30. *Thunk.* A car door slammed. *Thunk.* Another door shut, followed by a drunken, "Shh, you'll wake her up" and then laughing. Clumsiness up the wooden steps and a command to open the door led to fumbled keys in the deadbolt, an opened door, and dragging across the carpet. A heavy weight smacked the couch and footsteps faded in the distance.

"Thanks, guys," she yelled.

"Welcome," two men slurred in unison.

Betty Lou slid to the bed's edge, folded to her knees and crawled. Because rainstorms locked up her knee awfully bad, walking wasn't an option. She smelled the beer and kerosene on Jack Miles long before reaching the couch. Good thing she wasn't smoking.

His shirt came off easily. The trousers were another story. Betty Lou tugged at the soaked denim until it gave up the fight around his knees. Rolling the clothes into a ball, she crept away with them cupped under her arm as he snored. In the bedroom, she examined the articles, dipping a different finger into each spot on the black t-shirt. One stain was blood; obviously not his. *Jack*, she thought, *what you gone on an' done?*

He disappeared like this the same night Mark Williams was killed; a convenient "poker night." Something about his stories never jived. She could always calculate a significant gap in time between lies.

Fearful, she crammed the clothes into a paper bag and shoved it under the pile in the clothes hamper. Later that day, when he left for work, she planned to put the items in a safer place. The less he knew she'd figured out, the better.

Only hours later, as the first signs of morning appeared, did the stubborn-as-the-dead structure completely flame out. Wood and stone debris clung to one another, charred, wet and on the cusp of collapse, while white flakes of ash floated in circles. Like buzzards around a carcass, media members circled the area for story tidbits.

The place had been firebombed – that much was clear – and the perpetrators were obvious. Faced with the familiar question whether or not the offenders were squad members, Chief Riggins declined comment, though he himself suspected it. Evidence on Johnson, Watson, and Reifer was circumstantial. Regardless, the state gave them all paid leave to investigate.

After the scene died down, Georgie emerged from the row of bushes where she'd laid in wait since the fire. She approached the massive pile of debris. Regardless of the negative reports, she had to verify Darrion's death or survival for herself.

The hill towered high above her head, at least half its normal height, jutting out in every direction. Nevertheless, she pulled herself over the marked off areas and up onto the unstable mess. "Darrion?" she cried. The beam supporting her bare left foot collapsed. She dropped down before finding another foothold. "Mother Kelley? Darrion?"

Georgie's lungs burned from the smell and her hands, knees and feet bled. The footing gave way and she fell again, this time onto the muddied ground. She gazed up. The debris formed at her feet like a cave and tunneled from the ground out. She muttered a quick "thank you" prayer and crawled forward. Halfway down the makeshift passageway, her knee banged against something small, rectangular and hard. Georgie reached back, retrieved the object and gasped. *Violet's notebook!*

She crawled free, clutching the book like a lifeline. Weary, wet and sorrowful, she treaded home through the stew-thick mud by the roadside to protect her feet. Her stockings were torn up to mid-calf and large dirt spots coated her dress. On the verge of collapsing, she climbed her porch stairs and opened the door. Frantic, Livvie sprang up from the couch and swallowed her soiled baby sister in an embrace. "C'mon," she said, fondling her sister's hair. "Hop in the bath and I'll take you to breakfast."

"Not hungry, Liv," she sniffed. "Darrion could still be out there. I have to go back."

"Well, if you don't eat, I will, and you watch me. *Then* you can go back. Do it. Go on!"

Georgie did as she was told, making sure she did not tread mud on the carpet. Instead of a bath, she showered beneath a steady stream of warm water. Afterward, she washed her hair free of ash and the aroma of smoke, which reminded her of the previous night's downpour. Georgie wept for Darrion and the still uncertain outcome of his survival.

With a change of clothes and clean hair, she admittedly felt like a new woman. Livvie left the children with Raul and the sisters were on their way. At the luncheonette, they ordered eggs, bacon and raisin toast. Behind them sat a Negro woman with a gorgeous ponytail and a white woman whom Georgie swore she had seen before.

"Joséphine, Gal, look at this!"

The morning edition of the *Herald*, along with every respectable newspaper in Black Mountain County, carried similar headlines, photos and stories trumpeting the demise of a home at the edge of the Negro boundary line. Well before Charlie flipped the newsboy change to purchase the daily, the breakfast counter already buzzed with the news.

Joséphine swabbed the egg yolk off her plate with a biscuit half. Ten o' clock in the morning was too early to handle an excited Charlie. "Dang, that's all that's left of it? Ain't much to look at, is it?"

"The remains of Kelley James, 52, were found in the blaze," Charlie read. "while excavation will continue today for any other survivors." Wonder if anyone else's in there?"

"Darrion," said Georgie loud enough for Charlie to hear. "Darrion James."

Joséphine turned to look at the dark woman behind her but didn't recognize the face. Georgie repeated the name again and Livvie stopped shoveling food into her mouth.

"Yeah, Cheri? And how do *you* know?"

"I *know*," she said nonchalantly. "I know it."

"How, Darlin'? Gimme the scoop," asked Charlie.

"Wait." Joséphine's fingers snapped. "I know you. You came to me."

"Yes. You should be happy. I got the book."

"Who's she?" Livvie asked, with a mouth overflowing with food.

Something inside Joséphine screamed with joy. "The *book*? You have it?"

"You told me to separate him from it."

Livvie rudely elbowed Georgie. "Who is she?" she muttered in Spanish. "What foolishness are you talkin' about?"

"Nobody, girl, alright? Quit elbowing me."

"*She's* the one with the guy and the book?" Charlie pointed in the Cubans' direction.

"So, what are you going to do with it?" Joséphine's interest piqued. "Let me see it."

"I'll figure it out once they find his body."

"Body? Don't think he's *dead*, Cheri."

"Yeah," Charlie said, gnawing on one of Joséphine's bacon strips. "Me, neither."

"What are you talking about? The paper says right there that…"

"All the paper say is what them white folks want you to believe. He's alive. I can feel it."

Disturbed, Georgie rose to confront her. "Then why don't *I* feel it?"

"Maybe you're not supposed to," Joséphine said.

"Look here!" Georgie jabbed a finger into Joséphine's face. "Who do you think you are? How are you going to tell me what I feel and don't feel? That he's alive when the paper says he's *dead?* Liar! How dare you give people hope like that?"

"I know the truth," Joséphine said, still not making eye contact with her accuser. "You believe *everything* you see?"

Though the two women were the same age and dressed in similar fashion – she in a sleeveless lavender dress and Joséphine wearing a periwinkle, white lily patterned skirt and cream blouse – a nonplussed Georgie felt so much younger than her confronter.

"Of course, who doesn't?"

"You tell me. You're the confused churchgoing girl."

Georgie turned away. "Livvie, you finished?"

Olivia erased every last trace of food from the plate, licked her lips clean and smiled. Georgie passed money across the counter and the two departed.

Charlie munched the last bacon strip from her partner's plate. "All that over a *man?* That lil' girl's breath still smell like breast milk. Why'd you mess with her like that?"

Joséphine plunged a fork into the film covering her grits. Even though Mark's murder soured her, half the things coming from her mouth as of late were mysteries. Once sweet as hot milk, cinnamon and honey, she now cut down others with her words, even paying clients. "It's different, Marie." She never used Charlie's real name in public anymore. "He's not a John."

"What is it then?"

"The book, that man, it all – something inside me won't just leave it alone. But he's not dead, that I know."

The dance started with a blood red teardrop *cha cha-ing* in the dark of Darrion's subconscious, blossoming into a bachata firing into consuming festive ginger and sunburst. Quiet and calming, the dance turned fierce with spins and leaps, spiraling out-of-control from corner to corner of his childhood home, blazing trails on the floor from its birthplace, leaving charred skeletons in its wake. The heat skipped behind him and licked his heels.

Darrion twitched and writhed in bed, tearing the main sheet form its corner. In his dream, he barely beat the inferno upstairs to the master bedroom, where Kelley kneeled and fervently prayed. "Come on," he yelled, but no sound came from his lips. "Please! Get up!"

The raging fire consumed her kneeling body, but now, next to it burned a second body. In an instant, he was transported from the door into a kneeling position, alongside his incinerated mother's skeleton. Darrion screamed and raised his burning hands.

Breathless, he sprang up and looked for something to identify his surroundings. Whitewashed walls, worn azure carpet, sheets as rough as concrete, dirty vanity mirror – all unfamiliar and cheap looking. It was Miss Parsippany's boarding house. The place's emptiness encouraged the mid-morning nap. The last tenant had moved on a while ago, so his hysterics went unnoticed. But it was just a matter of time before the Zyonne grapevine ran its course and the congregation found him, expecting him to do *something.*

What could they possibly want me to do? They were all victims of a color system. He'd understood it, previously benefitting from it, now in condemnation of it. If he'd reconciled with Jayne, none of the past two months would have happened. Kelley might still be alive. That thought alone inspired a kind of rabid frustration.

Hours ago, after escaping the cellar, he'd dragged Whitehead's body to a safe location away from the chaos and began tending to it. Darrion clenched his eyes and gritted his teeth. The book's hard cover swelled in his rear pocket. *It is the notebook's fault.* He removed it.

His mind eddied with images of Jayne, and his mother, still alive and burning to death. Beside him, Whitehead's blood oozed. Behind him, congregation members were being beaten.

He wound up and threw Violet's notebook. It carried in the night air higher and further than he thought possible. He watched it fall as best as he could around where the kitchen used to be, 20 or so yards from the spot where he stood.

Whitehead stirred, his unclosed eye staring a clear message. "What have you done?"

At least his mind quieted for a moment. But now, things were at "pot bottom black," like Kelley used to say, and when you're that low, she'd say that there wasn't any other way to go but up. The wisdom helped him to dress and force himself over to the site. Barely more than twelve hours after the blaze, the first misgiving arose in him. In essence, he'd bartered his life and Violet's work for a pile of ashes sure to have been blown away by now or watered into clay.

From afar, he imagined that the grayish frame skeleton would look like close up; large, broken segments sacrificed on a flaming pyre. As he drew closer, hope sagged from his shoulders. Doused, half-bulldozed and thoroughly picked over, nothing remained. If the *Lost Testament* or Violet's notebook lay beneath the removed destruction, he stepped on them now.

Through the fog, he spotted a body in the distance on his left. No telling its identity; the smallish figure suggested it was a woman or diminutive man. He intended to avoid whoever it was, but he was noticed. Darrion proceeded. A purple dress flourished out from the person's legs.

"Darrion?" Using her hands for blinders, Georgie called out tentatively. She beckoned him again, louder.

He leaned forward and squinted. The voice resembled Georgie's.

Tossing away the hardness Livvie encouraged her to possess if given the chance to confront Darrion again, she sprinted the remaining distance and bounded into his arms. "I thought I lost you last night," she whispered, trembling.

"In a way, you did," he responded. Darrion released her. "After everyone else, and they were still chasing...I couldn't help, or do much. My mother is *gone*."

"I'm so sorry," she said with true remorse. "Why didn't you phone or come over? Where have you been? And look at you, your clothes... you're a mess."

She was right. Even after a full shower, wearing the same sullied clothes made his skin itch. The mud streaks ingrained in his woolen slacks were set in and his sweaty shirt reeked of smoke. "*The Lost Testament*, I need to find it."

"Reverend Whitehead's in General. He's asked for you. I didn't know what to tell him."

Somewhat dazed, Darrion began poking through the rubble. "I think I threw Violet's notebook...around the kitchen, which means it's around here somewhere."

Georgie's cheeks flushed red. "Are you even listening to me?"

"I'll go see Whitehead," he said, scanning the ground. "I'm happy to see you. But if it or the translation still exists..."

"Don't you care about *anything* else?" she interrupted, clearly hoping he mentioned her.

"There is nothing else!" he exclaimed. "Kelley is dead. There *is* nothing else!"

She fussed with her pocketbook. "Reverend Whitehead may not be the best pastor in the world, but he's polite. He's not nasty or sharp with folks, even when he wants something out of you, and he knows how to say thank you." Georgie thrust Violet's notebook into his chest. "I found it this morning. Take it. It's yours."

Out of shock, Darrion tripped over his words. "I'm..."

"Save it." Georgie muttered in Spanish and stormed off.

SEVENTEEN

EARLY MONDAY MORNING, SEPTEMBER 3, 1962

BACK and forth, Betty Lou hobbled, bad knee creaking and popping like the floorboards beneath the bedroom's wafer-thin wine carpeting. Devious machinations popped up all over her curl-filled head. Jack Miles' late night adventures were no longer a mystery. Everyone he cavorted with had blood on their hands. *Something must be done.*

She didn't need the Creole gal to read the signs. Covering up the truth must have been easy: start out with a phony thread, straighten out the stories, and weave the falsehoods into a shroud of lies covering the town. Despite obvious holes, even the media bought into them, but everything criminal-minded Jack Miles involved himself in was two seconds from hitting her front porch. She'd either have to distance herself, or don a white hood herself.

Betty Lou unearthed the evidence from the laundry basket, bent over, rolled back the carpet, removed two floorboards, crammed the bag into the space and replaced the wood. The spot had been loose for years and she saw no reason why her husband would repair it now. She'd use the clothing to leverage him into a divorce, money and the house.

If the newspaper articles proved true, racial violence was drawing attention all over the south, including the state and small towns like Zyonne, which typically went unnoticed. And threats sent Jack Miles running. He'd give her all those things and the moon, if she asked him to. But she couldn't be stupid. Jack Miles was dumb but he wasn't stupid. He'd come after her.

She removed the barely-used .38 special from his hiding place and stuck it in her underwear drawer beneath the packaged things he swore he'd never touch. She limped to the kitchen and formulated the bare bones of a plan over scrambled eggs.

Later that morning, about 6:00 a.m., with legs astride a grocery bag, Betty Lou clutched a half-empty glass of wine in her left hand with a fully-loaded pistol in her right. A Lucky Strike dangled from her lips. When a key invaded the deadbolt lock and twisted, she cocked the pistol's hammer, quivering inside.

Jack Miles stumbled in with a quarter-full bottle. "Hey Bets."

She concealed the firearm behind her back. *"Jack."*

"Sit down, why don't ya? Take a load off. What's with the dress?"

"No, thanks," she said, leaning against the living room wall. She wore *the* dress; the same one he shattered her leg for purchasing years back.

He plopped down in the rocking chair and chugged a little booze, wiped his mouth clean with his black and red checkered lumberjack sleeve. "What you drinkin'?"

"Poison, same as you. 'Cept it ain't killin' me like it is you."

"What you *tryin'* to kill this time?"

"Every evil part of you that ever got inside me. You gonna give me a divorce and move out, but pay the bills. You owe me way more, but I'll settle for that like I settled for you."

"Yeah, right. Over my dead body! Talk about owing folks, *you* owe *me* for that cigarette and the others you been smokin' behind my back."

Betty Lou whipped the pistol from behind her back, aimed at Jack Miles' feet and fired before she had time to second guess. The bullet ripped through his left boot top and sole, nicking his big toenail. He jerked forward, coddled the foot with his hands and screamed obscenities. The second shot embedded in the armrest below his hand. She steadied her hand. "Is that the way Negroes jump 'fore you kill 'em?" She popped off two more shots, intentionally missing.

"You got two more bullets, Bets." His voice bubbled with ill intent.

"Just takes one good one."

Jack Miles thrust the bottle sidearm at the wall adjacent to Betty Lou. Glass shards and whiskey spattered all over her. She shrieked and unloaded a round on reflex. Jack Miles flinched. The two looked at each other for a few minutes, speechless, breathing hard, searching for words. Betty Lou shed the straps from her shoulders and dropped the stained outfit to the floor.

"I want no part of you Jack Miles Everham. It's *over*."

"You ain't that smart. You don't know who you foolin' with."

"You right. Might not be real sharp, but you done killed me slow every day for years and I ain't dead yet. Ain't nothin' ya'll can do you ain't already done. Force yourself on me, beat me up real bad and laugh, steal my happiness, kill my joy, what more can you do? I'm still here!"

Jack Miles charged. She fired off the last shot at his head, much closer to killing him than she'd counted on. He groaned and covered his grazed temple. Before he had a chance to recover, she landed the wineglass across the crown of his head, followed by picture frames, knick-knacks, paper weights – anything in the immediate area. As he cowered in distress, she reloaded the gun and fired at the floor, driving him scrambling backwards toward the door.

"Alright," he submitted, face bloodied along the brow and ears. "Alright. I'll get the guys to come for my things."

"Wrong. Tell 'em we split up. There're two suitcases on the porch with everything you need. Come anywhere near *my* house and Black Mountain County'll haul you off 'fore you can think to run, get it?"

"How do I know something's in the bag?"

"You don't. Cross me and you'll find out. I never see you again, on purpose, by accident. If you see me, go the other way. Keys?"

Jack Miles rummaged in his pocket for the house keys and tossed them onto the floor. He stumbled to the porch for his bags and drove off into the approaching darkness, cursing everything under the sun the entire way. Betty Lou let the handgun fall to the floor and relaxed, the iron shackles around her feet and wrists finally unlocked.

Suspension from the force meant Geary, Kludd, and Gaston drowned their sorrows in booze, poker and television nonstop from the time Riggins said, "Get out." On this particular afternoon, the trio, plus a surly Jack Miles, gathered at Reifer's house. Out back, Gaston and Kludd dipped snuff and shot the breeze, while Jack Miles and Geary played card games and drank whatever Frankie brought in front.

Jack Miles eyed Geary. "Still miss Schiffler, don't you?"

"Ain't right the way she went, Hawk." He swigged deeply from the beer can and placed it next to others. "On the train tracks? Jus' ain't right."

"Well, she's a Jew," he said bluntly. "Least she ain't get gassed."

"You're not helping."

Jack Miles lit a cigarette and blew smoke rings in Geary's direction. "Betty Lou kicked me out. Think you can put me up for a while?"

"She *finally* did it, huh?" he snickered. "You should have told her… gotten her into it."

"Like you did with Schiffler?" he shot back. "Seemed like it worked the same, either way. No way Betty gets in on this."

"Then you *force* her, ain't that what you tell me?" Geary resented Jack Miles for giving him advice that never worked, Jack Miles didn't follow it for himself, but he always had some.

"She's got my clothes from the last job."

"No, Hawk, you're not that sloppy. We've got an investigation up our butts and you *kept* your clothes? Do you *want* to get caught?"

"You're one to talk!" Jack Miles voice raised loud enough for Gaston and Kludd to circle the house. "Burn yourself half to death an' tell Riggins half-baked lies like a kid. And Frank Abraham made that call, right? I know his kin. They still live over on Hoss Road. Frank

Abraham is dead. Don't believe me, go to the cemetery, dig him up and ask him."

Geary cursed and chucked an empty can into the street. Frankie dropped a full one over his shoulder and retrieved it. "So, what's a dead nigger and a burnt down house to me?"

"Then we did it for *nothing?* We were set up Geary. If it's the same people doing your investigation, we're all going down."

Geary pointed at him. "Not gonna happen. We'll lay low for a bit and it'll all blow over."

Darrion straightened the poorly-fitting, out-of-style clothes before ringing the doorbell. A day after the fire, Whitehead arranged for him to rummage through Higher Ground's clothing donations, which is where he came up with his current ensemble; a powder blue short sleeved shirt two sizes too big and a pair of polyester pants so long he had to roll them at the cuffs. When he thought to complain, he remembered they were clean and appreciated Whitehead's generosity.

While he waited for the door to be answered, the poorly patched, bullet-sized holes in the woodwork and the front door caught his attention. These must be some of the alterations the advertisement in the newspaper was referencing. Admittedly, he was not the most skilled at home repair, but he hoped he'd get a fair shot. He needed the money; rent was due yesterday. Ms. Parsippany gave him an extra day on his word and the recent loss of his mother.

"Yes?" Joséphine's eyes met Darrion's. "I remember you. You helped me once. Come in."

He entered the living room, which was garishly decorated with various bottles, relics and colored scarves. "I'm Darrion James. I came about the advertisement in the paper."

"My fiancé was murdered by white people," she said somberly. "I read about your mother. I'm so sorry, but you must know the pain I feel."

"I do."

"Look around. There are some things I need that women like me can't do by themselves, you know?" Joséphine moistened her lips. "How good are you with your hands?"

Darrion paused at her question's undertones. "Sorry?"

"Do you know what it's like to have every eye in a room looking at you? Every man who has come here to be hired wants up my skirt for no good reason b'sides they think there's some secret thing there. Can't offer a drink without getting stared at."

"Your white friend hasn't helped you find someone?"

"She don't mind exchanging favors for favors. *I do.* I fix the house up as best I can, but I need help. I don't know nothing 'bout no pipes or woodwork, and I'm not strong enough to push and lift things. You're a reverend, right? Maybe I'm safer in your hands."

Darrion thrust his hands into his pockets and jingled some change. "I don't know. I'm not so handy after all and I don't know if that would look proper."

"Of course it would…unless you're like the others, which I know you're not. Where are you staying these days?"

"Miss Parsippany's on Carriage," he responded.

"From the looks of you, looks like you might need a lil' change to your name. Let me pay for your room for a month or so, while you help me fix my house. If it ain't lookin' proper to all them church folks then you can stop helping me and you owe me nothing but a goodbye."

Something about the whole scenario didn't appear on the up and up, but his options were limited. Working for Joséphine would give him something to do besides translating, as well as prolong his stay in Zyonne, so he could prayerfully figure out his next move. In the meantime, it presented an opportunity to share the Word with her.

"Don't the Bible say something about helping widows and orphans?" she asked, unfolding bills from a wad of cash.

"But you're not a widow. Do you have children?"

"No, but still," she persisted. "Can you help me?"

Despite the inner nagging, Darrion consented.

Joséphine extended a hand. "Thank you so much. When can you start?"

"Today, I suppose."

"Good." She offered him a few bills, enough to cover rent for a month. "Show up at 9:00 every day, you can leave at 5:00. It's almost 2:00 now. Fix my faucets and we'll call it a day."

When Darrion returned to the boarding house after replacing the washers on Joséphine's sink and bathtub, which took him all of two minutes after he figured out how to do it, two white men sitting on the porch stood up. Both wore black suits, white shirts, thin black ties and carried briefcases. "Mr. James, we have business with you."

The three men entered the home and reconvened in the sitting room. Miss Parsippany offered the men something to drink. All declined but Darrion and she disappeared after serving.

Darrion shook hands with both men. "How can I help you?"

"Joshua Freedman," said one with a short nose, pallid skin and impeccably combed brown hair. "Your mother used me as counsel regarding her estate."

"Reginald Michaels," said the other. He was chubby, tanned and sweating profusely. "Gormean Insurance."

They spoke freely but all understood that Miss Parsippany was eavesdropping somewhere.

"The home at Seven Superior Place, your mother's sole asset, was willed to you. She also left a safe deposit box at Zyonne Bank. Present identification and they will open it for you."

Darrion sipped his drink. He assumed all this information before.

"The fire insurance policy on the house was canceled last month because she couldn't make the payments," said Michaels, "but she kept up her life insurance. Sign these."

Michaels pushed a quarter-inch thick stack of paper-clipped papers across the table to Darrion. He fast scanned the documents and signed them one-by-one at the bottom where necessary. "Is this amount correct, $15,000?"

A plate shattered in the kitchen.

"The largest Negro estate settlement in Black Mountain history," Michaels said.

Nothing could replace Kelley, but with money came options. He finished signing and showed them out. After subtracting final bills and their fees, he could expect a check in about three weeks. Given the lack of privacy at the boardinghouse, he'd pick up the money downtown.

"Who was that?" Miss Parsippany played dumb. "What'd they want?"

"Settling my mother's business."

"Well, just know the rates don't change here, same as they always was. Won't ask you for 'nother extra penny, no sir. Say, what you gone do with all that money anyway, Boy?"

He was off the front porch and on his way before Miss Parsippany's phrase of fake concern and last question. Fifteen blocks later, he rang the bell to Joséphine's like a madman.

"What's wrong?" she asked in half-Creole. "Change your mind?"

Darrion grabbed her hand and pulled. "C'mon Boss. I need help."

"Wait, wait a second, I don't have shoes on."

"Well, hurry up. This is important."

Joséphine slipped on whatever shoes she left on the floor mat and locked the front door. "What's so important? Where are we going?"

"A little further on the west side."

"Wrong answer." She pulled away. "Hardly know you and it's too late for all that."

"It's a beautiful day. We've got time. It's barely half past 5:00."

That much was true. The overcast sky parted, exposing a daisy yellow sunburst. "Okay." He wanted to share the vision God had given him: millions of lost souls reaching and crying out to Heaven for Christ and he, who no longer looked himself but more like Christ, stretched an open palm toward them with the *Lost Testament* in it.

Those people crawled from behind the cross one-by-one and ate the pages from his palm. As the people ate, they turned into quiet lambs.

Minutes into the trip and tired of the silence, Joséphine spoke up. "If we're gonna die today, don't you think I deserve to know why I'm goin' to the grave so young and pretty?"

"You're not going to die, Joséphine," he deadpanned.

"Then why all the mystery, Cher? I ain't the surprise kind of gal."

"There's something I have to know," he responded, making sure his company understood that he didn't desire to be questioned further.

Somewhere on Zyonne's west side was a large building he'd seen in another vision, but Darrion had no clues to direct them there – besides numbers emblazoned in his consciousness, *3-1-2*. Every street on that side of town owned a 300 block, so he relied on his mind's residual images and his spirit.

Joséphine submitted and followed Darrion's confident lead. She detested everything Christian, but the mysticism surrounding the religion made it tolerable to her. The reverend let a few Biblical tidbits slip out while he fixed the faucet, a couple verses and theological explanations "to make small talk," he'd said.

She knew better. All the men she'd ever encountered wanted something from her. This angle was different. The others were after Joséphine for her desirable body. Darrion James was after her soul. The pair hopped on the 144 bus, rode it to the route's end and disembarked on Hoghoba Street.

"Alright, I'm here. Now you're gonna have to hold my hand."

Darrion accepted the shaking hand she offered. "We're safe."

"Tellin' me not to worry. How do you *know* we're safe? And don't give me none of that God stuff, you hear me?"

"Right, no 'God stuff'."

Joséphine smacked his shoulder hard. "Don't you dare laugh at me!"

"How many times can you die, Joséphine?"

The question was the first move in a game of religion versus religion that she'd no intentions of playing with the reverend. "I don't know and I certainly ain't no coward."

"Listen, even if you believe in coming back as someone else, the body you're in right now has to die. It can only die once. But if you walk around afraid of everything all the time, you die a little more every day. Cowards die a thousand times before their deaths."

"Who said that, *Jesus*?"

"Shakespeare."

Joséphine wrenched her hand free. "I'm no coward."

"I'm just saying you don't have to be afraid."

"So, why ain't you afraid?"

"Because if I do die, I know where I'm going afterward."

"That's enough for me, Bible Man. Are we almost there, you know, wherever it is you're taking me that I'm not gonna die?"

Darrion brushed soot from the top right hand corner of the street sign. Hoghoba Street, 300th block. His spirit bubbled over like boiling water. "Yeah, we're almost there."

At a distance, he saw the numbers *312* on a brickface warehouse-looking structure. It was the tallest around. From outside, the building looked sturdy and soundly constructed.

"Why are you looking at that building like that?"

"C'mon, let's go inside."

Her eyes bulged. "You know what's in there?"

Darrion rattled the dust-covered pewter handle until the steel door groaned open. Spider webs decorated the rotting doorjamb. "Rats, roaches, horse and dope fiends, murderers…"

"There ain't enough light in here."

"Sure, there is."

Sunlight broke through the rear window to light the floor area and the bottom third of the walls near the spare mechanical parts and paint cans stacked along the shelves. A rickety staircase in the upper left hand corner of the room led to a second storage floor, where the pitter-patter sound of tiny feet could be heard.

"Alright, hurry up, Reverend," she rubbed her arms in discomfort. "Miss Joséphine don't do rat holes. Why'd you bring me here anyway?"

Darrion followed the impulse to open the translation to the blank pages at the back and sketch the vision. He licked his pen tip and started drawing the pulpit; the raised platform occupying a fourth of the room wall-to-wall; a lectern in the center, represented with a rectangle, royal purple carpet beneath, and choir stands to its left. Next to those things would be a piano and organ (he represented these with two large boxes) and...a drum set – (miniature circles and straight lines). Had anything so elaborate ever been done before?

Aisles and aisles of folding chairs, stacked as close as possible. It was snug, but not another fire trap. This was more spaced out. Even with this unique setup, he figured the crowd attending this service would exceed the building's occupancy limit. It was an issue that he'd have to take up with the fire marshal.

"Hey," Darrion said half-distracted, pen flying across the page, "you ever heard of a tent revival? My mother...used to tell me about these awesome all-night church meetings underneath a tent propped up a block or so from here at Hoghoba Street Park. Can you imagine 200 people accepting Christ in one night – hookers, alcoholics and dope addicts leaving clean? Can you imagine something so incredible, something like that, in *here*? After it's fixed up, of course. A little dusting and some paint would do it good."

Joséphine's demeanor fouled. "You're gonna do that here?"

Keeping the conversation civil amidst opposite spiritual positions was a tightrope act, but he did it hoping that she may find salvation.

Something within Joséphine stewed. She coughed and gumbo fragments surfaced, which she expelled as ladylike as possible. *No worries. Darrion didn't notice.* According to Freedom, appearances were everything, especially in front of attractive men. "Yelling and screaming for God to show up. Does He, or She, or It? If God exists, I don't think it even listens. It's all an act, like a high-priced picture show, or theatre act."

Disturbed, Darrion put his things down. "Why are you so angry?"

Joséphine clenched her teeth. "Mark believed in your God and what did it get him? Those white people hanged and burned him like an animal! He went to those godless tent revivals, threw away the money he bled for, cried, danced and came home broke and tired. You call it an 'offering' when you give up something you want, right?"

Darrion reached out for her. "Joséphine, please."

"No!" she yelled, backing away. "Why'd I have to offer my soul, my life? *God?* Is that what you're going to tell me…that He's got something to do with it? Don't you dare preach that to me! If I can die like an animal believing in God, I can die like an animal without Him."

"Don't you care where you'll spend eternity?"

"You don't get it. You preacher types never do. Heaven ain't worth waitin' for, Reverend, if you struggle to get halfway through today on the way to tomorrow. Hell ain't half as scary when you live like that."

"I never thought about it that way," he said, somberly.

"Nobody's gonna buy what you're sellin', if you don't."

Darrion swallowed the jab and backed off. "Jo, I think this just might be the right place for a godless tent revival."

"Suit yourself. Nothing's stopping you."

EIGHTEEN

SATURDAY NIGHT, OCTOBER 27, 1962

WITH darkness creeping in along the still poor-lit west side, the saints fearfully left for their own homes, leaving Darrion to add finishing touches to the warehouse sanctuary. They reunited quickly after a chain of calls describing his intent to pastor a new church there, as Reverend Whitehead was still unfit to preach.

Minus years of dust and industrial debris, the place looked respectable as a church might look after almost a month of work. Grape carpet cloaked the pulpit and livened up the whitewashed room when the ceiling light reflected off it and the white fold-up chairs. And, after a major tune-up, the old heating unit still worked. He'd swept, mopped, nailed down and scrubbed for as long as possible without it, but forced himself to turn on the heat when the temperature plummeted into the low 40's.

Tomorrow morning, he'd hold the church's first service at 10:00 a.m. Following much begging on his part, Georgie agreed to lead the choir and perform the original compositions she'd previously been forbidden to sing. And, as tradition dictated, the church mothers planned to sit two rows from the front in the center, with a chair painted black in Kelley's memory.

Darrion dropped the broom and strolled up to the front. He'd been a presiding pastor before, but this was totally different. In his former position, he'd labored under the church board's collective thumb and political shadow – even being pressured to handwrite his sermons, so their content could be approved or changed prior to him preaching it.

"I will stand upon my watch," Darrion yelled, fists on hips, "and set me upon the tower, and will watch to see what He will say unto me, and what I shall answer when I am reproved?" Fixated with the pure beauty of a divine vision conceived, birthed, and finally coming to pass around him, he puffed out his chest. "And the Lord answered me, and said, 'Write the vision and make it plain upon tables, that he may run that readeth it. For the vision is yet for an appointed time, but at the end it shall speak, and not lie: though it tarry, wait for it; because it will surely come, it-will-not-tarry!'"

"Am I interrupting?" Joséphine shouted from the warehouse door.

"No, not at all." He stepped down into the cleared middle aisle to meet her. "Just a few finishing touches!"

"You ain't been by in a few days. I know you got all that money, but I thought we had a deal – that you'd finish out the week at least?"

"You're right. I'm sorry. I'm not so good at managing my time."

By this time, they were within normal speaking distance.

"It's about *that book* again, isn't it? That's what's keeping you busy these days?"

Darrion ignored the guilt trip. "Not this time."

"What is it then? Why don't you have time for me?"

"I feel the presence of God inside me. Sometimes, I feel like I can do everything. Sometimes, I commit myself to too many things because I believe I can handle it all. Other times, it's pride, I guess, because I don't want to admit my weaknesses and disappoint people. I have a duty to preach the Word of God. It's why I'm here in the first place. But as a man of God, I also have to keep my word. Things are about finished here. It's nothing I can't get up and do early tomorrow. Can I walk you home? Maybe fix a few things for you?"

"No," she said, playfully. "Not tonight. Too late for all that."

"No? I thought you wanted me to help you?"

"I hate givin' in easy, but alright. If you let me take care of the *Lost Testament* for you. That's the deal."

"Sorry." Her request alarmed him. "Why do you want it anyway?"

"What's the big deal, Cher? It's just a *book*. I'll make you a late Creole dinner, while you work. It'll take your mind off things."

Darrion shut down the furnace and breathed deep, convinced that he'd overreacted. After the fire, the *Lost Testament* hadn't left his side. He returned to Joséphine and admitted it.

Joséphine slid a warm hand into his. "How 'bout a shrimp Po' Boy and some sweet potato pone? Hot tea and lemon pound cake?"

He'd been so busy, his body must have mistaken its hunger for purposeful fasting. "Sounds delicious, but if I give you the *Lost Testament*, you have to read it."

Joséphine paused. "No way."

"Stakes too high for you? If you're not going to read it, why do you want it anyway?"

"Fine." He offered her the text and she snapped it away. "I'll take a nap and if I can't, I'll just do some looking here."

"It's a religious text, Ma Chérie, not Reader's Digest."

"Same ole thing to me 'cause I ain't about nobody's religion. And don't speak Creole again. It don't sound right." She dug her arms inside Darrion's jacket and buried herself in him. Uncomfortable with the sudden affection, he walked rigid, pretending the cold was bothering him and not his company's actions.

"Something wrong, Darrion? I just caught a bad chill."

"Oh," he said, embarrassed. "Of course. I knew that. Me, too."

"Course, you did. You thought I was diggin' on you."

"You're still wearing your ring."

Joséphine stared at the small band on her left ring finger. "Didn't you wear yours for a while after Jayne left you?"

"Yes, but to remember the good times, the fun times, I guess. I didn't want to let go."

"What, your *Bible* don't give you good thoughts?"

After a month, her flippancy was beginning to irritate his nerves. "Even Adam needed an Eve. Sometimes, I need the Word and sometimes I want someone in the flesh to talk to."

"Well, I wear mine 'cause it's the one nice thing I got. I love wearing pretty things, sounds selfish, but it's true. Mark worked hard for it. He let me know it, too, but I ain't mind so much. I miss him. Ain't a day goes by I don't. Think 'bout him all the time – the way he smell and the things we used to do together. Every day, it feels like my heart's gone out my chest and my body's goin' only 'cause it's too dumb to go on an' die." Emotion poured forth, saturating her trembling voice. "I've gone all these months hopin' it was a mistake, thinkin' maybe they grabbed another Negro and my Mark's on the loose somewhere, waitin' 'til things smooth over so he can send for me."

Darrion wrapped Joséphine a little tighter in his arms. As they headed out, she shivered and welcomed the added body warmth. "They left him hanging there all night. I woke up and I still don't know what time I did. There was a knife in the shed. I wanted to use it on myself, but I took it, walked out to the orchard and climbed the tree he was hanging from. And we talked…and then I cut him down," she sniffed. "The body burnt so bad and so long, it became a pile of dust when it hit the ground and then it blew away. I buried the rope in the backyard."

Darrion added the fragments together. "*That's* why they couldn't find the body?"

"They ain't *want* to 'find the body.' If it was still there, they'd have cut it down and gotten rid of it before I did. Them devils ain't nobody but the police. Tis why nothin' ever happens to the Klan 'round here."

"There has to be something we can do, or someone we can notify."

"Ain't no one care 'bout this town, 'specially 'bout no Negroes livin' and dyin' in it. They killed us 'fore you got here and they'll do it long after you gone."

"I don't believe that, Joséphine. Somebody has to care."

"Accept it or don't, it's the truth. We in a bad way as Negroes, if we prayin' to a dead white man, beggin' Him to get the white man an' to come rescue us from the white man."

They turned the corner to Sesame Drive and Darrion relaxed his grasp. "Jesus is not white."

"Well then, what color is He, Preacher Man?"

"What difference does it make? You're not praying to Him, are you?"

Caught off-guard by his snappy argument, Joséphine quieted.

"So where will you go when the house is done?"

"I want to move to Paris and be a singer." Between all the recent lies, her childhood dream sounded ridiculous even to her.

Darrion muffled his laughter. "Why Paris? Can you sing?"

"Freedom named me after Josephine Baker because she loved her singing voice. You know her story? She was adored abroad, but they never respected her here in the States 'cause of her color."

"Right, kind of like Nina Simone."

"Who?"

"Nina Simone, a jazz singer. Similar story. Your beauty and talent would be appreciated more there. Here, you might end up as just another Negro with a pipe dream."

Joséphine wilted beneath the compliment. "You think I'm *beautiful?*"

"Out of what I said that's the only thing you remember?"

"And I'm talented. You ain't even heard me sing. Swear you ain't diggin' on me, brother, not just a little tiny bit?"

Darrion grinned, remembering Kelley's old tactic to avoid questions. "I ain't tellin' and I ain't lyin', neither."

Joséphine hugged him with all her strength, chest pressing close to his midsection and beating a strong steady rhythm into his body. The flattery brightened up her otherwise bleak day. "Thank you, Cher."

Midway to the house, the familiarity and closeness started bugging Darrion, so he pretended to cough and drew back. He maintained his distance and Joséphine stayed her own path, a good three feet away.

"You the first man I seen in a while who ain't want his hands on me."

Darrion said nothing.

She searched inside for the voice that spoke when she counseled people about their pasts. Since the moment she touched Darrion's hand, Joséphine heard nothing. Even worse, she couldn't concentrate on it. Things she usually picked up second nature were more difficult to call out and terribly off-base, which bugged her to no end. "Give me your palm," she spat out.

"What? Why?"

"I want to understand more about you. What's your birthday?"

"What does my hand or my birthday have to do with it? If you want to know more about me, just ask."

"Do you always have to know *why*?"

"Not always, but asking for my palm is not an average request."

"I want to see some things about you. The way you argue, you must be a Gemini. You're birthday's in May, right?"

"I told you that I'm not into this consulting stuff. It's not godly."

"Why not? Don't you want to know the answers to questions you could never answer? I can give them all to you."

His gait slowed. Something about Josephine had noticeably changed. She refused to look directly at him.

"You can give me the answers?"

"Yes," she said in a nonchalant tenor. "I can. I know a lot about you, Darrion James."

"But I know nothing about you," he played along. "Who are you? Where do you come from?"

There was no response. Joséphine shifted and squirmed. "I've been around here for quite a long time. Don't you recognize me?"

"Joséphine, let me help you."

She waved the *Lost Testament* at him. "You've helped me already. This is the second time you've given this to me. All of you are the same. You all hurt the same."

Darrion's heart froze. He imagined Joséphine's past littered with sketchy characters who'd left painful fingerprints on her life, asking for her trust, abusing her naïve dependence, violating her innocence, and forcing her into a life she'd never intended to live.

His heart broke over the Creole beauty's change in temperament. A minute ago, she sauntered down the street without a care in the world. Now, her behavior reminded him of a story he once read. "Jo, do you hear me? Look at me."

Joséphine displayed a wicked grin. "You're not gonna let me walk away like Jayne, or *die* like your mother in the fire?" The maple tree by the roadside lit with flames at its tendrils when she focused on it. "Remember it, Darrion? Her flesh melted like hot butter, like that tree."

Darrion redirected his focus inward. He couldn't be distracted by anything, including the absence of the *Lost Testament*.

"You let her die and might as well have lit the match yourself."

"There is no condemnation to them which are in Christ," he responded, "who walk not after the flesh, but after the Spirit."

Burning leaves dropped from the overhead branches and furiously ignited pot-sized fires in the area around the duo.

"Because of you, Kelley died in a fire just like this. I can kill you the exact same way. Burn you and this precious book."

"Thou shall not bear false witness against thy neighbor. Whether I live, I live unto the Lord; and whether I die, I die unto the Lord: whether I live therefore, or die, I am the Lord's."

Amongst the rapidly rising heat, Joséphine shed her dress and stood before him in underclothes. She strutted up to the reverend and rubbed her hands lustfully up and down her body. "How long has it been since you touched a woman, Darrion? How long has it been since a woman's touched you and you felt like a man?" She approached closer and stroked his midsection. "Come be with me. I'll do anything you want me to…be what you want me to be."

Darrion's hand found Joséphine's face and gripped it tight around the cheeks and jaws. "Destruction," he called out.

She pointed to the *Lost Testament* lying on the pavement next to her dress and its cover began to smoke.

"Bitterness!"

"You can't get rid of us," she said between gnashed teeth.

Darrion braced his arm behind Joséphine's back to keep her from struggling. "Lust! Anger! Deception!"

"No! No, no, no, no!" Joséphine dug her nails deep into Darrion's throat and dug its flesh away.

"Witchcraft! Murder!"

"I'm warnin' you, James. Stop! You'll die for this!"

"In Christ's name, *be gone!*"

Still in bed 13 hours later, Joséphine reviewed everything she remembered about last night and her encounter with the reverend, starting with a walk from the warehouse on Hoghoba Street. Darrion smelled of old dust and musk cologne, and his hands were rough and calloused, like Mark's overworked fingers used to be.

Sometime later, she ended up in bed with just underclothes on and no concept of how much time had passed between their conversation and the present or how she'd become undressed. The reverend surely hadn't been with her. *Maybe it rained, or I'd vomited all over myself?*

Pots and pans clanging together in the kitchen alerted Joséphine to the fact she wasn't alone. *It has to be him. No self-respecting interloper would create so much noise.*

She donned the peach satin nightgown hanging on the closet door and tip-toed barefoot into the kitchen, where Darrion unsuccessfully attempted to cook. Joséphine sat at the kitchen table, propped her chin up with her fists and watched.

"You know," he said in a coarse voice with his back turned, "you could help instead of watching me struggle."

Joséphine gasped when he faced her. "What happened to your neck?"

Gashes clotted with black and maroon blood covered the skin beneath his faint beard. "I couldn't find any bandages or alcohol."

"You got attacked by some wild animal, is that what happened?" She retreated to the bathroom, freshened up, and returned robed with cotton balls, witch hazel, gauze and tape. "Look, Cher, ain't no time for guessin' games. What happened to you?"

"*You,*" he winced in pain, as she blotted and dabbed. "You weren't yourself last night. What time is it?"

"Then *what* was I? Stop tryin' to look at the clock and hold still."

"Do you believe in evil spirits, Joséphine?"

"Of course. There's always a balance. Where there's good, there's evil, too. Why? Quit movin' so much."

"Sorry, it hurts. There's no easy way to explain this."

"Well…" She attacked a scab and swabbed it until the blood around the spot disappeared and the ragged skin flaked off. "It's okay. Explain it to me in God-talk. However you can, I'll live."

"You asked to do your fortune-telling thing with me. When I refused, you changed. You were angry and attacked me."

"I see." Joséphine's heart skipped a beat.

Darrion set down across from her and explained it all in 15 minutes – creation, human beings and their inner need for God, salvation, the Spirit's presence, or in His absence, demons.

Joséphine listened and absorbed it all from beginning to end, including his mind numbing story about a clinically insane woman from whom he'd cast out several devils. Out of respect for her beliefs, Darrion kept it as short and uncomplicated as possible, expecting huffs, sighs and rolled eyes from his atheist audience. There was no such thing.

Joséphine folded her hands and barely moved, except to nod. As he spoke of last night, its memories flashed back to her in violent spurts. Everything sounded irrational on one level in her mind, but altogether sensible on another in the pit of her stomach. "Thank you for what you did," she said full of emotion. "Don't know anyone who'd do somethin' like that for me. You sure you ain't diggin' on me, Reverend, not even a little?"

He took her hands. "I ain't tellin' Joséphine and I ain't lyin', neither."

"Call me Jo, again. Like it when you call me that."

He obliged.

Joséphine's fingers tensed in his. "Tell me what I need to do."

Darrion bowed his head and led her to the Lord.

NINETEEN

EARLY SUNDAY MORNING, OCTOBER 28, 1962

AFTERWARDS, Jolene rose, feeling fresh and renewed. She combed through her tousled hair with her fingers, but to no avail. Knotted hair, offensive morning breath, red eyes – Darrion had seen it all, including more cleavage and leg than she'd wished to reveal. She left him in the kitchen and scooted to the bedroom for real clothes. Although she'd been seen unkempt, there was no sense in staying that way. Freedom taught the Courtiér girls better.

When she returned well-groomed, her company continued to fumble around the preparation area. Jolene shooed Darrion away, opened the refrigerator and removed several containers and a paper parcel.

"So, what are we having?" Darrion grinned. "I'm starving."

"Eggs Ponchartrain, bacon for you, toast, orange juice."

"How do you feel *now*, Jo?"

Jolene's hands worked the ingredients. "Like a new woman. Don't ask me what I'm cookin' up now. Go on and eat it. You'll like it."

Darrion sucked his teeth. "How are you so sure, Miss Courtiér?"

"You'll like it," she said, playfully. Bacon sizzled in the pan. "You'll *love* it. You'll just be too stubborn to admit it to me."

The two continued talking and laughing so loud that neither heard the front door open, the approaching high heel clicks, or the Tennessee twang coming toward them. "Joséphine, you won't believe the night I had," said Charlie, hands full with paper bags. Shameless cleavage tumbled from Charlie's open white cotton blouse and her skirt was wrinkled and twisted. "You know what John did? We were in the living room and we was..."

"Charlemagne!" Jolene reserved full names for exclamations.

"What?" She entered the kitchen. "Oh!" She cursed. Darrion's brow furrowed at the flustered white woman. "Sorry, oh God, sorry! Gosh! Ain't know you had company."

Jolene introduced the strangers. "It ain't like that. *Reverend* Darrion James, Charlemagne Marie Evans, I told you about her, remember?"

Religious church folk boiled over Charlie's insecurities like hot milk. One look into her eyes and Charlie was positive that a flashcard showed on her forehead, listing every sin she'd ever committed. As "Marie," she disrobed by choice, but no one undressed Charlie by force since her first. Anyone with a Bible and an opinion after him did the same with examining eyes.

"Hey," said Charlie, nervous, sure to avoid Darrion. "H-hey Joséphine, I'm kinda sore about that. You makin' Eggs Punch an' Chains without me?"

Jolene and Charlie kissed one another on the cheek. "Have my half. Ain't quite feelin' it right this mornin'. And it's 'Jolene' again."

"He's cute," Charlie whispered into her ear.

"Who you tellin'?" she mouthed back. "We need to talk."

"Say ladies, it's getting mighty lonely over here."

"Almost done, Cher. Three minutes."

Charlie nodded toward the pastor and spoke in a subdued tone. "Is it 'bout *him*? You diggin' on him?"

"Can't consult, Charlemagne. Not no more. I'm sorry."

"Please tell me you ain't one of them church folk now? Joséphine, all them people is hypocrites – tell you one thing, live another. This cat prolly one of them, too. Done convinced you to do somethin' you ain't need to do. C'mon, Joséphine, *think*! Think 'bout this! What about the *money*? Since when did *Jesus* start payin' bills?"

Jolene dressed the plate, served Darrion, and dragged Charlie by the elbow to the other side of the kitchen. "Go on an' eat, Cher. Be with you in a second," she said, nodding in his direction. Darrion nodded back and then busied himself with chewing.

"Charlemagne, look at Darrion's neck."

She poked her head around Jolene's shoulder. "T'was wonderin' how he got them scratches. Look like he done wrestled a wolverine."

"I did it. *I* scratched him."

Charlie shook her head. "You?"

"I ain't believe it neither 'til I washed my hands this mornin'. My nails was bloody and had clumps of skin under them…his skin."

"You done lost it, Darlin'? Why'd you do it?"

"Sit down and eat. He'll tell you why."

By the time Charlie and Jolene joined him, Darrion had already devoured everything on his plate but the silver fork. Charlie dove into hers, while Jolene nursed a glass of water and presented Darrion the opportunity to share "the Word" with Charlie.

"Charlemagne, you seem like a woman who knows the game."

"I like to think so, Rev," she mumbled between bites.

"So there's no reason to beat around the bush."

"None. Give it to me straight."

Darrion simplified it as much as possible; everything from God to Satan and demonic possession, but the explanation was hardly straightforward. Every reason and detail inspired Charlie to ask more questions, which resulted in Darrion giving more reasons, more details, and then her asking more questions. The exercise lasted a full ten minutes before Charlie submitted, exhausted by all the mental posturing.

"Okay, now. I'm confused. You sayin' there's *one* God?"

With fingers massaging his temples, he signaled yes.

"And one God is *three different people*?"

"Right. Father, Son, Holy Ghost."

"One of 'em died. You said He died for me…just me or everyone? Why? And since He died, that means there's two now?"

"Jesus gave His life, so everyone who believes in their hearts that Jesus died and that the Father raised Him from the dead can live forever. Jesus is in Heaven, with the Father, and the Holy Ghost is in all of us who believe. Still three persons and still one God."

For some reason, the lecture sounded reasonable. "Tell me more."

Jolene rose, stretched and yawned. "No time. It's 8:30. I'm gonna bathe. Charlemagne, you'll drive us to the west side?"

Charlie was captivated with her thoughts. "Huh? West side?"

"Church, Cheri."

Charlie used God's and Jesus' name in vain plenty, but it never occurred to Jolene she may have wanted to tag along. When Jolene shuffled off to the bathroom, Charlie's eyes moistened. Darrion dabbed away the tears rolling down her cheeks and she collapsed onto his shoulder, sobbing. She was unsure why the thick emotional walls she'd erected so well brick-by-brick for 38 years were crumbling down so thoroughly. The debris drained out in painful coughs, sniffles, huffs and hysterical sobs. Darrion patted Charlie's back and embraced her with his free arm. She clung to him, as if she feared drowning beneath herself.

She remembered it all, every scab, scar and broken bone of the past and where they came from. She wept for the ugliness. She needed healing. And whatever this beautiful man was selling, she intended to buy it all.

Jolene wished for a long, soothing shower, where the water dribbled indiscriminate trails along her milky cocoa body and relaxed its muscles. She'd stroke the wet soap bar along her skin like a fiddle playing a symphonic interlude and hum along to pass time. But not today. Darrion was on a schedule and far be it from her to make him tardy. Freedom said handsome men should wait for a gorgeous woman, but not too long, for even the longsuffering have limits. Besides, since he'd refused to leave some clothes at her home like she'd asked, Charlie would have to drive across town to the boarding home, wait for him to dress and motor out to the church. With no traffic, the trek might take 45 minutes total, leaving Darrion nearly ten minutes short.

It still sounds strange to call a storage warehouse a church, she thought, while toweling off. She was ashamed to admit it to the reverend, but the converted warehouse was her first visit to a sanctuary. Freedom's mother Hannah was a voodoo priestess and forced Freedom to believe as such. She, Annie and Nona were forbidden to go within blocks of a church.

Things were different now. She was a Christian, or at least she imagined so. *Isn't that what Darrion said I am?* He called her "Jo," which she loved for its playfulness, and "sister" a lot. Deep in her heart, she resented that. "Sister" sounded sterile to her, like "Jolene" used to before he started calling her that. She wanted to be more than a "sister" to the pastor.

She glanced at the wall clock: 8:45 a.m. She mummified her head and body from chest to mid-thigh in towels and exited the steamy washroom. It was quiet enough for a pin to drop. She wondered whether Darrion had beaten Charlie to death with his Bible. Curious, she poked her head around the corner. Charlie and Darrion were holding hands at the kitchen table. Charlie brushed aside her dyed blonde curls and looked at her old friend with mascara-smeared eyes.

"Don't look at me," she said. Charlie massaged her reddened face and bowed. "I look horrible, just horrible."

Jolene walked over and gave Charlie a smooch on the forehead. "No, Cheri, you a new person. Can't get no more beautiful than that." After she dressed – nothing complicated, a navy blue sweater, long-hemmed matching skirt, white high heels – – the trio shot over to the boarding house. From the time Darrion shut the automobile door and ran up the stairs until the moment he reappeared in an impeccable charcoal suit (ten minutes tops), Jolene and Charlie discussed the things in their former lives and how things had to drastically change.

Later, the trio eased into the refurbished warehouse which was crowded well beyond their expectations. After all, the Bible study group started with 20 people, a number which swelled to 100, then doubled at its crowded peak right before the fire. Now, standing before them was 500 people, chatting and sharing fellowship, including a small, grim-faced, white contingent at the sanctuary's rear.

"Great! Thought I was gone be the only one in here!" Before Charlie moved too far toward them, Darrion caught her by the wrist.

"Don't sit over there. Those people mean nothing but trouble."

It was foolish to believe something this positive involving this many believing Negroes could be free from enemy attack, but Darrion believed the visitation was for observation purposes – to feel out the atmosphere. Once the church services progressed over time, he figured these intruders were likely to report back to their superiors. But it was no time to think so far into the future. There was a word he needed to deliver and everything today seemed to be distracting him. If it wasn't the subversive whites, there were the errant, uncontrollable thoughts and the "preacher pursuers," as Jayne used to call them; women who threw themselves at him.

Jayne gravitated toward her husband when one of them came around, like the way Jolene moved closer to him now. Darrion whispered into her ear and took to the pulpit, refusing to be deterred further.

"What did he say to you?"

"Sit in the front row and we'd see the seats."

Sure enough, between the newly-appointed church officers were two chairs. Jolene sat down practically in front of Darrion.

"I can't believe her!" Georgie elbowed an alto and shot a stare Jolene's way. The woman's ears wanted more, but Georgie converted her complaints to passionate Spanish.

"Joséphine, you sure we supposed to be here?"

"Right here, in these seats." She patted Charlie's thigh. "Ain't you used to folk starin' at us by now? Be easy. And it's *Jolene*."

"Change your name one more time," Charlie said, "and I'ma start callin' you John, so I don't have to remember your name either."

Georgie turned her back to Jolene and signaled the choir to rise. Inside, she persuaded herself to believe that she formed and led the choir for God's approval and not a man's. When Darrion had asked, she couldn't resist him. Something about the lingering sadness in his face and the humility broke her resistance. She hugged him. It was something she swore she'd never do again.

The organ and piano preludes drowned themselves in the rafters. Georgie trained the singers to focus on her direction and not the music's tempo, so her hand patterns had to be perfect. She counted time with her right hand and directed the voices with the left. Georgie had no idea how to write music for drums, so she entrusted the former drummer of a famous rhythm and blues group to improvise a good beat. He did. If it weren't for him, the first couple measures would have been a confusing disaster.

The soloist belted the first verse of "Save Me," the first religious song Georgie had ever written and the first to be performed. The bassist and drums grooved a catchy bottom, like the kind in the music on the radio, and the congregation members stood up one by one and clapped. "Hallelujah" and "Jesus" shouts popped up around the place. Once everyone caught onto the singsong chorus, they sang along. One animated woman hopped into the aisle and almost pounded a hole into her tambourine, while another flailed around and screamed.

Bewildered, Jolene just observed and politely clapped. Charlie, too. Neither had seen anything like this and despite their new status as "saved," they were reluctant to partake in it. *Perhaps God Himself was motivating these people to do these things? If we don't feel Him too, then we should wait until we do.*

Still, it was difficult for both women not to move. They didn't know if it was God they felt through the music, but it was *something*. Charlie was the first to start clapping – although way offbeat. Jolene absorbed the downbeat and clapped, but outright refused to dance. When she danced, Mark said no man alive could resist her.

The musicians and choir vamped on the song for several minutes before Georgie cut it off and directed the second selection, "Give Him the Glory." Like "Save Me," the song was upbeat and rousing. More folks clapped and danced this time, even some of the men and children. Jolene showed Charlie how to clap on the downbeat and watched her fail miserably at it. *At least the old girl gave it a shot.*

By now, Darrion emerged from the old manager's office in the back, which he'd converted into a study. Jolene smiled and Georgie nearly forgot to direct when he walked behind her. Beneath the brand new black with white trim vestments that the congregation had given him as a surprise, Darrion wore a high-collar black shirt. At first, the cotton didn't itch his wounds, but combined with sweat and the scabs the material felt like steel wool against his skin.

Unable to take the pain anymore, he reentered the office and reappeared near the song's end shirt free. Anyone within a few dozen feet of the pulpit gasped at the grotesque marks on his neck. He tried to imagine the pointing and mouth covering away, but as the word spread, it had become yet another distraction. After the music ended, Darrion assumed his position at the podium. "Good morning Church," he nervously laughed.

"Good morning," came the scattered response.

"Guess you're wondering what happened to my neck here," he said, pointing at his scars. "I'm in church. I can't lie. So, I'm not telling you."

Jolene snickered at Darrion's joke. Her sardonic humor had rubbed off on him after all.

There was silence. *Either they're convicted or offended*, he thought, *but definitely not amused.*

"Welcome to the…Hoghoba Street Mission…Church." Darrion reviewed the church name he invented on the fly in his mind. *The Hoghoba Street Mission Church – not too bad for at the last second.* He held a mason jar in his hand and lifted it high so it could be seen. "If you can understand the meaning of what is in my hand, today you'll see God move like you have never seen Him move before."

Heads wagged in confusion.

Isn't that just a mason jar in his hand?

"Understand its meaning?"

It's an empty mason jar. What's there to understand?

"After today's message, you will desperately want to be what's in my left hand. You will want to be God's empty jar. Repeat after me: I'm God's empty jar."

"I'm an empty jar for God!" Charlie yelled aloud. The rest of the congregation was silent. Charlie shouted it aloud again.

"I'm not gonna move on until you start saying this with me. I'm God's empty jar."

"I'm God's empty jar," some murmured.

Darrion repeated it a third and fourth time and the congregation bellowed it back.

"This message is going to change your life forever. Let us pray."

TWENTY

SUNDAY MID-MORNING, OCTOBER 28, 1962

"**F**ATHER, open up the eyes of our understanding and allow Your people to see Your truth," Darrion prayed. "Give Your servant the ability to speak this word clear and plain. Forgive us for any sin blocking Your movement in our lives. In Jesus' name, Amen."

"Amen."

Jolene lifted her head, feeling an immediate difference in her heart.

"Friends, family, and enemies in the rear, I would like to greet you in the name of our Lord and Savior Jesus Christ."

The white contingent didn't move or respond.

"Today, I'd like to talk to you about being an empty jar for God. Please open your Bible, if you have one, to Second Kings, Chapter Four and rise, as it will be our custom here at the Hoghoba Street Mission Church." His voice still halted over the impromptu name.

"Now there cried a certain woman of the wives of the sons of the prophets unto Elisha, saying, 'Thy servant my husband is dead; and thou knowest that thy servant did fear the Lord: and the creditor is come to take unto him my two sons to be bondmen.'

"And Elisha said unto her, 'What shall I do for thee? Tell me, what hast thou in the house?' And she said, 'Thine handmaid hath not anything in the house, save a pot of oil.'

"Then he said, 'Go, borrow thee vessels abroad of all thy neighbours, even empty vessels; borrow not a few. And when thou art come in, thou shalt shut the door upon thee and upon thy sons, and shalt pour out into all those vessels, and thou shalt set aside that which is full.'

"So she went from him, and shut the door upon her and upon her sons, who brought the vessels to her; and she poured out. And it came to pass, when the vessels were full, that she said unto her son, 'Bring me yet a vessel.' And he said unto her, 'There is not a vessel more.' And the oil stayed."

Darrion opened the now-complete translation of the *Lost Testament*. A cool shiver traveled the length of Jolene's spine. The door to the warehouse had opened and an icy breeze shot through the aisles and chilled the front. She turned around far enough to see Betty Lou in a dark blue dress and high heels limping toward the first unoccupied row of seats. The group of whites, Frankie included, stared her down.

"I'd like someone to tell me something about this jar. Anything."

"It's empty!" Charlie yelled, excitedly.

Darrion pointed to Charlie. "Empty. Thank you, sister. What else? What else do you notice about this plain old mason jar?"

"It's round," said Jolene, "kinda like..."

"You can drink from it, too," Georgie blasted over her.

"Why isn't it a square, or a rectangle, or a triangle? Why didn't the jar maker form the jar into another shape?"

"It's a *jar*." Jolene looked puzzled. "Ain't no good if it ain't the shape it is. It just is what it is. It's a *jar*."

Darrion stepped from behind the pulpit. "There are people in this audience who at one time or another have questioned why God shaped you the way He did. Why did he make you fat? Why is your hair kinky? Why is your skin copper, high-yellow, darn near white, like mine, or so black, you're almost purple? Why are you Negro, *period?*

"God shaped you a certain way for a certain reason. I'm not talking about figures or color. I'm talking about you being you and I'm telling you, Negro or white jar, you ain't no good if you ain't the shape you are. You are the way you are for a reason. God put something inside you and you couldn't hold it if you weren't the shape you are! So stop praying and asking Him to change you around!

"Let me suggest to you this one thing and then we're going back to the real message. The reason why so many of you are uncomfortable being the way you are is because you don't know who you are. Children of God, listen. Your name isn't who you are. It's what you're *called*."

"He got that from me," said Charlie, elbowing Jolene. "I been sayin' that very same thing for years."

"Your parents may or may not be able to tell you who you are. They may not know who they are, or who you are. If you don't know what's inside you, what God placed in you, you're constantly going to try and find it. And if you think it's something unlike God inside you, you're going to confuse yourself."

Darrion wanted to slow down so the people wouldn't be lost, but the wisdom of the *Lost Testament* was coming forth like a rushing river and he felt helpless to stop it. Besides, it appeared through their faces that they were soaking up the entire sermon and thirsting for more.

Jolene's mind raced. She didn't know who she was, so much so that she used a different name and redefined herself again into someone she thought she wanted to be. More or less, Freedom instructed her about how to act, while Mark and Charlie taught her survival.

She knew little about God and whatever it was He put inside her, so Jolene wrung her hands, hoping Darrion would somehow tell her more. Charlie's moist hand found hers to let Jolene know that she wasn't alone in her anxiety. *What time we have wasted!*

Betty Lou almost passed out when the preacher spoke about not knowing who she was. He defined her life in a sentence. All her life, she'd been who someone else wanted her to be.

Helen Graham needed a steady replacement for her estranged husband and her daughter provided it. Jack Miles wanted a housewife who tended to his husbandly desires. She did that, as well. The more Betty Lou thought about it, everything she accomplished was a collage of desires expressed by various people who had passed through her life at one time.

"I'm not telling you God wants you to be something," the pastor continued. "That's like saying I want this to be a jar. It can't *become* a jar. It *is* a jar, regardless of what I call it. God does not want you to *become* a jar. He wants you to realize that you *are* His jar!"

Betty Lou stood to her feet and hollered, drawing the attention of several people in her immediate area. But she didn't care. She hollered aloud again and clapped her hands.

"In the Scriptures, we find out the widow has two boys and owes a debt that she cannot pay. Because she is unable to pay her dead husband's creditors, they are going to take the boys away as bondmen. The law that God gave to Moses said the boys could work off the debt in trade, but the creditors were going to make them slaves. There will always be someone in the world willing to abuse the law for their own good, and trying to make you their slave.

"The Scriptures also say the widow's husband was a God-fearing man. This gives us the basis for what the widow does next. By faith, she approaches the prophet Elisha. There's a word I want to use here called 'liaison.' A liaison is a person who links one person or group to another person or group. If you want to talk to a man who speaks a foreign language and you don't speak it, you need a liaison between you and the man who speaks that foreign language to translate.

"In the Old Testament, God didn't speak to the people Himself. He used his prophets as liaisons. Prophets went before God on behalf of the people, received God's Word straight from Him and communicated that Word to the people. The widow goes to Elisha by faith because she believes in this circumstance that God is able to do something.

"We know she's going to Elisha by faith because she could've put her hands in her pockets, went home and let her sons be taken away. Also, Elisha is a prophet and doesn't have enough money to pay off the creditors, so she is expecting the answer will come another way. She is expecting God to do something because her husband feared Him."

Darrion paced to the end of the altar, a fine-crafted wooden construction complete with varnish and a high shine, received a glass of water from an usher and devoured it entirely. The group of white people moved up into the section on his right, a row behind the last section of Negroes, which was empty, save for the frail white woman.

"Whatcha doin' here, Betty?" Frankie nudged Betty Lou's shoulder with a fist. "Ain't you s'posed to be out spendin' up all of Jack's money? Ain't right what you did to him."

"Ain't right what he did to me, neither, Francine. Let me mind my business and busy my mind and tell your white hood buddies they can all go to..."

"Warnin' you, Betty," Frankie interrupted, "best for you if you stay away from these niggers. God knows all that'll happen if one of 'em sees, I don't know, 'nother fire."

"Leave 'em alone. You all ain't gone get away with this forever." Betty Lou limped across the row to an unoccupied seat far away from the small white mob, close to a bulky Negro usher.

"The widow has faith," continued Darrion. "Faith starts as a seed God plants inside you at birth. Everyone has faith. Everything surrounding you: life, circumstances, trials, tribulations, hurts, and joys. We experience these things to help that seed of faith grow into great, mature faith. We decide whether it grows or stays small.

"Take the widow's example. Again, she could have put her hands in her pockets, went home and let the creditors take her boys as slaves. It takes no faith to allow what looks like it *could* happen to happen instead of going against the grain and trust God when the situation looks hopeless to change. She, however, decides to trust God and rely on the prophet Elisha.

"Elisha asks her two questions. First, he asks 'What do you want me to do?' Please understand that God knows every thought, desire, or wish you have, have had or ever will have, so there's no point in lying to Him. Elisha asks the question because although the Lord knows what you need and wants to provide it for you, He wants you to ask Him. In many cases, we don't have what we need because we don't ask.

"The second question he asks is, 'What do you have in your house?' If you have a need, God often multiplies what you present Him, but you won't give Him what you don't know is there. And if you don't have faith, you will say to God that there's nothing in you, His jar, because you don't think it can be multiplied or used.

"Jesus multiplied the two fishes and five loaves, and the seven loaves and few fish *after* there was a need and the disciples presented to Him what they had. They had something and submitted it to Jesus. The disciples have faith in Jesus because they have seen Him work with a little bit. The widow has faith in what God can do because of the example her husband set in being a God-fearing man."

For the past 15 minutes or so, the warehouse was pin-drop quiet. The musicians had laid down their instruments a long time ago. Just the snare drum rattled in response to Darrion's voice.

"Catch onto this. Elisha asks the widow what she has in her house. Here, we see two things. One, she has something in her house, big or small, and Elisha knows it. Two, Elisha knows the widow knows what's in her house. Elisha wants to know, if *she* will give the right answer.

"Elisha's question is designed to test the limits of her faith and trust in God. She demonstrated a little faith in coming to Elisha. Now, he wants to know what she is willing to submit to the Lord for Him to multiply. God has already planned to multiply the oil. All she has to do is tell the man of God the truth to receive provision.

"Everyone has something, but not everyone will hand it over. God can work with a little something, ya'll, but if you don't give Him *something*, He cannot multiply what you're saying is not there."

Jolene covered her mouth. Four months in the country and Darrion caught himself trying to have a Carolina accent. She teased him about his perfect English because when he used southern slang, it sounded as if he were an old monk trying to use his first cuss word.

"Ya'll have to wake up. I'm an empty jar for God!" Betty Lou said it aloud for the first time, almost as loud as Charlie. Everyone else drooped beneath the overzealous temperatures the heating unit continued to pump out and gave a half-hearted reply.

"To be an empty jar for God, you must have the faith to humbly come to Him, present Him with whatever it is He's given you, big or small, and trust Him when He tells you what to do with it. Humble people admit needs to God. Prideful people go around thinking that they can do any and everything, and never admit their weaknesses."

Right then, after the words left his mouth, Darrion experienced a sharp pain in his chest near the heart. *Weak people like me.* The Word was cutting him, too.

"The widow," he said, clearing his throat. "The widow comes to the 'liaison'; the man of God, with her problem and when he asks her what she has in her house, she says a little oil. Elisha commands her to ask all her neighbors for many empty jars. This requires humility to ask someone else for something you need. He commands the widow to close the doors behind her and her sons. Some miracles, some works of God, happen in crowds, while others occur in the intimacy of our own lives.

"Then Elisha tells her to pour oil into all the empty jars and once they're filled, put them to the side. If I'm the widow, I'm thinking I go and grab as many jars as possible. The man of God told her to pour out oil into all the vessels, indicating that there will be enough oil to fill however many empty jars she can find."

Impatient, Charlie wriggled in her chair. She understood everything from the first thing he said, and not because she heard this before just an hour ago. The "Bible stuff" those church folk in Tennessee threw at her helped Charlie feel worthless and hell-bound. This "Bible stuff" cut and soothed her, instead.

"The oil does not stop until all the jars are full. If you want to be an empty jar for God, you must do a few more things. You must allow God to empty you of all the stuff you've been carrying around inside;

all that hatred and anger, the bitterness toward your enemies. You have to confess to your sins and repent. You must be saved.

"Once you are saved and empty, you must realize that God has deposited His Spirit inside you in the form of a gift. This gift is not meant to just sit there inside you. It must be poured out and multiplied to help other people. As you pour out this gift into others, God will refill you so you can pour it out to more people. When you want your gift to benefit yourself, you keep it to yourself, and you remain full. And when you stop pouring, God stops refilling you."

The people stood and applauded – Jolene, Charlie and Betty Lou included. They clapped until Darrion waved for them to sit.

"Paul writes in Romans, Chapter Twelve, that God has given to everyone a measure of faith. Faith is the promise of things hoped for and belief of things not seen. So, if you believe what your unseen God says without seeing evidence of it, you are blessed and have faith. Be not just a hearer of the Word, but also a doer. *Hear* what He tells you to do and *do* what He tells you to do regardless of the impossibilities you see in front of you."

The round of applause fueled the rumbling fire in his belly.

"Let's go back to the widow. In the physical realm, there was no way the little oil she had would fill all the jars she gathered and she knew so in her mind. It was impossible. Other people around her would think that, too, and might have said so, which is why Elisha told her to close the doors. To do what God is calling you to do, you have to sometimes push some folks away and close the door so He can work. The widow understood the physical impossibilities, but spiritually she opened herself up to the possibilities of multiplication."

"Preach, Pastor, preach," Georgie yelled from the choir risers.

"Do you believe God for miracles, or do you *talk* about it? Are you one of those people who are satisfied with just a little bit? Can He use your weaknesses to glorify Himself, or are you so stuck in old, traditional ways that He has to do it the old way or no way?

"Can He tell you to build a boat for a flood when it never rained before, or fill 55 jars with slow dripping oil? Would you be a little upset if He messed up your life a little bit and told you to do things no one in your family has ever done before? Or are you afraid you'll never be filled again?"

The organ piped up several invigorating chords. Betty Lou screamed, "God" at the top of her lungs. Charlie hopped up and down like she was in a hopscotch game and the reserved Jolene tossed her head back and yelled something in French.

"See, many people start out wanting God to multiply their oil; what they have, but stop because it's difficult, it's a problem, or they're tired of the challenge, or believing for the physically impossible.

"Terah, Abram's father, set out with him, Sarai and Lot for Canaan. Perhaps he got too tired, or the journey was too hard or great? Maybe he liked the place around him and didn't want to go closer to the land so beautiful that it brought Eden to mind? Perhaps he didn't want to be too radical or the people occupying the land were too frightening? For whatever reason, Terah stopped along the way in Haran and died there."

"See, Jesus set the standard when He submitted to death. Will God ask you to go through something you don't like to get where He wants you to go? Absolutely! Joseph went from his father's house to slavery to jail. Jonah had to preach salvation to people he wanted to see destroyed. Paul was beaten, jailed, shipwrecked, and had to endure sickness. Peter was crucified upside down and John was exiled to a foreign land.

"If you want to save your life, you will lose it, but if you lose your life, you will save it. They did it. What makes us any better than them? Don't die in fear! Follow their example and surrender all to gain it all! The doors of the church are open."

Darrion stretched out his arms, as he'd seen Whitehead do before. "Some of you are tired of feeling empty, like there's something missing in your life. You tried the booze, the man or the woman, the clothes, the money, but you still feel empty. God wants to fill you with His presence today. Come down this aisle right now."

Betty Lou had no idea if what the reverend was saying was true, but she sensed a little tug in her gut, like there was a handle attached there and someone was pulling it forward. She stepped out into the aisle and limped as graceful as possible. If Jesus didn't work, *He* couldn't be worse than life with Jack Miles.

Darrion received Betty Lou first and then a light-skinned woman came forth. After those two, men and women flooded the altar until they pressed Darrion on all sides. He led them in prayer as a group and then said a short individual prayer with each person, all 150 of them. After an hour and a half, everyone settled back down in their seats in silence and Darrion collapsed into his chair. He was empty.

TWENTY-ONE

SATURDAY NIGHT, NOVEMBER 24, 1962

THERE, on the front page of the *Zyonne Herald*, was yet another photo of the Creole girl Geary coveted and *him*. In a black-and-white photo, he looked white, though a careful investigation into the text of the article revealed that he was Negro – a half breed. First, she had Williams, and though Geary had left an indelible impression upon her, she now chose a genetic mule over him. In just under four weeks, Darrion James built the largest Negro ministry in North Carolinian history. If it had stayed a religious matter, he might have left well enough alone, but James began beating a drum calling for a more thorough investigation of Klan activity in Black Mountain County, particularly the recent murders of Mark Williams and Kelly Nixon James.

He and the others had been recently cleared of any wrongdoing and reinstated onto the force. This was not by accident. Geary was sure something on his property implicated him in something. However, he caught several of the investigators glossing over the contents of his garage. He meant what he said to Jack Miles about the Klavern "laying low" and James wanted to shine a spotlight on them again, endangering himself more than anything else. Every white man worth his salt in Zyonne knew James' face, where he slept and the warehouse's address. Someone could have his head before breakfast Sunday morning without him lifting a finger.

Geary sucked down the rest of his beer and tapped the empty glass twice against the polished wood. The bartender refilled it in a flash and returned the mug to its place by his elbow. According to the article, the crowd at the Hoghoba Street Mission Church neared 1,000 people in any given service: Negro and white. Whoever *heard of Negroes and whites in church together?*

His stomach bubbled at the thought. After emptying the glass again, he placed a bill under it and set about devising a plan.

Outfitted in an olive cotton dress with a rose scarf tied around her neck and a matching ribbon securing a long ponytail in place, Jolene was almost ready for church. Her shoes, which she waited to put on at the last minute, looked good but hurt her toes something awful.

"You writing another book in there?"

Darrion struggled with his necktie in her bathroom. No matter how he seemed to knot the goldenrod silk material, the thing came out two inches too short or four inches too long against his dark blue suit. "You're too funny for words."

Curious, Jolene claimed the foot of the bed for a seat and opened the *Lost Testament* to a random page. Darrion's handwriting was neat, florid, almost mechanically perfect, but appeared rushed. "Hey."

"Yeah," he said, still struggling.

"Can I ask you a question?"

"You can ask me anything."

"There was a certain man," she read, "who took a flea, placed it in a clay jar and covered it. Day after day, the insect heartily leaped up and down in an attempt to escape, but kept striking his head against the top of the jar. One day, the man removed the cover and expected the flea to jump out and escape. He leapt up and down, but continued to fall short although the lid had been removed."

"So, what's your question?" Darrion's tie was finally correct.

"What does this mean? It just sounds like a story to me."

He kneeled beside the bed next to her shiny butterscotch legs. "Parables are stories with unclear meanings. You have to dig for it. When you don't understand a Scripture, what should you do?"

"You told me to take it piece by piece, not altogether."

"Right!" His eyes lit up. "Tell me who you think the man is."

"God, ain't it always God, or Jesus, or one of them?"

"If God is the man, then who is the flea?"

"Us, we, someone. I'll say me." She smiled, coyly.

"Okay, 'flea,' why would the man or God cover the jar?"

Jolene thought for a minute. "Trying to keep me from gettin' out. If it's God, I guess He might be keepin' me from somethin' 'cause I can't take off the lid. I can only jump. Guess if I'm buttin' my head up on the lid, there's somethin' I ain't gettin', like He's tryin' to tell me somethin' and I'm too mule-headed to listen, so I keep on hittin' my head."

"Okay, what else?"

"If I done hit my head so many times, I prolly don't want out anymore, even if the lid is gone. Jus' tired of jumpin'."

Darrion affectionately slid an arm across Jolene's shoulder. "I thought you said you didn't understand?"

She caught Mark's photograph on the bureau mirror and jumped up. "We, we gotta go. Charlemagne will be here soon…in a minute."

"No, she won't. Saturday service doesn't start until 8:00 and it's not 7:00 yet. Keep going."

"I don't want to keep goin'. That's the problem. I'm goin' too many places too fast. Doin' too many things. It's just too fast."

"Jo," he said, putting his hands up. "Slow down. It's alright."

"No, it ain't alright. I'm engaged…an' you diggin' on me. Don't care what you say 'bout lyin or tellin' no truth."

Darrion bowed his head. Jolene was beautiful and alluring. She must've noticed something in his eyes – a flicker, warmth, tenderness. He'd tried to hide, kill or bury it.

"Won't happen again." He solemnly opened his palm. "Friends?"

Jolene's heart dropped to her knees. She was "diggin' on him" and felt every bit as guilty for being attracted to a man months after her husband-to-be had been brutally killed. Whether she liked the man or not was never the point. Out of respect and reverence for Mark, the flirtation had to end. She shook his hand. "Friends."

"Hey!" Charlie busted in. Since last Sunday, she'd straightened up her wardrobe a little and wore a respectable taupe dress with a caramel handbag and matching pumps. "Seems like I'm always interruptin' somethin' between you two."

"Nonsense," said Darrion in a stern voice. "Let's go."

"Jus' to let y'all know," Charlie said, as they walked out, "I got Betty Lou in the car, too. She needed a ride."

"Oh God, Charlie, you know I consulted that woman!"

"Be easy, Doll. Ain't no biggie. Shucks, we ole girlfriends now. She ain't holdin' no grudges, so you don't worry."

Jolene dreaded sitting in front of the meek little figure in the backseat, wearing the same navy dress she wore to the first Sunday service. To avoid detection, Darrion always sat in the back. As far as they knew, he was a marked man already.

"Hey, Jolene. Good to see you again!" Betty Lou patted her on the shoulder with a white-gloved hand. "How you been?"

"Jus' fine, Betty Lou. How you been?"

"Makin' it along jus' fine. Thanks for pickin' me up, Charlie. Hey, Reverend James, good to see you, too. Lookin' forward to the sermon."

"Jolene read the passage," he said bitterly, "so maybe *she* can teach it to you. Right, friend?"

"I'll do no such thing," she responded. He sounded so frigid. *Some men act like babies when they don't get what they want.* "Teachin' is your thing. Mindin' my business is mine."

Betty Lou and Charlie had the same crossed look on their faces. Something else was at work here and it wasn't a Scripture.

"You know, Jolene, I'm speaking about that parable tonight."

"That so, Cher?" She guarded her speech. Darrion was about to blow.

"I was wondering if you could give me a little *friendly* advice."

"Darrion!" Now she was ticked off. "Stop it."

"What's goin' on 'tween you two? Jolene? Reverend?"

"Nothin'. Nothin's goin' on, Charlie. Nothin' at all."

"She's right, Charlemagne. Nothing is going on."

No one said another word until the car pulled into the reserved parking spot on the warehouse's east side. Charlie exited first, followed by Darrion, who opened Jolene's door. Jolene slammed it shut, said something malicious in French and eased past him to Charlie and Betty Lou. The three women walked in together.

Darrion preferred being alone right before he preached, but not this way. He was wrong and Jolene deserved an apology. "Jolene, hold on for a minute please."

She stopped and rolled her eyes. Betty Lou and Charlie kept going.

"Listen. This was a mistake."

Is it so wrong to want love again so soon? "Darrion, I..."

"Wait, let me finish. We've been through a lot in the past few months and you're right, we were moving too fast toward something."

Jolene wanted Darrion to stop talking before he vowed to do something she never intended for the reverend to swear off.

"Maybe it was loneliness, you know," he said, scratching his beard. "I guess that's what it was, well, for me. And you, I couldn't ever let..."

Jolene's heart swelled with emotion. "Please, Darrion, there's something I gotta say."

"I couldn't ever let something else happen to you. You're a good friend, Jo, such a good friend. And I want you to know..."

Jolene stepped on the alley's curb, propped herself on her tip-toes, closed her eyes and leaned forward in one motion, pressing her lips against his. They were soft, comfortable and warm. She tilted her head and hoped with all her heart that he'd respond. Darrion forgot his station, his whereabouts, surroundings and duties and artfully massaged Jolene's lips with his.

"Friends?" he asked, between peppering her lips with short kisses.

"Friends."

Oblivious to the fact that they had a small audience for their first kiss, Darrion and Jolene strolled into the warehouse hand-in-hand. At the door, they parted company with a long glance. Darrion bee-lined for the office and Jolene joined Charlie and Betty Lou on the front row.

"Say, Jolene," said Betty Lou. "What shade lipstick you wear? Or should I ask Reverend James? Maybe he could tell me?"

Jolene blushed beet red, and whipped out a miniature mirror and lipstick tube. Charlie and Betty Lou cackled.

"Ya'll two are evil. It's Cinnamon Sunshine. You should know."

"We think it's great, Darlin'. You two need each other."

"Wish Jack Miles was half the man he is, tell you that."

"There." Jolene snapped the mirror shut. "Ya'll happy? I'm back to normal, alright? Stop playin' 'round."

"Why you so uptight 'bout it, Gal? It's just a kiss. Dang."

"It's not just 'a kiss', Cheri. It's *more* than that."

"It doesn't have to be unless you make it that way."

"Darrion James is not a *John*, Charlemagne Marie," she said between clenched teeth. "It ain't the same thing!"

"Whoa. Did you have to use the full name?"

"It's not just about the touch, or the kiss or tinglin' I feel in my legs," she muttered low enough so Charlie could hear. "You hold back so much so long and you don't wanna give out anythin' 'cause you think a man's gonna take somethin' from you. He already took it, Darlin'! You ain't free 'cause you ain't wanna be. Jail door's open and you sittin' in the middle of the floor on your big behind!"

"Now, you wait just a second. Since when are *you* judge and jury over me? And my behind is not big! It's full, I think, kinda healthy."

"I'm not judging you Charlie. I jus' want you to be happy, not just existin', I think of you like family, only family I got here."

"I know you do." She smooched Jolene's cheek. "So, pray for me, *Christian*. And don't start smellin' your pee jus' 'cause you got kissed either."

"Felt it down deep in my soul, Charlie," she whispered to her friend. "Ain't no one ever kiss me like that before, not even Mark."

"I'm sayin'," Betty Lou blushed. "Your *legs* tingle?"

"What ya'll two grinnin' and skinnin' about?" Georgie approached the trio, while the choir assembled. Recently, the exchanges between Georgie and Jolene had become exceeding catty. Every service, Georgie walked past the trio in the front row to reach the choir stand, although there were at least four different paths she could have taken.

She started with Jolene, who continued and ended it most times. "Alright gal, I'm 'bout sick an' tired of you. We sittin' here, ain't hurtin' nobody, and here you go again."

"I don't like the way you use people, especially Reverend James."

"Hold on. Wait a second. When I was doin' what I was doin', *you* came to *me*, I ain't twist your arm or nuthin'! Ain't no one botherin' you or talkin' to you. You just come on and poke your big ole head in our talkin' and say whatever you wanna say. So talk, Chatty."

"Ya'll two makin' a scene." Betty Lou was shocked by the animosity.

"Quiet." Charlie smacked Betty Lou's hand. "This is gettin' *good!*"

"Talk Georgie! 'Tis why you always come over here. Say somethin'."

"Why'd you have to take *him*, huh? Look at you. You could have any Negro man in Zyonne and you picked *mine*. Why? What did I ever do to hurt you? What? All I wanted was a lil' happiness for myself." Georgie stormed off, pounding her heels hard into the carpet.

Charlie and Betty Lou snickered. Jolene followed her gut instinct and trailed the choir leader to the risers.

"What do you want?" Georgie's tears flew wild. "Ain't you done enough to me already?"

"I ain't do nothin', Cheri. Me and Reverend James are *friends*."

"What was that outside then, huh? If that's 'nothing' and 'friendly,' I hate to think what you think 'somethin'' is."

"Okay, so maybe it's a little more than nothin'," she admitted. "But no one planned it and no one meant to hurt you. Those things I said before about you were lies."

Innocent belief coated Georgie's face. "Then why couldn't I keep *him?*"

"You ain't gotta try so hard. If a man s'posed to be with you, he'll find you. You ain't gotta run after nobody. If you runnin' after someone, you ain't got him. You fooled yourself. Freedom always taught me that and she ain't never lie to none of us."

"How can I believe you? How do I know you ain't lyin' now?"

"*The Lost Testament.* I've been reading it."

The revelation darkened Georgie's heart. Darrion never let her be involved in his ministry.

"S-so," she stuttered. "S-so what? Y-you puffed up about it?"

"No." Words scrolled through Jolene's mind's eye. "God'll bring you to the man you s'posed to be with, it says. He shaped Adam from Himself and the ground. Eve was taken from Adam. Adam recognized Eve as his missin' part after God brought her to him."

"I don't get what you mean —missing part?"

"It's simple, see. God formed the animals first. He created male and female animals. Now, this is just ole me talkin', but I think Adam saw the animals and was thinkin' he should have someone, too. And that's why God said it ain't good for a man to be alone. So, you see, I ain't the only one. If you meant to get a man, you will."

Georgie threw her arms around Jolene's upper back and squeezed. "Thank you so much. Don't know I understand all what you said."

"Welcome," she managed. "It'll come when you ready. Now go on up there an' sing somethin'."

"What was that about?" asked Charlie when Jolene returned.

"Tell you later."

Three songs later, Darrion entered the pulpit with the grin of life on his face. Jolene giggled like a schoolgirl and blushed when she gazed her way. Charlie, Betty Lou, even Georgie picked up on their faces and smiled. It was about time those two experienced some joy.

TWENTY-TWO

JANUARY 4, 1963; FRIDAY NIGHT

UNSHAVEN and cherry-eyed, Jack Miles examined his ex-army buddy for *it*.

It could be the sharp, confident jaw line constructed to intimidate and piercing, unforgiving aqua pupils. It might be the way he appeared serious and focused now, even when he laughed.

Whatever *it* was, it now separated the two men, who used to run together thick as thieves. As the Grand Nighthawk, he served as right hand man to the Exalted Cyclops, an iron fist extension of the Exalted Cyclops' strength. No matter how violent, he carried out orders with cold precision and ordered the rest to follow suit. Now, Geary did all those things without his best friend. It shot his confidence to pieces, worse than Betty Lou divorcing him.

"You got a staring problem, 'Hawk?" Geary stared back.

"Nope." Jack Miles redirected his attention around the auditorium. Klansmen crowded wall-to-wall, all uniformed. The group multiplied exponentially since October, though he was sure the spike in membership was a one-time thing. Still, Geary would amount to nothing without Jack Miles and one day, he intended to prove it.

"You alright, Jack?" Frankie rubbed his shoulders from behind and spoke into his ear. Since their former affair, she teased him on a regular basis despite her husband's misgivings.

"Why you ask?"

"You starin' at Geary like you look at me sometimes. Somethin' you wanna tell me? You ain't one of *those*, cutie, are you?"

"It's just...what is it about him lately? He walks around like he's a god, like the world owes him somethin'. C'mon, Frankie, don't you ever get tired of hearin' him go on and on about mixin' whites and niggers and how the Bible says we shouldn't mix races?"

"Jack, c'mon, give it a rest."

"You don't get it, do you? My life is crap! Why am I even here? Geary does it all now. There're hundreds of us around here that ain't screwin' up their lives. They still got their wives, still gotta life and a pot to pass water in and a window to throw it out of."

Frankie sat next to him and stroked the renegade gray in his sideburns. "This Betty thing got you on a rope, don't it?"

"Daggone right it does. Eats at me like locusts. Can't eat or think right. Makes me wanna stop livin'. Jus' ain't worth the work. And you said she found God or some other nonsense?"

"That nigger James done cornered the market on tonic, that's for sure. Bible don't do nothin' else but make 'em think they feelin' real good and I know some ways to do that without crackin' a book."

Jack Miles smirked. Frankie always brought a smile to his face.

"Cheer up, sweetheart. Cykes's got this big plan."

"What about?"

"Shh." Frankie's slender fingernail teased the grizzled mustache above his upper lip. "Stand up."

Kludd led the pledge. It was a swearing of allegiance to the great white Christian race – a promise to oppose niggers and niggers mixing with whites in any way, and a vow to preserve the earth the way God intended it – whites in power with everyone else as their subjects.

"What do we want?" Geary screamed. Though his speech improved, it was still difficult to understand.

"White power!" The auditorium echoed the boisterous response with pumping fists.

"When do we want it?"

"Now!" An electric silence settled like dew over the people.

"You're probably aware of the growing threat among us." Geary tried hard to reign in his diction. "And that threat is located at 312 Hoghoba Street, led by Darrion James. His father was half-white and his mother was Negro – mixed blood! This is not God's way!"

The riled-up Klansmen roared.

"He passed for white up north. Now, he's come here to stir up trouble 'round the niggers, who ain't give us trouble 'fore now. We burned his house down, but he lives. Here, we shoot niggers and nigger lovers that don't die right in the skull. That's how James will die – one good shot to the head. Then, we'll burn him. The niggers will see him die and they'll listen to us again.

"This is what we do. Scare 'em. Fellas, we know what to do and how to do it, so let's give it to 'em right! We'll get rid of James for good and scatter the rest. Tomorrow, we stake claim on Zyonne for the good, white people and drive the niggers out!"

The meeting recessed and everyone returned home, except for the core group which reassembled at the Reifer's for pizza pies. After a few rounds, the boys loosened up their conversation.

"So, Cykes," said Gaston. "Where'd this change come from all of a sudden? A month ago we were laying low. Next thing I know, we're recruiting."

"Who cares, Gaston? It's not important."

Snickers followed. "What's important then?"

"What's important, Jasper, is the agenda. A month ago, we were sitting around, drinking beer and playing cards like a bunch of gossiping housewives. We didn't do anything but burn a house down, kill an old woman and hang a couple niggers. That's disgraceful."

Frankie's body tightened up at the *housewives* crack. Gaston, Reifer, Jack Miles, Kludd and Geary all knew it was the truth.

Geary dropped his pizza slice and stood up at the table. "There's a nigger out there in burnt up West Zyonne drawing out *our* Christian white people and what are we doing? Sitting here eating pizza pie and drinking beer! Where are the cards, huh? Where are they, girls?"

"That's enough," Jack Miles said. "We're supposed to be laying low. It's over. Sit down!"

"It's 'over' when that mule is dead and his blood runs over my hands. That's when it's over – then and not before!"

"I bet it's about that Creole gal," said Jack Miles. "It's not about the niggers at all."

All eyes trained on Geary, who fumed. "Is that what you all think?"

Vacant looks surrounded the table, as they had little knowledge of his preferences. Geary eased confidently into a chair. He'd beaten Jack Miles again.

Jolene jittered with nerves.

Tonight wasn't a "date." She and Darrion established that days ago when he proposed they synchronize their hunger on Friday night and drive ten miles outside Zyonne to Rell's Rib Shack for barbecue before service. With her savings low and the con game caput, he volunteered to pay, but she promised to do her part by bribing Charlie into letting them borrow the car.

Turns out, it didn't take much convincing. For all her sexual exploits, the Tennessee girl was a diehard romantic at heart. She even offered to complete Jolene's makeup, which turned out to be a true blessing since her friend struggled with fidgeting. "Stop blinking so much. Can't get this dang eyelash stuff on!"

"I'm trying, Charlemagne. Tell you, I am."

"Why you so nervous after all, it's not a 'date', right?"

"No," she said tersely. "Not at all."

"Well, he's paying, *and* he's driving, *and* you goin' alone, so why ain't it a date? And why's he callin' you Jo?"

"'Cause I like it when he says it," she giggled. "When he says Joséphine, it sounds like he's about to scold me or somethin'. He talks so proper and such, sound like he ain't hardly Negro."

"He's smart," Charlie said, swabbing Jolene's cheek with rouge. "Ain't like me and you. We can't talk right. Ya'll gonna have lil' babies wit' pretty eyes, light skin, straight hair and smart, too."

"Ain't no one talkin' babies, Charlemagne. We goin' to dinner 'cause he needs a break and I got me a taste for some ribs."

"Still think ya'll crazy for crossin' the town line that way. You know they watch it. Whatchu gonna do if someone follows you?"

The one road to Rell's Rib Shack was bordered by open corn fields several feet too high for a vehicle to pass through, even at high speeds. Negroes dubbed it, "Death Run." White men harassed the Negroes who traveled it because the cattle chute road had no escape. Most claimed harassment was a small price to pay for Rell's ribs. Each season, Rell and his sons dug a pit six feet deep and barbecued four pigs in it every Friday and Saturday night unless snow covered the ground and prevented them from doing it. The juicy meat fell from the rib bones and Rell's special sauce was finger-sucking good.

"Will you at least let me drive ya'll, Joséphine, please?"

"Absolutely not. Darrion ain't havin' it. He's a mule stubborn man. B'sides, it's just a 20 minute drive down Death Run. It's dark and it's *your* car. How many Negroes you know drive an auto like that?"

"You gotta point, I guess." Charlie surrendered the Cinnamon Sunshine lipstick tube and Jolene applied several coats.

"I think it's sweet – you two diggin' on each other."

Jolene fell silent, guilty for feeling anything. Charlie laid a hand on Jolene's shoulder. "He'd want you happy, you know. Believe that much and stop actin' up so."

"Thank you, Cheri." She fought off tears. "But Mark was a fighter. He ain't want me with nobody else, even if he is gone. Want me all to himself like a chile with a handful of penny candy."

"Rev is good for you, Darlin'. He's real fond of you, and the way you tell it he saved your life. Don't he deserve a chance?"

"Don't feel right 'bout it. Feel like I'm betrayin' Mark or somethin', like I should stay off men forever and a day."

"You ain't been on men long enough to stay off 'em. And trust me, stayin' off of men is the last thing you wanna do."

"That's so nasty. We ain't doin' that, he's a *reverend!*"

"Honey!" Charlie set a hand on her hip. "A rev ain't nothin' but a man in a suit and a robe. He got him wants and needs like any man. You touch him along the neck right here an' see what happens."

Jolene nonchalantly studied Charlie, who stroked a strategic trail from the earlobe down the nape to the collarbone.

"Aww, you ain't payin' me no mind, forget it."

"No," she covered, "it's not that. I think I hear him knockin'."

"You ain't hear nobody knockin'. You blushin'." Charlie pointed to Jolene's left hand. "And for God's sakes, take it off already."

"This ain't a date," Jolene argued. "He ain't my man and you ain't my momma and I ain't takin' off my engagement ring!"

"Well, at least think 'bout turnin' it around. Ain't nothin' sorrier in the world but a woman markin' time in her past when she need to get to her future and she watchin' life pass her by 'cause she too scared to grab it by the horns and ride it."

Jolene's eyes drifted down. "I...I do think I hear him now."

Charlie kissed Jolene on the cheek. "Have fun, Gal, an' you better bring me back some ribs since you got me stuck here an' all."

"Do my best, Cheri. Can't promise they'll survive the ride."

"Sure you can," she winked. "Occupy him. He won't be thinkin' 'bout no ribs, if you touch that neck and plant one on him!"

Jolene slipped into a grey wool skirt, eggshell blouse, and black sweater with black flat shoes. With her hair in ringlets and earrings sparkling in her ears, she looked about 18 again.

Darrion entered the bedroom with ease, as he did so many times when he came over the house. On the bed's edge in her brassiere and slip because of the overactive radiator, Charlie sprung up, covered her breasts with crossed arms and left the room.

"You know, Rev," she said, coyly, "if I ain't no better, I'd think you tryin' to cop a peek at my goodness comin' in here like that."

"Nice to see you, Charlemagne." He smiled.

"Why you call me my full name all the time? Charlie's fine."

"Because it sounds elegant." Darrion poured on the charm. "'Charlie' sounds like a greasy mechanic's name. Charlemagne is the name of royalty, beauty, grace, and charm. It fits you."

"Aww, shucks," she said. "Jolene, you in trou-*ble*!"

"Do you happen to have any butter left for me, Reverend?"

Darrion eyed Jolene head to toe. Even dressed in simple outfits, the woman was show-stopping gorgeous. "You take my breath away."

Jolene was taken aback. She expected a compliment, not heart-stopping praise. All Mark ever told her was that she looked "good."

Charlie gushed inside the bathroom. It was a date.

"W-well," Jolene stammered. "Y-you look mighty fine yourself." It's all her brain could cook up on such short notice. He'd served her the choice filet mignon of compliments and she presented him with an underdone frankfurter on a stale roll.

The man's charcoal gray wool slacks with razor-sharp creases, button down sky blue shirt, and navy blazer with pearl buttons deserved better than a "mighty fine." Not a hair was out of place in his thin goatee, sideburns, or atop his neatly-trimmed head. Darrion's stunning proclamation caught Jolene off-guard and never one with words, she struggled to equate his eloquence. "Mighty fine." She smacked her forehead. "You look wonderful, and I love...*like*, I *like* your outfit. It just goes together with mine."

"Thank you."

"And your hair, I mean, is great. Makes your head look better. Not that it looks bad, but you know what I mean, Cher, it's lovely."

"Shut up," Charlie whispered. "You're killin' the moment."

"Shall we go?" Darrion crooked his arm. Jolene rose and took it.

"Good night, Cheri. Make yourself at home."

"I'm 'bout to make myself right at home with those leftovers and sweet potato pie you left in the refrigerator, that's for sure," she said through the bathroom door. "Good night, Reverend."

"Good night, Charlemagne." They put on the coats and headed out.

Death Run was deserted. Neither Darrion nor Jolene spoke, while the car traveled down the road at a steady speed. Halfway down the road, a car with its headlights off followed it about ten car lengths away.

Jolene reached for Darrion's hand and almost squeezed it numb. The other car picked up speed, but Darrion didn't accelerate. When the car was four car lengths away, he broke the silence.

"Do you trust me?"

"With my life," she responded.

"Take my blazer," he said, while retrieving it from the back seat. "Put it over your head and pretend you're asleep. Lean under my arm close to me and don't move a muscle. Try and stay still."

"I'm scared, Darrion."

"Don't be." He cocked a hat over his face. "Just do as I say."

The sedan's engine gunned behind Darrion and tapped the rear bumper. Jolene almost screamed but kept quiet beneath the wool mask. Soon, she sensed the car slowing down and wondered why Darrion didn't make a run for it. At least then they had a chance of staying alive.

Four white men, two on the driver's side, two on the passenger's side, approached Darrion and Jolene with rifles. When the first man saw Darrion's complexion, he backed up a little and waved for the other men to fall back.

"What you doin' down this way, son? Niggers travel this road."

Jolene buried her shaking hands in her ribs.

"Oh?" Darrion acted surprised and resurrected his best southern accent. "Me an' my girl, she done gone sleep. We goin' this way 'cause it's the only way I know. Any of ya'll got a way to the Valley?"

"The Valley? Ain't never heard of no Valley."

"Sure Brian," said one of them while pointing to the end of Death Run. "It's right round about Mount Nebo, 'bout five miles west of here. He's right. Ain't no other way up there by auto on this here street."

"You be careful, son. We thought you was someone else."

"No hard feelins!" Darrion shook the man's hand. "Hey, we gone be awright comin' back this way in a few? We ain't wantin' no trouble."

"Ain't no niggers comin' back 'til at least 11:00 when ole Rell close up his rib joint. You best be comin' back 'fore then. We'll remember the car, hear?"

Darrion put the car in gear and drove off. The men returned to their vehicle, did a U-turn and reassumed their post at the halfway point.

"Is it safe yet?"

"Not yet," he said. "They turn on their lights, they'll see you."

Jolene exposed her face from beneath the coat. "I don't know what to say. You sounded like a country white man."

"My father was the son of a country white man."

"So, you tryin' to be like him?"

He sensed her eyes examining him. "I'm not trying to be anyone."

"Then who *are* you?"

"Who do you think I am?"

"Five minutes ago, I'm thinkin' this is a man I admire 'cause of who I see you to be. Then, you go and shuck and jive so those crackers don't kill us and I think you ain't no better than them Negroes that bow and beg for the white man. Almost think it'd been better if they'd beat us and we go on to Rell's like the rest of 'em."

"You want me to go back, map them a family tree and prove to them I'm half-Negro so they can beat us half-dead? I'm not doing that. As long as we're together, I'm going to protect you and do whatever it takes to do that."

"Hmph." She crossed her arms. "Heard that one before."

"What does that mean?" He missed the connection.

Jolene wanted to regain the respect she'd lost for him, but didn't know the first thing about the process. *Maybe he's right?* She was wrong and Mark had sacrificed himself unnecessarily. "Why did Mark have to die?" Jolene's question injected an uncomfortable silence into the conversation. "Been trying to figure it out for months now and since you got this God connection, I figure He might tell you."

"You have the same God connection I do."

"But you had it longer, so you understand Him better. Darrion, answer me if you can. I can wait on it."

Her sweet, innocent disposition didn't do a thing to simplify the situation. Darrion exhaled, turned into the gravel parking lot behind the restaurant, placed the gearshift in park and shut off the engine. "I can't tell you why he's gone, other than some hateful human being wanted you and Mark dead. That's all the answer I got."

"And you think I can be at rest with that?"

"You have to…because if you don't you'll think about everything you could have possibly done differently and drive yourself crazy. Don't do that to yourself, Jo. It's not worth it. Jayne loved me and Mark loved you. We have to keep living today and not in yesterday's past."

Jolene remembered Charlie's wisdom, about taking life by the horns. She crawled into the reverend's space and clutched him tight about the ribs, forcing her face to nuzzle close to his heart.

TWENTY-THREE

THURSDAY NIGHT, JULY 4, 1963

ONCE the state stopped snooping around the civil servants in Zyonne, Police Chief Riggins began sniffing around, first around Geary, then Reifer, Kludd and Gaston.

At the station's Fourth of July celebration, an event he insisted his deputies and their spouses attend each year, he forced small talk with Frankie. "What've you two been up to these days, Francine?" he asked. "Haven't seen you around much anymore."

"Stuff, Chief, nothin' big. We're still newlyweds, you know."

"Right, right." He sucked down a glass of lemonade. "Whattya think 'bout that Negro thing on Hoghoba Street? We havin' a devil of a time tryin' to control them crowds."

"Oh?" Frankie refused to bite on Riggins' bait. "Try harder."

Just like that, he'd been dismissed and denied. It was the holding pattern for police investigations as of late; Negroes beaten, terrorized and threatened and his policemen turned up nothing – no evidence and no suspects.

Suspecting an elaborate cover-up, Riggins supervised every investigation aspect, from interviewing to combing the area for clues. The neighbors never gave him anything beyond a horrified or irate look, or they slammed the door in his face. When Riggins found any physical evidence, he placed it in a bag and added it to his locker of random puzzle pieces, with no clear idea if they fit together.

He still believed in a cover-up, but was unaware of how to uncover it. Every search for answers ended the same way; Riggins, frustrated, digging into his jacket for the metal flask he swore he'd never pick up again, while Geary, Kludd, Gaston, and Reifer silently celebrated.

After the rally that night, almost a full six months passed to assemble the plan the way Geary wanted it done and low profile enough to avoid detection.

The warehouse on Hoghoba Street became more church than warehouse with three services; one at ten o' clock in the morning for the housewives and children, another at midday, attended by those on a long lunch break or who worked third shift, and the last at eight o' clock at night for families. Each was standing room only, holding 700 to 1,500 people per service, with chairs jammed into every available corner.

His first inclination was to goad the fire chief to fine Darrion for violating the capacity limits and shut the warehouse down. The move backfired. Somehow, the reverend pulled the money together for the outlandish fine and brought the building up to code within the 24-hour window he was given. Now, with the improvements, even more people flocked to the place and there wasn't a lawful thing to prevent it. Those who didn't fit inside the building erected a large white tent beside the warehouse parking lot and sat beneath it, hoping to catch the highlights of the service through the windows.

After Darrion became apprised of the situation, speakers were set up outside to connect the overflow to the service. Although the temperature never dropped below a humid 70 degrees in Zyonne on a good summer evening, the tent never stood empty.

The failure fueled Geary's fire, giving him new thoughts and ideas; ways to eliminate the Negro problem quicker and much more efficiently. For starters, *everyone* had to bear arms, even the squeamish. Geary forged gun orders staggered all around in everyone's name but his, even Jack Miles, whose attendance had become spotty.

The opportunity was coming soon. Darrion's time was almost up.

"What is it that you fear, saints of God? Is it a *who* or is it a *what*, a *person* or a *situation*? Do you fear a *thing?* Is it a thing you fear? Or is it fear of a person you think is controlling something you're unsure about? Who do you think that person is? And if you say it's God, are you afraid that He's going to let you down?

"See, here's the thing. There's a certain lot of people who wear these white hoods and robes to intimidate you. They're beating us and whipping us and hanging us and we fear them! We fear them because God is supposed to protect us. When we let go, He's supposed to catch us.

"For a long time, I trusted that as long as I had the *Lost Testament*, God was supposed to protect me, which He has, but not because of a book. Our Father's protection doesn't mean we will never go through anything. First Peter, Chapter One says our faith will be tried by fire. The Spirit of the Lord is an all-consuming fire.

"Therefore, through trials allowed by the Spirit, our faith will be tested and proved so God may find glory, honor and praise in it. Our faith is a seed that must grow and produce fruit called action. Faith comes by hearing the Word and it grows through this testing. But if our faith never grows, we're not effective."

In the front row, to Jolene's left, Betty Lou wondered if her faith was growing. She buried Jack Miles' pistol as deep in the ground as her arms would allow. And, in a true mark of Christian charity, in her estimation she'd insisted the alimony be enough to cover the home expenses and give her a reasonable allowance, minus tithes.

On the other hand, Jolene marked her spiritual growth in a diary on Darrion's suggestion. There was growing done and growth still to do, but she wasn't where she was, which Darrion said she should remember. Her entries were inconsistent ramblings – scriptures, advice, memories, and expressions of guilt over her growing love for Darrion.

She'd first told him a month ago, on an unseasonably frigid Saturday night before service. The radiator was on the blink and while he finished fiddling around with the machinery, she started humming a pretty, discordant, almost haunting song.

"What's that you're singing?"

"A lil' Jacques Brel tune, Cher. Song of my life."

Darrion placed a towel under the radiator's release valve and wiped his hands clean on a towel. "It should be fine now."

"Darrion?" She almost never called him by his name.

"Yes?"

"Can I sing it to you now?"

He appeared honored. "If you'll dance with me."

She took his hand and placed the other in the small of her back. She backed up enough to gaze into his eyes and sing the song. Between the first and second verse, all sung in French, a tear fell on cue. Darrion caught it with his thumb and smudged it away. More fell, well beyond what his fingers could deal with. She ended the song repetitively singing what he presumed was the song's title.

"I don't know what to say."

"Don't say nothin', Cher," she sniffed.

Confused, he scrambled. "What's 'Ne Me Quitte Pas' mean?"

Jolene broke down. "It means…'don't leave me,' that's what it means, don't leave me…it's necessary to forget…everything you need to forget…which is already over."

"Jolene." He clutched her tight.

"Forget the times of the misunderstandings," she cried, "the lost times to know how. Forget the reasons why the heart is full of joy."

"Jo."

"Don't leave me. Darrion. I love you."

Those words frightened, exhilarated, and thrilled him. He knew she felt duty to her deceased fiancé and conflict over the new feelings. After all, Mark had not been gone a full year. His responsibility as a pastor took precedence over his social life, but the prospect of new love free from lies quickened his pulse. "I love you, too, with all my heart – for real I do."

Her faith in God, the source of love and her love for the man delivering the Word grew day-by-day, service by service. She served in every way possible and found joy in tending to other people and fulfilling their needs, particularly Darrion's.

"So what does this mean for us?" Darrion continued in the sermon. "What are we supposed to do – sit down and let these people beat us like dogs? Should we be violent and take up arms against our foe?

"Those who live by the sword, die by the sword. If you pick up a gun and point it at a man, be prepared to shoot it because if not, he will shoot you. But, if you shoot in violence, also understand your life will be cut off by violence. Saints of God, our Father gives us weapons against fear, but in order to use them we must be willing to see the enemy holding the fear and we see them by closing our eyes."

Charlie, who sat in her customary spot next to Jolene, struggled to mentally understand these types of messages. Inside, though, the logic was perfect. Later, when she'd pondered the sermon's main points, understanding would fall like a cool mist over her mind.

"Elijah challenged Baal on behalf of God to pull Israel over the commitment fence and won. The Israelites killed 450 false prophets because of it. Jezebel found out and threatened to kill Elijah. And this same man of God, who called down fire from heaven and ordered these false prophets killed, ran away in fear.

"We have to choose which side we want to be on. If we want to fear, then *fear*, but if we want God, we must choose Him and not fear. God is perfect love and perfect love drives out fear. We can't have both.

"Throughout Scripture, the Father and the Son command us not to fear. Fear paralyzes us into believing something opposite to the Word of God. When we choose the devil's lie over the truth, we become ineffective and God cannot use us. They cannot kill us and due to that fact – due to the fact they cannot kill us – we cannot fear them."

Elbows, heads and arms stirred restlessly.

"So we got this strange fruit hanging from our trees. We got battered, bloodied Negro bodies submerged in Meuller's Lake, so Police Chief Riggins can't find them. And here you got some fool in a robe preaching scripture you never heard about telling you we can't die, we can't be killed. I assure you, I ain't crazy.

"With Christ, there is no death. There is no sting. When God raised Jesus from the dead, He set the example for how life would be for those who believe in His Son. Jesus did die, but nobody touched Him until His time. The Jews tried to stone Him several times but failed.

"What does this mean for us? God is our shepherd. He is *Jehovah-raah*. Our God will protect us and we will not die before our time. This does not mean that we will not be beaten or harmed. If we were never hurt or harmed, we would never know God as a Healer and He wants that!

"You ever meet a child who's been babied all their life? Their knees ain't even scratched up 'cause their mommas kept them from falling. When they go five minutes without something they want, they don't know what to do with themselves.

"What you got on your hands is a little boy or girl in a grownup body, but the disposition determines the maturity, not the appearance. God looks at the heart, the inner man, not the outer man."

Betty Lou realized for the first time that her pink and white clothes were all about holding onto the past. Since her mother died and she married, her maturation process became a complicated mechanism she'd had no clue how to jumpstart.

"The Word says we should fear the one with the power to kill the soul and sentence us to eternal damnation. No Klansmen can touch your soul! They don't even believe you *have* a soul, Negro! If you fear them, I have news for you, you're already dead a hundred times!"

Shakespeare, Jolene thought.

"So, stop fearing them. Stop crying. Stop begging for what God has given you the authority and power to make happen yourself. Stop crying, Elijah. Stand still and see the deliverance of the Lord!

"What do you have to lose, your *life*? What kind of life is it to walk with your head down, shut your door to company and look over your shoulder everywhere you go? Isn't that how you've been living… all this time? Stand up and reclaim your privileges, kings and queens!

"*You* are the righteousness of God. *You* are the head and not the tail. *You* are the chosen elect. *You* are the remnant God set aside for Himself, *His* peculiar people, *His* pride and joy! Do not fear!"

Never one for "whoopin' and hollerin'," as old church folk called it, Darrion jumped down off stage and waved his arms around, as if shadowboxing some invisible pest. The Spirit stirred up the church, touching each person in a unique way. Fussy children were quiet and the quiet worshippers broke from their staid behavior and shouted. A few women sprinted around the church and 40 or so people fainted. Everyone outside the church committed themselves to prayer so fervent and powerful that the tent poles shook and threatened to collapse.

Meanwhile, Jolene, whose eyes were fixed on Darrion the entire time, became preoccupied with the process taking place inside her spirit. At first, the feeling resembled anticipation or excitement. It leaped up inside her, kicked and turned like an unborn child. She raised her hands toward the sky, expecting to receive whatever it was that God intended to give her.

Immediately, a fist-sized ball of flame alighted on Jolene's forehead in her mind's eye, sending electric-like tingling through her pores, nerves and muscles. Her tongue lifted on its own and started articulating foreign words and phrases her spirit translated to her mind.

Betty Lou also experienced something, a bubbling in her gut. If the encounter were physical, she'd have taken seltzer and saltines to counter it. But while the sensation resembled nausea, it was pleasant. She placed her hands over her stomach to quiet it. There was a heartbeat inside it; not hers, as the two were on different rhythms, this life's tempo beat much faster, four to five times as quick. She hopped up and down with joy over her answered prayers. She wasn't pregnant, but took it to mean that she could be. Despite what the doctors said, the possibility existed again. And her leg no longer hurt.

Next to Jolene, Charlie cried – over what, she wasn't sure. She remembered her father and cried for the pathetic sob. She wept over her first love, their child, who she'd sacrificed "for his own good," and her used-up body that had been handed out too many times for nothing. Now, in hysterics, she yanked out small platinum tufts from her skull in grief. Her pastor witnessed the wreck and stopped in his place.

"Charlemagne," Darrion called loud enough for her to hear. She didn't respond, still buried in piled-up pain, distress and nerves. "Charlemagne!" He approached. She shook her head. "Charlie!" Darrion sandwiched her teary face with his hands. "Everything tormenting you must go. Release her *now* – in Jesus' name!"

He stroked her forehead with his fingers and continued rebuking her memories. Charlie's entire body trembled and crumpled to the floor, what the Zyonne Negroes called "knocked out in the Holy Ghost."

He unzipped his robe and cloaked her legs with it. Before long, others joined her on the floor at the altar. Jolene spoke in foreign tongues for an hour straight and Betty Lou flipped off her heels and pranced freely around the sanctuary in her stocking feet. Save for the choir, the musicians, whose members were worshipping or stretched out on the church's wooden stage, played a series of dynamic chord progressions on their instruments. From the pianist to the bassist, all looked asleep – their bodies limp, unresponsive, save their fingers, which operated the instruments.

The sounds awakened those on the floor like a clarion call to the dead. The people rose slowly and stood, united, focused on their pastor; their leader. Darrion's moist skin glowed under the now flickering lights. He unbuttoned his shirt, tossed his tie to the side, undid his French cuffs and rolled up his sleeves. "Somebody in here is tired of being under bondage to fear."

Betty Lou, who found her seat, hopped up and down, screaming with joy. Still talking in tongues, Jolene outstretched her shaking hands. Charlie's face resembled a boxer's stare-down of his opponent before a bout. All three women recognized the true enemy now and wanted to fight.

"Somebody in here is tired being bound by fear!"

In a tight sequence, hands, both white and black, raised from the church's left side to its right.

Darrion raised his free hand. "When Jesus came to set you free, He did it once and for all – for good. The way you become a captive to fear again is if you allow Satan to slap the handcuffs on you and lie you to death. He'll lie to you, and when you believe Him you put your sword down. The Word is the weapon God gives you to take off Satan's head."

Darrion lifted his Bible into the air and invited the others to do likewise. "Raise your sword up. We're doing warfare here tonight!"

They obliged, hoisting their Bibles into the air. Spare Bibles were passed to those who had none. The music crested and swelled louder.

"Before you go to war, you gotta have armor on. If you're not saved, you're not the righteousness of God and your faith is not active. Your heart's exposed and Satan can still kill you. You can't go. If you don't believe in what I'm saying, you doubt the truth. There is no shield and you can't win the fight. Your spirit must be aligned with the gospel of peace, or else you're not ready. Stop the music."

The musicians paused.

"If you're ready for war, repeat this warfare prayer after me." He paused. "Father!"

One strong clear voice repeated his words in sync.

"Clean me! Make me perfect in your sight! Forgive me and help me forget my sin! In Jesus' name!"

The people swallowed and regurgitated the words in a verbatim chant.

"Arm me with Your Word and might! Father, arm me with your Word and might! Teach me how to fight the devil!"

Betty Lou, Charlie, and Jolene rather their burning arms drop off from the sockets than to lower them.

"For your Word says don't fear! I believe the truth and reject the lie! I demolish strongholds and cast down imaginations. Right now – I cast every devil out of my life in the name of Jesus!"

The musicians started playing again, softer this time. Darrion opened his arms in a V shape and the crowd imitated him. "Now Father! I have room to receive your blessings!"

The warehouse window fixtures rattled loudly from a strong wind whirling outside. The worshipers beneath the tent propped up the tent poles with their bodies to withstand the blast. It was warm, and forceful, but comforting, like a mother's embrace or father's strong reassuring hand.

Darrion spoke several phrases in an unknown tongue and continued. "I reclaim everything the devil took from me in Jesus' name! Peace is mine! Joy is mine! Protection is mine! Healing is mine!"

The gushing air blasted the windows and metal doors open and swept through the place. Fans and random articles of clothing took to the air and circled like a funnel within the building. Everything else remained picture still.

But no one dared opened their eyes to the supernatural experience except Darrion, whose forehead was hot, as if it were aflame. But its skin was intact and there was no pain. Harmless fire engulfed every member's head from the neck up, making each congregation member resemble a human-sized brown or white candle.

Then, just as quickly, the wind withdrew, dropped the personal effects back in their places, slamming the doors and windows shut. The fire bundles dissipated, followed by complete silence.

TWENTY-FOUR

FRIDAY NIGHT, AUGUST 23, 1963

CHARLIE stood up and self-consciously smoothed the shimmering silver dress down her body, so not too much cleavage or leg showed. Hiding generous C-cups was no small task. She wore a transparent eggshell silk scarf around her neck, which seemed to highlight her breasts rather than detract attention from them. It didn't help that the brassieres she owned shaped her bosoms into plump man-seeking missiles. There was a day she desired that effect, but not today. All eyes needed to be on Jolene. This was her moment.

"You know, Rev," she said, raising a full champagne flute. "I'm fightin' mad at you 'cause you takin' my girl from me tomorrow. But ain't nobody deserve to be happy more than ya'll two. All the buttin' heads ya'll done 'cause ya'll both two stubborn jackasses."

"Charlemagne!" Darrion half-smiled. Jolene blushed.

"Well, ain't God say to tell the truth, an' the truth will make you free? It's alright, Rev. I'm freein' ya'll right now. And God created the jackass and He told Peter not to look down on His creation."

Charlie paid attention in service after all, Darrion thought.

"Joséphine Jon Marie Courtiér soon-to-be-James, you been a sister to me." Both Jolene's and Charlie's eyes welled with tears. "An' you gone make me cry...you the only family I got, don't care what color you are. I love you like Eggs Punch N' Chains in the mornin'. And I love you too, Rev, wit' your fine lookin' self. God bless You both."

The engagement toast was everything Darrion had hoped for and more, when Charlie "volunteered" to be Jolene's maid of honor mere minutes after he'd slipped the quarter carat ring on her finger and she'd said "yes" just weeks ago.

Inside, he envied the closeness that Charlie and Jolene shared. Between teaching the *Lost Testament* and spending time with his fiancée, he failed to cultivate meaningful relationships with other men, at least close enough to designate one of his brothers-in-Christ a best man.

He theorized that his mistrust had originated from the splintered family unit he was raised in. His father barely paid him any mind and his stepmother busied herself with tending to her husband and doing everything possible to try and give him another child. Turned out, she was barren. Thus, Darrion did not naturally gravitate to friendships with either men or women. Instead, he chose to be alone and delve deeper into his studies. Jayne was as studious and emotionally disconnected from her socialite parents as he was from his parents. There, the mutual attraction began.

But it'd been years since then. Jolene had broken down his shell and here he was, engaged to be married tomorrow morning. There were no lies this time and no secrets. He chose a brother from the congregation, Ezra Hairston, a 45-year-old early graying gentleman especially helpful in the ministry, to be his best man and Darrion was happy. His true best friend sat to his right anyhow.

That disconnection, plus his first marriage, still worried Jolene. He didn't talk about Jayne on account of a pact they'd established to let the past stay buried. Charlie told the two loners only God Almighty could resurrect the dead and divorced, so they shouldn't try anymore. If Mark ever loved Jolene, he'd want her to be happy.

For all her serrated edges, Charlie delivered advice like a finely woven silk thread and the soon-to-be-newlyweds, both stubborn as the day is long, hated admitting when the Tennessee firebrand was right. "Oh, I ain't done, fixin' to say one more thing." Charlie sprung back up, as quickly as she sat down. Thankfully, the wedding party was familiar with her quirky personality. "Rev...Darrion, you've been a father to me, though I'm a lil' older than you are. Owe you my life," she choked up, "and I'll never forget it, 'tis long as I live. Make my girl happy."

Darrion and Jolene were both in tears by the time Charlie sat down on Jolene's right after her fourth or fifth outburst.

"I have something to say." Darrion stood and tilted his glass. "Jolene, I adore you more than words. I count the ability to love you as both a privilege and an honor. And your love for me is a gift I learn to cherish more and more. It's a precious jewel I learn to look at in a different way each and every time I take a breath." Darrion practically pried Jolene's clammy hand from her thigh. "I look forward to growing old with you and seeing your love and tenderness..." Jolene's hand trembled. "And our children..."

"I'm sorry." She bolted from the room, tossing her hands up and rambling in a mix between French and English.

Darrion followed her. Charlie wanted to go also, but Ezra secured her in place with a hand on her wrist. "Let them work this out, Charlie," he said. "Better that way."

Jolene put a corner of her shawl over her shoulder and was halfway outside the restaurant door when Darrion stepped in front of her and prevented her from going any further. "Wait, wait, Jolene, wait!" She struggled to leave, but he refused to let her get away. "What's the problem? Whatever it is, we can..."

"Don't even fix your mouth to say we can 'fix it!' We can't 'fix' this! *This* ain't gettin' fixed. It is how it is and I ain't goin' through this heartache mess a second time. Now move out the way!"

"Fix *what?*" Darrion was flustered and Jolene was almost in hysterics. "What are you talking about? You ain't makin' sense. What's going on? What's all this about? Talk to me, please!"

"Here." Jolene wiggled her finger out of the engagement ring and planted it square in Darrion's hand. "Ain't doin' this all over again. And I ain't tellin' you twice to get out my way." Jolene thrust her hands into his chest and barreled through, rumbled into the restaurant parking lot and strode intently into the summer night.

Before a shocked Darrion regained his bearings, Charlie brushed past him. "I got it, Rev. Stay put," she said, waving a hand.

"Charlemagne, I..."

"I said I got this," she blurted out, not breaking stride or turning around. "Trust you me. Gal ain't goin' nowhere but to the altar tomorrow morning."

Darrion crossed his arms in defiance. Ezra massaged the groom's shoulders and urged him to return to the dinner table, which he reluctantly did.

"Joséphine!" Charlie stumbled on a rock. "Dangit, stop already! Joséphine! Joséphine! Will you slow up a tick or somethin'?"

"You the one always say keep going when life gets rough," said Jolene over her shoulder, about five yards ahead. "Can't stop now."

The sky opened up and dropped wet pennies onto them.

"Just how far you intendin' to go?"

"Trouble don't aim to last always. Ain't that what all them folks say? If trouble don't last always, it can't follow me forever."

"You'd be surprised, girl."

Jolene stopped, whirled around and stormed back to Charlie, who refused to back down. "And what do *you* know? Ain't no man want nothin' from you but what's goin' on underneath your skirt."

Charlie chewed up the criticism and spit it out. "Least I ain't runnin' 'round with a snotty nose and baby milk on my breath, pissin' and moanin' 'bout everythin' when happiness hangin' from my roof. And Honey, huh, what's under my skirt done seen some happy daggone days."

It's impossible to hold a serious conversation with Charlie, she thought, *especially when she's intent on cheering me up and digging to the sore root of the issue in the pouring rain.* Jolene forced herself to stop giggling. "Forget you, Charlie."

"Forget you, too. You need to forget whatever's bugging you, get your narrow behind back in that restaurant and start actin' right."

"You better quit talkin' to me like that, 'cause you ain't my momma," she said, pouting like a spoiled child.

"Somebody need to momma you right now – might as well be ole Charlie. So, tell me what's the problem, or I'll beat that attitude straight outta you like Freedom shoulda done."

There was seriousness to Charlie's glare that Jolene feared putting to the test. "Been dreamin' these terrible dreams 'bout him."

"What kinda dreams? Him leavin' you at the altar or somethin'?"

"No," Jolene said, somberly. "Not that. Worse."

"What about then? Spit it out."

"He's all dressed up in some fancy suit and he gets up stage, like he always does, and preaches. Then, these shots go off and he falls back. There's blood all over."

"Oh Darlin'," said Charlie. She anticipated it getting more horrible.

"I see myself go to his side, while the guns still going off and I got all his blood on my hands," she continued, speaking with her hands covering her eyes. "Then there's this laughin' – somebody laughin' – worst laugh I ever done heard in my life!"

"Darlin', it was just a dream. Every dream don't mean somethin'. Quit eatin' that fancy French food after 8:00 an' you'll be alright."

"No, that ain't it. This ain't no regular dreamin'. I wake up and it's like I feel *death*. I smell the gun smoke and I hear that laugh over and over and over again. It's gone happen, Charlie, and that's why I can't marry him. I can't lose two loves that way in one life!"

"So if you ain't marryin' him, you gone figure out how to stop lovin' him, too? 'Cause if you can't do that, you gonna be worse off 'cause you still love him and you gave up your chance at bein' happy – even if it is for a short while."

Jolene pondered these things and wished Charlie weren't so profound.

"Say it *is* true. You'd be better off livin' like it ain't. Love him while you got him 'cause tomorrow ain't promised to you, neither. You goin' back in there or what? We soakin' wet. I ain't finish my chicken or salad and Ezra was makin' nice. You know me, I don't give up good food or fine men for nobody – 'specially you."

"Done embarrass myself in front of our people like that. I ain't goin' back in there, lookin' a mess like this. Can you make up somethin' for me and drive me back to the house?"

"I oughta make you run behind the car," she said under her breath. "Stay here. I'll be right back."

Jolene sought out dry refuge beneath the trees abutting the parking lot. A few minutes later, Charlie exited the restaurant with a tall gentleman holding an umbrella. As the couple approached, Charlie's tense body language indicated that it wasn't Ezra, but Darrion. Jolene silently prayed for a hole in the earth to open up and swallow her whole.

"Here." Darrion thrust the umbrella into Jolene's hand and secured her fingers around its handle. Even the rainfall cascading off his black Fedora couldn't hide his displeasure with his fiancée.

"Darrion, I'm sorry. I..."

He stormed off toward the car. Charlie put an arm around Jolene. "C'mon. Let a man be a man."

After asking Charlie to drop him off at the church, Darrion said nary a word the entire trip. Jolene studied him from behind Charlie's seat and attempted to decode the feelings buried beneath the cruel look chiseled onto his face. Darrion caught her staring at him in his peripheral vision. "Problem?"

She froze at his response. "Darrion, I...we need to talk...in private."

"Say it here, say it now. You tell Charlie everything anyway."

"That's not true and you know it. Why are you being so mean to me?"

Without a word, Darrion produced the engagement ring on his pinky finger.

"I'm *still* your fiancée," she said.

"Not without this you're not, and we both know who decided that."

The car stopped abruptly. "Ya'll get in that church and settle this before service 'cause ya'll gettin' on my last nerve," Charlie said.

Darrion exited the car first and Jolene followed him into the sanctuary, past the choir risers and the practicing musicians, and back into his office. She gingerly shut the door behind her. "Can I say something?"

Darrion sat down in his desk chair and crossed his arms. "Why not?"

"I never meant to hurt you, Darrion. I love you."

"Love shoulda brought you back inside," he spat out.

"'Twas bein' full of pride and I'm sorry. God knows I'm sorry. But there's somethin' I have to tell you and I need you to listen to me."

Darrion relented. "Go ahead then."

Jolene explained what she saw in the dream and it pricked Darrion's spirit in a strange way, which she detected in his facial expression and body language. When she spoke about the shooting in particular, she exploded into a crying fit. Darrion kneeled before her and enveloped her face with his hands.

"I need you so much! I can't stand the thought of losing you, too! Let's run away, Cher, far away from here – together, you and me!"

"You know as well as I do that we can't outrun God's will."

"Don't you dare say that. I don't care what God tells you. You don't say mess like that to me right now, you hear me? You say something to help me and not no chapter and verse."

"Forget tomorrow. Marry me tonight."

Jolene sat back and snaked her head. "Uh uh. All the things we done to get ready for this, we doin' this right – tomorrow. Been thinkin' 'bout this thing for a long time. You had the big ceremony an' all I was gonna have was a Negro preacher and a couple witnesses. Uh uh."

"So what then?"

Charlie was right after all. No matter how astute the reverend was, he didn't have the first clue into navigating the labyrinth that was Jolene's female psyche. He'd needed to be led, instructed and taught these ways in repetition, so their channels would never be crossed. "I never wanted to call the wedding off. I just wanted to understand what I was dreamin'. Without teachin' me, can you explain why I'm dreamin' these things?"

He wished Jolene forgot dream interpretation was one of his spiritual gifts. "The vision is incomplete. There's another part."

"Do you know the other part? Will you tell me?"

"No, but it's not for me to know, that's for you."

Jolene sulked. "Then hold me tight." She rolled forward into Darrion, who pulled her close to him. "...and tell me you love me."

"I love you, Joséphine Jon-Marie. You'll never know how much."

"Wait here."

Jacob "Kludd" Watson faked an emergency and stole out of the Klan rally to meet Jack Miles around the corner and take him to see Betty Lou. Against Kludd's wishes, Jack Miles left the Klavern before the plot against the Negroes reached its zenith.

There was a fight going on inside him and no matter how much he drank or what he smoked, his relief came when he listened to and obeyed his inner conscience instead of his mind's desires. He left the Klavern and now, he'd had to warn Betty Lou tonight about Darrion before he left Zyonne for good on the 11:30 train.

Kludd let the Ford's engine idle beside the weed-covered whitewashed picket fence at the driveway's edge. A van blinked its high beams twice in the distance, but Kludd thought nothing about it. "Hurry up, Jack, 'fore someone notices where we are."

Jack Miles trotted around the holes and puddles up the mud driveway to the porch steps. Betty Lou opened the door with a bag full of decorations in hand and dropped it upon sight of her ex-husband.

"That's it, you broke the deal. First, I hear you quit the plant and you ain't pay no alimony this week, now this? I'm calling Riggins."

"No, no wait, Betty. This is important and I'm not here to cause trouble. This ain't about me and you. This is about your Negro reverend. He's in danger."

"What kinda danger, Jack?" She was incredulous.

"The *worst kind*, day after tomorrow."

Betty Lou gasped with horror. "Why?"

"Bets, please, just listen. I'm tryin' to do the right thing here. Get your Negro reverend to leave town as fast as he can. Geary's got this plan to pop him. Warn the Negroes, too. I'm leavin' town, but you stay real low until this thing blows over."

Sympathy crossed Betty Lou's face. "Then you're in danger, too?"

"None of that matters now. Take this." He handed her an envelope and identified its contents before she even asked; his last will and testament, his term life insurance papers and his entire paycheck minus the cost of a one-way bus ticket out-of-town. "There's just one thing I want from you, Betty Lou." He then explained his need for Betty Lou to forgive him for everything wrong he'd done to her for the past 19 years. She forgave him without hesitation.

"I don't wanna die, Betty Lou – not now, not like this."

She persuaded him to give over his hands. "Will you pray with me right now, Jack?"

He humbly nodded. His ex-wife led him in a prayer for salvation, which he repeated, wholeheartedly and verbatim. After they finished, eyes watering, Jack Miles thanked her for giving him complete peace.

"Thank you, Betty Lou. Thank you."

"Thank the Lord, not me. Who brought you here?"

"Kludd's out near the fence in the Ford, but Betty, I want you to be careful. Just phone your pastor or something. You need to be safe."

A white van sped toward the driveway. Jack Miles waved for Betty Lou to go back inside in a hurry.

"Go turn off all the lights and hide. That's Geary. If he thinks you know something about his plan..."

Betty Lou's voice trembled with worry through the screen door. "What about you, Jack?"

Jack Miles slammed the front door, pretended to lock it and strolled over to the passenger side of the van where Geary sat.

"I knew I couldn't trust you, Hawk." Geary stuck a pistol outside the window and pulled its trigger. Two men jumped down from the side doors, grabbed Jack Miles' limp body by the hands and feet and carried it toward the woods behind the Everham home. Three others followed the Grand Cyclops to the front door. "Find her." He wiped his fingerprints from the pistol with a handkerchief and handed it over. "Make it look like she did this."

Betty Lou prayed inside her hiding place, an old storage trunk. "Lord, deliver me from these evil men," she petitioned.

They forced the door open and began looking in every conceivable hiding place, under and behind furniture, inside the bathroom and closets, everywhere. According to Jack Miles' stories, Betty Lou wasn't the brightest bulb in the store, so they'd find her.

"She's not in the woods," said one of the two who disposed of Jack Miles' body in a briar thicket.

"Nothing," said the others. "She ain't here."

"Oh, she's here, alright. Jack was talking to somebody and she's got a bad leg, so she couldn't have gotten far. Check the bedroom."

Betty Lou continued praying and covered herself with a coffee-and-cream hand woven afghan which faintly smelled of her dying mother. Someone opened the trunk but failed to search through its contents.

"Close that trunk and stop wasting my time," Geary admonished. "Are you mad? She couldn't fit inside there."

The trunk door slammed down so hard it sent shockwaves through Betty Lou's bones. Six pairs of footsteps trailed off. She wanted to move, but didn't, thinking they could come back at any time.

After she'd counted from one-one thousand to six hundred one-thousand, ten minutes by her count but 18 in reality, she noisily emerged from the trunk and peeked outside from a window in the living room. The van was gone.

She snatched up her handbag, slipped on some shoes and scampered out to the fence where Kludd's vehicle idled. He was sound asleep.

"Jake," she rapped against the window, nearly breaking it. "Jake!"

"Huh," he stirred.

"Jake, did you see where they went?"

"Who went, Jack?"

"No," she managed. "White van…Geary…they drove here!"

"Geary was here? Oh God, no!" He feared the worst. Betty Lou's face confirmed it. Jack Miles had been murdered. "We gotta go to Riggins."

"What…you thought Geary was just gonna shoot ya'll some Negroes and leave it at that? Later for Riggins. I gotta go warn my pastor and you gonna drive me there."

Although the car was already started, Kludd cursed and turned the key. Betty Lou hopped in the passenger side. He drove double the speed limit, almost hoping to get caught in one of Riggins' infamous speed traps, but no one stopped him. He ignored the train's warning horn and continued toward the tracks. Out of nowhere, the white van appeared and swerved sideways behind the vehicle, blocking them from backing up. Kludd pressed the accelerator pedal to the floor and rammed into Geary's truck.

Now, stuck on the tracks sandwiched between two cars with a train approaching, Kludd tried to open his door and Betty Lou did the same. Both vehicles retreated, just before the train struck the Ford's left rear side, sending it into a vicious tailspin off the tracks.

TWENTY-FIVE

SUNDAY MORNING, AUGUST 25, 1963

JOSÉPHINE Jon-Marie James tapped her white heels against the church's floor. Betty Lou had been missing for two days now. Riggins discovered Jack Miles' body in the woods behind their home and his ex-wife was the prime suspect.

"Doll." Charlie's hand steadied Jolene's leg. "You troublin' me."

"Trouble don't last always, right, Charlemagne?"

"'Tis what the song says. She's alright, Darlin'. Don't you worry."

The best friends linked hands. Jolene barely had a day to enjoy with her new husband before he insisted on returning to the ministry, which infuriated her on several different levels. Aside from dramatically cutting down the physical intimacy and attention she craved from him, not to mention the drain on his energy, being in the church heightened Jolene's foreboding sense that the James' time together was indeed borrowed.

The night before, after a fight over dirty dishes, he'd tried. Jolene drowned beneath her husband and was content to let Darrion surround and suffocate her with love. She breathed him in, exhaled his beautiful essence and proclaimed hidden things from her spirit. The two became one, a painful adjustment, but harmonious in its continuous give and take. Jolene quivered inside and giggled, ashamed that she thought of such things in church, but Darrion said God extended grace over what happened in a married couple's bedroom because the marriage bed was undefiled. She wondered about the marriage kitchen and the marriage living room.

Charlie smacked Jolene's thigh. "Quit it, you in the Lawd's house."

"Sorry." Jolene shifted her hand back and forth and watched the sun shoot brilliance throughout her engagement diamond. She never tired of doing it, but tired everyone around her by talking about the ring. "You know what I like best 'bout this here ring?" she asked.

"Oh, Lawd Jesus, here we go. Hey Georgie, start the music, girl!"

Georgie turned around from the choir stand and smiled at Charlie.

"Darrion knows me so well. It's everything I wanted."

Right then, the beaming groom exited his office, strutted over to his new bride and kissed her full on the lips. "Hey, Sweetheart. I love you."

"I love you too, Cher."

"Oh, would you two c'mon? Stop, please, in Jesus' name."

They both laughed. Darrion practically skipped back to his office and Charlie busied herself with reading Bible verses, so Jolene would leave her alone. While she buried herself in Revelations, Charlie also started worrying about Betty Lou and whether her best friend's dreams were going to come to pass.

"This is it, men, no turning back."

Geary spoke freely, a white mask and rifle in his hand. All four hundred Klavern members gathered close around him. The demolished building site proved a perfect forum. Not even the paranoid Riggins would think of it. "If you are scared of white revolution, I offer you the choice to turn back. But be warned, Jack Miles Everham and his wife turned back. Jacob Watson turned back. And the Lord killed them because they were weak and only the strong survive. *We are the strong!*"

The Klansmen shouted in agreement and shook their guns.

"This is our moment, where we take Zyonne by the throat and snatch it way from the niggers. This is our time, where we eradicate this town of their stench and drive them back down into the dirty earth where they came from. Are you with me?"

"Yeah," they yelled.

"I said – are you with me?"

"Yeah," they yelled back louder.

Geary donned his hood and led the procession up several blocks to the church, drawing so much attention that several motorists traveling to service nearly veered off the road. When they arrived, about 300 crowded the doors on either side but didn't block them. The white hoods and robes prodded every Negro who looked like he or she wanted to turn away into the sanctuary amidst slurs and nasty comments.

"Wonder what's goin' on back there?" Charlie turned over her shoulder. "Folks look like they seen spooks or somethin'."

"You gotta mint? Stomach's been feelin' funny all day long."

"Told you 'bout eatin' that meat so late." Charlie handed her friend a peppermint candy. The word spread throughout the church like a virulent disease. Without saying a word, Jolene sprang up and went to Darrion's office, where he was perusing his sermon notes. "Darrion!" Jolene's face was panic-stricken beneath her white hat.

Her husband jumped up and scurried to her side. "What's wrong?"

"Outside...the Klan...they're outside."

"Is anyone hurt?"

"N-no, not that I've heard."

"The building is brick, they can't burn it. The windows have bars on them. Tell Ezra to have the ushers shut the doors."

Ezra poked his head into the office. "Pastor, they're already inside. Should we call the police?"

Darrion's insides quivered. For the first time since the pool hall, he feared dying. His hand found Jolene's clammy palm.

"Don't leave my side, even when I'm preaching."

She nodded in agreement. "On my life."

The James family, led by Ezra, entered the sanctuary. About a thousand Negroes were seated in the church, followed by a few hundred

Klansmen lining the walls. Darrion assumed a confident posture and reassured his wife, who released his hand just when necessary. She sat to his left and trembled enough that her hat noticeably shook.

Used to performing under pressure, Georgie focused and sang a stirring solo a cappella. The Spirit of the Lord touched each heart with so much peace and joy, most stood and waved their hands to the sky in praise. It was what their pastor called a "wave offering."

Darrion whispered something into his wife's ear and told her that she may not understand it now, but that the revelation would come later.

From the church's left side, Geary recognized the woman he'd violated over a year ago and anger burned inside him. *How dare she be with a half-breed over me?* She was responsible for the fire, his disfiguring burns, and skewed speech which doctors said would never return to normal. He resolved to break his own plan and send a bullet to her heart, but reconsidered when he saw James.

The offering, prayer and announcements have proceeded without a hitch, Darrion thought, because he wasn't involved. Aside from his wife, his nerves were the ones fried. The pair commiserated together and sucked down glasses of water like the world's supply was evaporating. Jolene didn't know what to think. The haze surrounding her dream blotted out most of its details. She didn't remember what they wore, how they acted, or who eventually gunned Darrion down. But she was by his side. That, alone, was a difference.

Geary anticipated the moment preceding Darrion's sermon and signaled Gaston, who communicated orders to the others by tapping his fist twice against his chest, as if he were coughing.

When the report about the Klan rally at the Negro church came down through the grapevine to the police station, Chief Riggins phoned Geary at home first. There was no answer. Frankie picked up Reifer's phone and said he had the flu and couldn't talk. Gaston didn't answer, either.

He assumed the worse about his deputies and put out three calls; to the Black Mountain County Police and the North Carolina State Police for backup, and another to the Zyonne hospitals to send ambulances. Riggins loaded his shotgun and service revolver, hopped in his police cruiser, blasted its siren and sped off for West Zyonne.

"The Lord has been dealing with me regarding timing; His timing. No matter what we think, saints, our God is the Master of perfect timing, for when we think things are destined to happen one way, He brings something forth in His timing which switches up the plan. Think of time like a thread. We see this thread cut up into pieces by the sun and moon's rising and setting because there are certain things we can do in the daytime, and others we can do at night. But what we do at night, we often cannot do during sunlight hours.

"The same is true about sunlight. Remember, Adam's purpose was to till the ground. Without the sun's light, he couldn't work. Therefore, his work was limited to the daylight hours. We find ourselves tired much of the time because the times God has designed for us to rest, nighttime and on Sundays, are times we work."

Gaston looked to Geary, who didn't signal to move yet.

"God does not see time like a cut up thread. He sees it as a continual thread with no divisions. There is no day or night in Heaven, just eternity – an everlasting continual thread with God as beginning and end. And since God has no beginning or end, neither does eternity. But, time as we know it, does.

"Being eternal, God sees you as He intended you, how you are, and what you will be. There is appointed unto man a time to die. You will not die before God calls you home, so it's useless for us to walk around afraid, if God has revealed things to us He will accomplish in us. Until He accomplishes those things in us, we will not die.

"Satan is not trying to kill you, saints. He's trying to kill those things God wants to do in you to produce for the kingdom."

Tired of waiting, Geary cocked his rifle and shot it twice at Jolene, missing both times and hitting the wall instead. She dropped faint to the floor beside Darrion, who shielded her with his body. Seats overturned and Negroes and whites alike scrambled toward the exits, but were blocked by Klansmen who fired at them with abandon. Several Negroes fought back or disarmed the Klansmen and used the guns to blaze a trail to the doors.

Ezra unloaded the rifle he'd commandeered and whacked at the padlock with the firearm's butt until the lock broke. He unchained the door and people burst forth into the street, falling over each other and scrambling for freedom. Through the chaos, he managed to drag Charlie outside and into the alley between the church and the next deserted building where it was safe.

Riggins swerved away from the rioting crowd and jumped a curb, abandoned his vehicle and fought his way inside, rifle in tow.

Still in the pulpit protecting Jolene, Darrion checked her body for blood, but the tailored white dress, a wedding gift from the deaconess ministry, was flawless. Her eyes drifted open. "Are you alright?" he asked.

"Yeah! Let's get out of here…now!"

Before Darrion could move, a shotgun blast tore into his back. Blood dribbled a dark pattern on Jolene's dress near her heart.

"Honey?" She fingered the wet mortality on her chest.

Another shot landed between his shoulder blades. Darrion's body shot erect and his eyes rolled back. The next shot punctured his heart and sent him sprawling onto the floor beside his wife. Jolene screamed, propped herself up and kneeled at his side, applying pressure to his chest wound. A thick crimson river flowed under his charcoal gray suit and soaked her knees.

Geary took to the stage, laughing the same maniacal cackle Jolene had dreamed about. He'd done it, taken down the Negro hope. If he could not have Jolene, no one else would.

"You ain't gonna die. God ain't gonna allow it. You ain't done yet! You gotta give me babies…I want four of your babies."

Darrion tried responding, but his respiration grew too shallow. Geary stepped onto the carpet gushing with blood. "He's going to die. There's nothing you can do."

I know that voice. Still compressing Darrion's wounds with her hands, she looked up and cursed him. "I should kill you with my bare hands for all you done to me, but you ain't worth the spit in my mouth."

Geary withdrew a revolver from his robe and Jolene closed her eyes, as he placed it at her forehead. A shot rang out. The gun fell next to her, followed by Geary's body. Riggins docked his rifle against a pew and ran to her aid.

"We need some help here!"

The church was almost empty now, save for the dead and injured. Ezra directed the medical staff toward the pulpit. Three white men, one with a black bag, maneuvered around the fallen and rushed to the stage.

"Gal, you gone have to move." The stocky paramedic forced Jolene into a corner, where Ezra and Charlie comforted her. Darrion's blood stained a straight line from her heart to her waist and large circular spots at the knees and legs.

"Looks like we got a goner here." The men lifted Darrion onto a stretcher, secured him down and wheeled him into an ambulance.

"You wanna ride in the ambulance, Miss Jolene?"

She nodded yes to Ezra, but collapsed in his arms.

About a half-hour later, Jolene came to in the back of Charlie's car. Still groggy, she could distinguish only bits and pieces of the conversation. "...said...'too extensive'...no chance," "Gal...through hell...goin' back through...," "...ain't...no suspect...typical," "...him Darlin'... they'll find...," "...gotta...funeral...few days," "I'll...ain't...no shape... nothin'."

"Ya'll quit talkin' 'bout me. I can still hear," Jolene muttered.

Charlie twisted around, her face piteous, red and make-up free. "Oh Darlin', I'm so sorry."

"Sorry for what?" For days, her life itself seemed like a dream.

"They did what they could, Darlin', but Darrion's gone."

The news grieved Jolene so much that she could muster nothing but a moaning wail from the deep recesses of her belly. By far, it was the worst sound either Ezra or Charlie had ever heard. Charlie entered the back of the car and held her best friend. Together, they mourned the man who helped bring healing to their lives.

Minutes later, Charlie composed herself. "We gotta take you in to sign these papers and get his things right quick. Alright, Doll?"

Jolene didn't respond, but moved slowly. The nurse's words flew past her blurred understanding, but she trusted Charlie and Charlie pointed wherever Missus James needed to sign. At the end, she handed Jolene a small bag. In it were Darrion's wedding ring, his wallet, keys, and his bloodstained crucifix. She slipped her husband's gold ring over her thumb and Charlie fastened the chain and crucifix around Jolene's neck.

TWENTY-SIX

TUESDAY EVENING, AUGUST 27, 1963

SINCE the county and state authorities designated the church a crime scene, Reverend Whitehead offered Higher Ground as a venue for Darrion's Wednesday morning funeral. The facility held less than a quarter of the people. Charlie suggested it be held at Darrion's church instead anyway. The officials claimed they could not promise it would be available, but that they'd "try."

Despite the timing conflict with Mr. Randolph's March on Washington, all the hotels and inns within a 30-mile radius of the hamlet were booked solid with media journalists and curious visitors from out-of-town, including Daniel Carpenter, his daughter, and even Freedom, who Jolene always referred to as if she were long dead.

The juicy story was golden copy to any writer who touched it, so much so that they dubbed Darrion, "a modern-day Negro Moses." An obvious comparison to Jesus was there, but no newspaper around would commit literary suicide by comparing a dead Negro preacher to Christ.

Media blitzed the James' home, forcing Jolene into further self-imposed reclusion – even from her inner circle. Charlie phoned every half-hour and Ezra must have stopped by ten times since yesterday and rapped his knuckles on the door until their blue-black skin bruised. As it was, she hadn't spoken a word since saying "goodbye" to Darrion's body. They asked her to identify it. She replied that it wasn't him, just a place where her newlywed husband used to live. Satisfied with the response, they covered him with a blue sheet.

These happenings rendered her numb; no grief or sorrow, no pain, no feeling. She draped herself over the exact spot in the bed where Darrion first made love to her on their wedding night and sank deep into the mattress. He'd smothered her with himself like that once.

Thoughts rampaged through her mind. *What about the Lost Testament...we are the Lost Testament...I miss him so much...am I with child, because my monthly is late, no my monthly is late 'cause I'm upset, but why am I upset, I'm going to see him again, but again is not now...I wanted a house, a new house, a new thing...I miss him...I hate him for leaving me, leaving us, us who...us me, us it, him, her, whatever it is...I'm carryin' his child...we are the Lost Testament...we are the Lost Testament...I'm not with his child, yes I am, no I ain't, yes I am, no I ain't, yes I am, 'cause I say it and it's so...*

For the first time in three days, Jolene slept soundly and dreamed.

The next day, bells chimed across Zyonne twelve times each hour in his honor. The morning burst through Jolene's window and she thanked God for remembering His daughter and waking her up. She readied herself for the funeral, phoned Reverend Whitehead and asked him over for coffee, which he was delighted to do. The beating left him with a limp, so it took longer than she expected for him to arrive, but he thanked God and noticed the remarkable changes and spiritual growth in Jolene.

She sipped, gave all glory to God, and mentioned her husband in the same breath as Jesus. A tear trickled out from her heart. Then she asked him, plain as day, and he agreed just as quickly. "Some church folk won't like it," he said, "but church folk is church folk, and some of 'em wouldn't like Jesus. So, you know what you gone say?"

Jolene paused. "Thinkin' 'bout somethin' good right now."

Reverend Whitehead drove away, and Charlie and Ezra pulled up a minute after he vanished down the road. *Them two been spendin' more and more time together,* thought Jolene. *They ain't hidin' nothin'.*

"You ready, Darlin'?" Charlie owned lots of black clothes. This dress masked her figure pretty well, but no one would ever know the way Ezra stared her down when she wasn't looking.

Jolene wore a dark gray dress which treaded a delicate balance between being too light for a funeral and too dark to be attractive. The outfit was V-neck, the way Darrion liked it, but not too revealing. She'd straightened her hair and donned her best jewelry.

In a plain black suit, matching tie, white shirt, and patent leather shoes, Ezra escorted the women into the church to their customary spots. Charlie wilted when he took her arm. But Jolene nonchalantly left them, strode to the pulpit and sat in the center chair without stopping to pay her respects to her husband. Whispers spread from pew to pew during the viewing. They called Jolene names. *"She ain't havin' no respect for the dead. Might as well spit on 'im and dance on his grave, disrespectful hussy."*

Passing the casket, Daniel Carpenter smiled, but an expectant Jayne expressed her grief openly with new husband Ben behind her. Freedom could care less what they said about her daughter, while Georgie's voice wavered too much to hold a single note steady.

At the appointed time, Jolene rose and stepped up to speak.

"When I look into the casket, I see with my eyes what you see. But see, I've been reading the *Lost Testament* an' now, I see things a lil' differently. When I look into my spirit, I see somethin' different. It's why you all wearin' black and I'm wearin' a different color 'cause I'm seein' things different now. Had it all wrong all the time. I'm speakin' 'cause I'm the one seein' it right.

"My husband whispered a word in my ear the morning he died. He said 'Read Ezekiel 37 and tell me what you think in your pretty head.' Well, Cher, I never got to tell you. I read Ezekiel 37 and this is what I been thinkin' 'bout. This valley of dry bones is like *you*. These bones ain't been buried like they should. And *you* ain't bein' buried like *you* should, like my friend over here, 'cause it ain't your time to go yet, either."

Charlie was so transfixed with the eulogy that she didn't notice Jolene pause and smile in her general direction. A soft feminine hand rested on Charlie's shoulder, startling her.

"Betty Lou!" Minus a few scratches and bruises, she was intact.

"Shh!" Betty Lou covered Charlie's mouth. "Tell you later."

Jolene stepped down from the pulpit and turned toward the casket.

"The Lord tells Ezekiel to say to the bones. 'O ye dry bones, hear the word of Jehovah. Thus saith the Lord Jehovah unto these bones: Behold, I will cause breath to enter into you, and ye shall live. And I will lay sinews upon you, and will bring up flesh upon you, and cover you with skin, and put breath in you, and ye shall live; and ye shall know that *I-am-Jehovah*.'"

"We'll know the Lord when the dry bones come alive, when the grave opens and they come up, when they return to the land, when they live and settle, have four babies, build a house and spread the gospel."

"Betty Lou," Charlie said, elbowing her friend. "What's goin' on?"

"Shh. Wait an' see! I got a good feelin'."

"Father, I thank You for hearing me," Jolene prayed. "So that they know You are God and You are with me, as You are with my husband, I ask that You hear me now."

Stunned by the unorthodox eulogy, many of the offended unceremoniously exited the sanctuary.

"Darrion, get up!"

Ezra, Charlie, and Betty Lou linked tense hands. Freedom yawned with boredom. Daniel and Ben looked dismissive and Jayne cried miserably. Reverend Whitehead stood up from the pulpit and looked down with curiosity.

Slowly, Darrion sat up and reached for his waiting wife, who embraced him.

THE END